ST. MARTIN'S

MINOTAUR

MYSTERIES

PRAISE FOR
RETT MACPHERSON'S MYSTERIES

KILLING COUSINS

"Torie is a warm, knowledgeable, and thoroughly American heroine."

—*St. Petersburg Times*

"Absorbing."

—*Romantic Times*

"A fine series."

—*Library Journal*

A MISTY MOURNING

"Unexpected and often amusing, another fine outing for Torie O'Shea and the oddballs she attracts without effort."

—*St. Louis Post-Dispatch*

"[MacPherson] is generous with her wit, and her descriptions of the landscape of Appalachia and the people who live there are especially evocative."

—*Publishers Weekly*

"Nothing, certainly not murder, dampens Torie's perkiness."

—*Kirkus Reviews*

"MacPherson once again displays her mastery of the cozy form, adroitly mixing charming characters (both new and old), a plot steeped in family drama, plenty of humor, and just enough grit to keep the story grounded in the real world."

—*Booklist*

MORE . . .

Killing Cousins

A NOVEL BY

RETT MACPHERSON

St. Martin's Paperbacks

KILLING COUSINS

Copyright © 2002 by Rett MacPherson.
Excerpt from *Blood Relations* © 2003 by Rett MacPherson.

All rights reserved. No part of this book may be used or reproduced in any manner whatsoever without written permission except in the case of brief quotations embodied in critical articles or reviews. For information address St. Martin's Press, 175 Fifth Avenue, New York, NY 10010.

Library of Congress Catalog Card Number: 2001048746

ISBN: 0-312-98325-5

Printed in the United States of America

St. Martin's Press hardcover edition / March 2002
St. Martin's Paperbacks edition / June 2003

St. Martin's Paperbacks are published by St. Martin's Press, 175 Fifth Avenue, New York, NY 10010.

10 9 8 7 6 5 4 3 2 1

FOR REBEKAH, ELIZAH AND DILLON.

For being my friends as
well as my children.

Acknowledgments

The author wishes to thank the following people for their help and advice:

Many years ago a group of local authors met at a science-fiction convention and decided to meet once a month to critique one another's work. I'm a member of that group and I just wanted to thank them not just for their support as writers, but for their wisdom and friendship. Over the years they have become my closest friends and have continually set standards for which I strive. Thank you, Tom Drennan, Laurell K. Hamilton, Debbie Millitello, Marella Sands, Sharon Shinn and Mark Sumner.

Also, my family, Joe, Mom, Nanny, and all the aunts, uncles, cousins, and in-laws who have put up with my little eccentricities. This book was particularly difficult for me to write because my father died of prostate cancer during its construction. My friends and family are the reason you hold this book in your hands, because without them, I'm not sure I could have ever finished it. A soapbox if I may: Guys, get your prostate checked. A simple blood test could save your life.

As usual, thank you to my editor, Kelley Ragland, who is never too busy to answer even the smallest question. And to my agent, Michele Rubin, whose voice has the power to uplift even my darkest moods.

Killing
Cousins

One

If anyone here has any reason why these two should not be married, speak now or forever hold your peace," the Reverend McIlhenny said.

I just want to state for the record that I did not say a word. I just stood there in my peach satin gown, holding back tears and waiting to hear my mother and the sheriff say the words "I do." Evidently everybody in attendance thought I *was* going to say something because the entire congregation looked at me. The reverend, my mother, the sheriff, everybody.

The breeze ruffled my dress, and I tried to think about the gorgeous weather on this August day and the pink and yellow roses that climbed up the trellises of the Laura Winery. My mother had picked the perfect spot to get married. High on a cliff, just north of town, the Laura Winery had attracted thousands of people for nearly seven decades. My mother had always said that if she ever remarried, she wanted to do it in the courtyard of the winery overlooking the Mississippi River. She got her wish.

It seemed like a full minute had passed since the reverend had asked his question and still everybody was staring at me. I couldn't help but wonder just how the entire town had found out that I wasn't real hip on this marriage. Well, I was all right with it now, but I hadn't been at first. My mother was marrying the sheriff. And let's just say that the sheriff and I have had a few disagreements in the past.

I have to admit that my soon-to-be stepfather, Sheriff Colin Woodrow Brooke, looked spiffy in his dusty charcoal-gray suit and spit-shined black shoes. He was a huge man, twelve years younger than my mother, tall and broad through the shoulders and just plain old big. No matter how many times I said we'd called a truce, I still couldn't help but think mean thoughts about him. Like, just how much food did he consume in one day, anyway? I imagined feeding him was much like feeding a horse. He probably bought his food in feed sacks rather than little cardboard boxes or cans. Did he use a trough or a plate? See, I can't help myself. What was my problem with him? Maybe it was because he was one of the few people who made me answer to authority. Yeah, that could be it.

So, there I stood next to my mother, who looked absolutely radiant in her ivory crocheted dress, imagining her soon-to-be husband on his hands and knees eating out of a trough, when they said the words "I do."

I looked over at Mom and thought that she was the most beautiful woman I'd ever seen. A splash of baby's breath graced her salt-and-pepper hair, and her large brown eyes were full of joy. The sheriff had to bend down to kiss her because she was in a wheelchair, having been one of the last polio victims of the 1950s before the vaccine was made public.

And so they kissed and now I had a stepfather who was the sheriff. How fair was that? I looked over at my husband, Rudy, who was the best man, and he winked at me. He looked pretty good in his suit too, I might add.

My mother and the sheriff made their way down the aisle, and Rudy came over and grabbed my hand. "Torie," he said. "Are you going to cry? You always cry at weddings."

"No," I said, as a tear ran down my cheek.

He smiled, squeezed my hand and kissed me. In the front row, my infant son Matthew wailed at the top of his lungs. I knew just how he felt.

•

After two hours of plastering smiles on our faces and posing just so for pictures, we all traveled back to New Kassel to the Knights of Columbus Hall in a long caravan of freshly washed cars. I was determined not to cry all the way back to town because my eyes would be swollen and everybody would know I had been crying; I was just determined not to do it. So I thought of the sheriff eating out of his trough again.

Once we were at the KC Hall, I was approached by too many people wanting too many things. The caterer wanted to know where to put the cake. My Aunt Bethany showed me the lipstick that my daughter Mary had somehow found in my purse and smeared all over her face. At least she hadn't gotten it on the dress, and at least she had waited until after the pictures. Helen Wickland wanted to know what to do with the party favors she'd made. *Chocolate* party favors. I told her to put them on the tables far away from me. Tobias wanted to know when he could start playing his accordion. I wanted to say never, but I just smiled and said, "In a minute." My grandmother insisted that I introduce her to the sheriff's sister. And there was no putting my grandmother off. It had to be done now.

In between carrying Matthew all over the room showing off his newborn son and keeping Mary from climbing onto the wedding cake, Rudy wanted to know when we would eat. And last, but not least, no less than a dozen people approached me and asked me just who the hell had invited my father.

My mother had. They were still friends.

I wanted to go home. Eat, cry, sleep. In that order.

3

Instead I smiled, raised my chin a notch and took care of everything, although not necessarily in the order that I had been approached. My grandmother came first.

A while later, my husband stood and gave a touching toast. It ended with "And she's the greatest mother-in-law in the world, and I don't say that lightly. Because my saying it means my mother isn't. So you take good care of her, Colin."

Great. More tears.

I stood in the corner, watching everybody, as the newlyweds prepared to cut the cake. Next, the music and the dancing would start. I thought I could blend into the deer-brown paneling, but I did not. My best friend, Colette, walked up to me and gave me a big hug.

Colette was thirty-five and still single. Not because she couldn't find a man, but because she couldn't find a *man*. She liked plenty of men, but she was usually too much woman for them. She was my height, curvy and buxom, with lots of hair. She couldn't help that big hair had gone out in the eighties, hers was naturally big.

She wore a Caribbean-blue dress, cut low enough to show plenty of cleavage and hemmed high enough to show plenty of thigh. She simply loved to give old men cheap thrills, and, well, she was thrilling them tonight. She was a reporter in the big city and I loved her like a sister, not just because I didn't have a sister, but because I have no memory of life without her. "B.C." in my life means Before Colette.

"I don't see you enough," I said to her.

"I know. I've got deadlines, you've got kids. I've talked to more women who say they really enjoy their fifties because their kids have moved out and their jobs are winding down and they can finally enjoy life," she said. "It's just not fair that by the time I get there my boobs are going to be keeping company with my navel."

"Ha. It's obvious you don't have kids," I said to her and smiled. She studied me a minute and then caught what I had said and

4

laughed. We laughed together a moment and then she regarded me cautiously. "You okay?"

"Yeah," I said. "I'm fine. This is a huge adjustment, that's all. Remember our senior year, when you were running for homecoming queen, and you said that you didn't care if you lost, just as long as you didn't lose to Cindy Lou Marks?"

"Yeah," she said. "God, she was my arch enemy. No, it was more than that. I hated her guts."

I gestured toward the sheriff standing beside the triple-tiered wedding cake. "Meet my Cindy Lou Marks."

"Ahh, I get it," she said.

"Really, it's not that bad," I said. "I hate to admit it out loud, but a lot of this is hormones."

"You been crying a lot since the baby was born?"

I ignored the question.

"Torie?"

"Yeah."

"Torie O'Shea, you've got the baby blues. You need to go to the doctor."

"Yeah, yeah, yeah," I said and waved a hand at her. I hate admitting that hormones actually play a part in my life. It just seems like one more thing that Mother Nature throws at women that men don't have to deal with, and therefore, most of the time, I refuse to acknowledge it. It's just not fair. But I suppose if you're a man and you live in proximity to a woman, then you'll have to deal with hormones after all. Maybe Mother Nature is fair in her own way.

"Okay," she said. "Maybe you just need to get back to work earlier than planned."

She was good. She always knew when to lean and when to back off. I gestured to my mother. "My baby-sitter is going to be in Alaska for three weeks. So, until she gets back, I'm kind of limited. I can't do the tours and such. Plus, I'm not sure I could fit back in

5

the dresses yet. All I can do is research, and then . . . Lord, Colette, have you ever tried to go to the library with three kids?"

"I try not to even be in the same room with three kids at the same time if I can help it," she said and rolled her eyes. "Oh, unless they're yours, of course."

I smiled at her.

"I guess being a tour guide would be really difficult with children," she said.

"You have no idea."

"Oh, here comes the wicked witch," Colette said and looked in the direction of my boss, Sylvia Pershing.

I stood up straighter, just because that's the type of behavior that Sylvia has instilled in me. Sit up straight. Put your shoulders back. Elbows off the table. She walked right up to me and, without even acknowledging Colette's presence, she said, "I've got work for you."

Sylvia owned half of the town and was president of the Historical Society, where I worked, giving tours and running things. The Gaheimer house was the headquarters, and she spent most of her waking hours there. It had once belonged to an old lover of hers, and the house was a shrine in his honor. The woman was in her nineties, and somehow she always made me feel as if I didn't do enough.

"What sort of work?" I asked. In addition to giving the tours, I was the one who compiled historical and genealogical data of the town, did displays of historical events or items, and that sort of thing. My job was also to play mediator between Sylvia and the rest of the town. The townspeople loved Sylvia's sister, Wilma, but they weren't nearly as fond of Sylvia. I think some of it was just a deep-rooted misunderstanding. She was actually a giving and honest woman. She just had no finesse at all.

"I'd like for you to write a biography," she said.

"Me?" I asked, thinking for a minute she meant Colette.

"Yes."

"Why?"

"Why must you always ask why?" she asked. The fuchsia-colored pantsuit she wore gave her aged-gray skin a nice healthy pink glow.

"It's my nature, Sylvia. You know how you swallow after you chew food? Well, I ask why when somebody says something," I explained.

"It needs to be about forty thousand words," she said.

"Why?"

She rolled her eyes and I found this funny. Sylvia was thin as a rail and wore her hair in two long braids twisted around her head every single day of her life. Wilma used to wear her hair the same way, until she realized that if she wore her hair down, it really irked her sister. Ever since, Wilma has worn her hair down.

"Because I said so," she answered.

"That never worked with my mother, and it's not going to work with you," I said. "I always asked my mother why and she always gave me an answer."

"It's a wonder your mother's not in the madhouse," she said.

"Hey," I said.

"For Pete's sake, Sylvia, just tell her why," Colette jumped in. "Before she has a stroke."

"You stay out of this," Sylvia snapped at Colette. She turned back to me. "If you must know, there's a small press . . . one of the colleges, and I thought it would be nice to compile a few histories of different things in Granite County. Maybe do a small biography on a few of the more famous residents—"

"Are there any famous residents of Granite County?" Colette asked.

Sylvia ignored her completely.

"—And on some landmark places. It would be just a small print run . . . maybe a couple of hundred books on each subject that we could deposit in different libraries. One of the people that has always fascinated me is Catherine Finch."

"Why?" I asked. Realizing I had—of course—asked why, I added, "Sorry."

"Once you start researching her, you'll understand. She was a fascinating woman," she said.

"I know who she is—"

"But obviously you know nothing *about* her."

"All right," I said. I was rather excited about actually having something to do that I could work on from home. "When do you want me to start and when do you want it finished?"

"Right away."

"Which was that the answer to? The former or the latter?"

"Both," she said, and walked away.

"The nerve of that woman," Colette said as she watched Sylvia disappear in the crowd.

"Yeah, but you gotta hope that when we're in our nineties, *if* we make it to our nineties, that we're as full of gusto," I said.

"More like full of sh—"

"Torie," the sheriff said, arriving just in time to cut her off. Sheriff. Colin. Dad.

"Yes?" I asked as I turned to him.

"I was wondering if you could do me a favor while we're in Alaska?" he asked.

"In addition to feeding your malamute, and your cat, checking your mail, watering your garden and . . . oh, yeah, making sure your malamute doesn't eat your cat?" I asked. "There's something else?"

"Yes," he said. "There's one more thing. And I'm afraid it can't wait. I'll gladly pay you for your time, since it's going to be pretty time-consuming, but I just don't know who else to ask. It really can't wait until I get back."

"What's that?" I asked, suddenly interested.

"I got the bid on an estate," he said. He had bought an antique store in town. It had been called Norah's Antiques, and so far, he hadn't changed the name of it. "I've been trying to get some nice

8

big estates to build up equity. When I retire, I'll have plenty of stuff in storage to haul out and sell."

Just the thought that I would be helping him to retire made me much more agreeable. "Okay . . ."

"Well, I put a bid in on this one estate. It was a doozy. Do you know who Catherine Finch was?" he asked. He was holding a clear plastic cup filled with beer in his left hand and fixing his boutonniere with his right.

"You got *that* estate?" I asked, impressed.

"What a coincidence," Colette added.

"Coincidence?" the sheriff asked. "What do you mean by that?"

"My next project for the Historical Society is writing a biography of her," I said.

He looked a little uneasy but went ahead with what he was going to say. "Yes. Well, evidently she was a famous singer back in the twenties," he said and smiled. "She's been dead for five years, but her estate has been held up in court this whole time. Just the fact that some of the objects were hers should bring in huge money when I resell them."

See, that's the problem with the antique business. How could he resell them? I couldn't bring myself to do it. When I buy something, it gets incorporated into my family heirlooms. How can people sell antiques? Everything old should be kept. "What do you need me to do?" I asked.

"I need you to go in and start throwing out the junk and cataloging the good stuff. You know . . . you can throw out her toaster and her toothbrush, for crying out loud."

"Why can't this wait for you to get back?" I asked. It sounded to me as if he just wanted somebody else to do the dirty work for him. I did realize that getting into her house and having access to her personal belongings would give me an immense edge in writing her biography. But if I didn't put up some sort of fight, Colin would worry about me.

"Because I didn't buy the house. Only the stuff inside. The house and the land is to be sold and split between her heirs, and they had to fight five years just to get that. No personal item of hers is to go to her heirs. Anyway, I think the house already has a buyer. Somebody here in town. They want it as soon as possible. How was I to know this was going to happen just as I was going to Alaska?"

"Yeah, right. You planned this," I said with a smile.

"Torie," he said plainly.

"Of course, I'll do it," I said and held my hands up.

"Great. If you could just throw out the junk and try to put everything in one room. Have Rudy move the furniture for you. And catalog it as you go," he said.

"Yes, I can do that," I said. "I can take the kids with me."

A grave look crossed his face. "Don't let Mary climb on anything."

"I won't." As if that were the most preposterous notion in the world.

"I'll give the key and directions to Rudy, since he has pockets. And thanks," he said. "I appreciate this."

Hey, what are stepdaughters for, right? "I don't need directions. I know exactly where it is."

"This biography . . ." he started.

I could tell by the look on his face that somehow he thought my writing a biography of Catherine Finch would interfere with his estate. Nothing could be farther from the truth. In fact, I thought the two tasks would aid each other. I was itching to get started.

"Yes?"

"Nothing," he said. He walked away to find my mother, and then the music started up.

Colette placed her hand on my shoulder and started walking me toward the dance floor. "You know, you've got what, ten or fifteen years before Rachel gets married? This may be the last time you get to dance at a family member's wedding for a long time."

"Yeah," I said.

"Maybe they'll play some Village People," she said, smiling.

"I'm more in the mood for Rage Against the Machine."

But there would be no Rage Against the Machine. The DJ started up with "Devil in a Blue Dress." Colette smiled from ear to ear, showing all of her pearly whites, and said, "It's not Rage Against the Machine."

I rolled my eyes. "Oh, like that's a surprise."

"So," she said as she grabbed my hands and yanked me hard. "Let's boogie!"

TWO

"I t was a good time," Rudy said in the car on the way home. It would only take two or three minutes to get home, we lived just a few blocks from the KC Hall. Which was good, since it was one in the morning. I smelled dampness in the air, which happens a lot when you live right next to a river. But this smelled like rain in the distance. The storm would cover miles before reaching us. "Yes, it was," I said. "A beautiful wedding and a happy reception."

"I want somebody else to get married soon," Mary said. "That was fun."

"Well, we'll see if we can't get somebody to get married just so you can have a party," Rudy said. He took something out of his pocket and handed it to me. "Here's the key for the Finch house."

"Did you buy a birdhouse, Mom?" Rachel asked from the back-seat. Rachel, who usually acted much older than her almost ten years, could still ask some pretty childish questions. And it never ceased to amaze me how she could hear the smallest details of a conversation that had nothing to do with her—in another room, even—and yet failed to hear me when I told her to take out the trash.

"No, Rachel. The Finch house is the Catherine Finch house. Not a house for finches."

"Who's Catherine Finch?" she asked.

"An old woman who used to live in that big mansion just south of town."

"Oh, with that big rock fence all around it?" she asked.

"Yes."

"Why do you have the keys?"

"Because I have to go in and separate her things for your new grandpa to sell," I said. "She died and he bought her estate."

"Oh." She was quiet a beat. "You mean you're going to go into that big empty house and go through a dead lady's stuff?"

I hadn't thought of it that way. Rudy turned into the drive of our own story-and-a-half brick house. "Yeah," I said. "That's exactly what I'm going to have to do. I was going to take you guys with me."

"No way," Rachel said. "Take Mary. Maybe a ghost will eat her."

"Nuh-uh," Mary chimed in. "Ghosts can't eat people."

"Nobody is going to eat anybody," I said, as Rudy turned off the car. "We're home. Don't leave anything in the car."

"I'll get Matthew," Rudy said. I had forgotten how with a baby it took twenty extra minutes just to get in the house and an extra half hour just to leave it. Just packing a diaper bag took more time than I was willing to give up in a day. So I packed it on Sundays and just replaced whatever I used from it throughout the week.

"You think your mom will enjoy Alaska?" Rudy asked as I unlocked the front door.

"She hates bears."

"And snow."

"It's August. There probably isn't any snow. I'm sure she'll have a good time just because she's with Colin. And, you know, that's really all that matters," I said as I felt around for the light switch. I found it, flipped it on and, as I entered my empty house, I was hit full force with the fact that I would never come home to my mother in my house again. I stopped for a second, allowing myself a moment of selfishness.

I walked into the kitchen, threw the diaper bag on the kitchen table, and reached for a glass from the cabinet to get a drink. I poured myself a glass of milk and turned around to find something sitting on top of my stove. I walked over and found a pan of my mother's apricot bars covered with Saran Wrap with a note placed on top of the pan. The note read: "*So you won't miss me too much. Love, Mom.*"

Apricot bars. My favorite. Oatmeal and brown sugar with lots of butter baked in and apricot preserves in the middle! Mmm mmm. I hadn't had any of these since last year at Christmas. A tear came to my eye as I tore off the Saran Wrap and devoured one of the scrumptious bars in reflective silence.

Rudy came into the kitchen with a satisfied look on his face. "Matthew is sound asleep. Carrying him in didn't wake him up, nor did the girls yakking and making noise. Hey, what are you eating?"

"Apricot bars. My mom is the greatest," I said, swallowing the last bite.

"Ooooh, she made apricot bars? You are so spoiled it isn't funny," he said as he grabbed one for himself and started eating it. "So now what were you telling Rachel about the Finch estate?"

I took a drink of milk, happy that he had changed the subject from my spoiled rottenness. "Well, if you can believe it, Colin won the bid on it. The problem is that the house has already been sold; he only gets the goodies inside. And evidently the buyer wants it cleared out fairly quickly, which Colin can't do if he's in Alaska. The good thing is, Sylvia came up to me and asked me to write a small biography on Catherine Finch. She's wanting to write individual volumes on the famous people of our county and some of the landmark places to deposit in libraries. A small press, small print run, so I can sort of kill two birds with one stone."

"What do you mean?" he asked.

"I mean, I'm going to be all alone in the woman's house. How many biographers get complete solitary access to the house and belongings of their subjects? Not too many. This should help me a lot," I explained.

"Huh," was all he said and reached for another apricot bar. "Is Sylvia paying you extra for this biography, or is she just going to pay you a weekly salary?"

"Probably just my usual weekly salary," I said.

"How many famous people came from Granite County?" he asked. "I didn't even know who Catherine Finch was until she died."

"I dunno. Let's see . . . there's that one actor who was always in all those bad B horror movies."

"Oh, *him*," Rudy said and smiled. "Yeah, I forgot all about *him*."

"Don't give me any crap," I said, eyeing the apricot bars, trying to decide if I wanted another one. Well, of course, I *wanted* another one. I just knew I shouldn't have another one. "I can't remember his name right now. Oh, and Judge Vogt."

"Oh yeah, forgot about him."

"And . . . and . . . Hope Danvers."

"The governor? She's from Granite County?"

"Yes, and I just saw a sign earlier this week that she's going to run for senator."

"Huh. Well, I'll be. Anybody else?" Rudy asked.

"Yeah, but I can't remember who they are. One became a famous architect. And then there was this woman . . . Eve something-or-other; she moved to London and became a writer."

"All from little old Granite County. Who would have thought it?"

I decided to eat another apricot bar after all and hoped that Rudy wouldn't notice. "I can't help but wonder who bought the house. You know—Catherine Finch's house? Why are they in such a hurry?"

"Oh, Bill bought the house."

I knew my face must have changed colors. "Bill. Bill Castle-reagh? Our Bill? Bill, the mayor of New Kassel, whose yard backs up to ours? That Bill?"

"Yeah. Why do you sound so shocked?"

"Well . . . well . . . I guess for one reason, I didn't realize Bill had that kind of money that he could just go and buy . . . Have you *seen* the Finch estate, Rudy? It's not a house—I mean, it's an estate. It's huge. It's three stories. The rock fence must travel a good mile. I don't really know how much land goes with it. There are out-buildings . . . I mean . . . come to think of it, I don't know how Colin could have afforded to beat everybody else's bid for the contents of the estate."

"Maybe he made really good investments," Rudy said. "It's not that hard, if you invest young, to get a good payoff in your forties. And he's never had a wife or kids or anything to spend his money on. He just puts that sheriff's check in the bank, and one day, boom, he's got a nice little nest egg."

"I guess so," I said, setting my glass in the sink, wondering why that strategy hadn't worked for us.

"Don't go getting all snoopy on my father-in-law," he said. "By the way, I have two now. Do I have to go fishing with both of them?"

"Oh, like anybody is twisting your arm to make you go fishing," I said.

Rudy laughed and leaned forward and kissed me.

"Why would Bill buy the Finch house? Why would he want to, and how could he afford to?" I asked.

"That's it. I kiss you and you ask about how Bill can or can't afford . . . Why do you think of Bill when I kiss you?" he asked.

"I was thinking of Bill *before* you kissed me," I said. Rudy had never learned that my mind never stops thinking. It never winds down. You ask a guy what he's thinking about when he's staring off into the distance, and if he says nothing, then that is exactly what he is thinking about. If you ask a woman and she says nothing, she's lying. "How do you know that Bill bought the house? Who did you hear it from?"

"Lord, I hate it when you interrogate me. I always feel like I'm snitching on my friends," he said.

"You are snitching on your friends. So which one of your friends did you hear it from?" I asked.

"What if I don't feel like telling you?" he said and put his hand on his hip.

"Fine. Good night. I'm going out to the Finch house early tomorrow." I headed up the steps to our bedroom.

"That's it? Fine? You just give up?" he asked, following me. "That's not like you. Are you feeling okay?"

"I'll find out sooner or later. If you want to play that way, I can go along," I said, sounding more peeved than I really was. In fact, I knew I could find out with no trouble at all, so if Rudy didn't want to tell me it wasn't that big of a deal. It was just fun to play along.

"It was Chuck. Chuck said that he'd heard from Elmer that the mayor had bought the Finch estate because of some project he had planned."

We reached the top of the steps. "It's okay. You don't have to tell me. Besides, if it went through that many people, it might not be that reliable."

"Chuck doesn't lie."

"Unless it's about his ex-wife," I said. "Whom he hates with a passion."

"He has reason," Rudy said, getting undressed.

"Well, whatever. I'm just saying that by the time the story gets through the fourth or fifth person, there's usually only a grain of truth left to it. I'll find out on my own," I said.

"Sometimes I don't know about you," he said, rolling his eyes.

"Yeah, well, hush up and come over here and undo my buttons on this godforsaken peach fluffy thing my mother calls a dress," I said.

Rudy came over and stood behind me for a minute. "There are no buttons on this dress."

"I know," I said and turned around and kissed him.

Three

Sunday morning broke with brilliant sunshine and a barge creeping up Old Man River. I rolled out of bed, took a shower, made breakfast—even though I was reminded by my children that my pancakes were not as good as my mother's and my eggs were too done—and got the kids dressed. Then I returned to my gingham blue bedroom upstairs and to my computer. Rachel and Mary went outside to ride their bikes, and Rudy and Matthew were downstairs watching the pre-pre-game show to some sporting event.

I had recently broken down and jumped on the information highway. I now understood the addiction to the Internet. It was incredibly convenient, and I could e-mail all of my scattered family for nothing, rather than pay the long-distance phone bills. Being the researcher that I am, I found the endless access to information (on any number of subjects) just too enticing to ignore. While doing research, I'd connected with people from branches of my family tree that I'd never even known existed. One man even sent me a scanned photograph of one of my great-great-grandparents whom I'd never seen a photograph of before. Amazing. And I had no idea at all how any of it actually worked. I just pressed this button and that button, and that's all I needed to know.

And yet there was still a part of me that really liked the personal touch of the handwritten letter, something that could be kept forever.

I logged on and that stupid voice declared, "You've got mail." I could see the little flag. I knew I had mail without the moronic voice telling me so. I looked to see whom it was from. Colette sent a Web address on postpartum depression to check out. I deleted it. My cousin in Colorado sent me an e-mail telling me all about her eighteen hours of labor. Luckily, Matthew had only taken about six hours to bring into the world. A friend of Rudy's sent something, and there was a note from Rudy's sister. As much as I have become accustomed to the Internet, since most of these people lived within a few miles, I had to ask myself the question: Doesn't anybody use the damn phone anymore?

I went to Google and typed in "Catherine Finch." Of course there were sites that weren't for my Catherine Finch, so I typed "singer" after her name. It brought up a few different Web sites, and I printed out the relevant pages. I didn't really have time to stop and read them right now. I would do it later. While the pages were printing, I got my camera together and found my notebook and pen. Once I had printed out what looked like about forty pages' worth of information from several different sites, I logged off, turned off the computer and went downstairs.

I grabbed my keys, slipped on the sandals that were sitting by the door, and kissed Rudy and Matthew each on the head.

"What about dinner?" Rudy asked before I made it out the door.

"What about it?"

"What are we having? Should I lay something out?"

"We'll go to Chuck's for pizza."

"Okay," he said.

•

Before I could make it out of New Kassel on this postcard-perfect August day, Eleanore Murdoch stopped me in the middle of the road, as she had a habit of doing. She just walked out into the middle of the road and then waited for me to roll down the driver's-side window.

"You know, Eleanore, I have an office in this town. A home, a telephone and e-mail. Why must you insist on stopping me in the middle of the road?"

Eleanore, a woman in her late middle years, top-heavy and broad, had a knack for being irritating. Of course, that was probably what she thought about me as well, so I shouldn't have been so quick to judge. She had a small gossip column in the town newspaper and fancied herself a literary genius. Which was hysterical because she often spoke like a thesaurus on acid. She and her husband, Oscar, owned and ran the bed-and-breakfast known as the Murdoch Inn. She always stuck her nose where it didn't belong, and she always thought she should be the first to know everything. There I go describing myself again. Why was it more irritating when she did it?

"This couldn't wait," she said to me, with her big purple plastic earrings clanking together. Eleanore loved costume jewelry, the bigger and brighter the better. And, it seemed, the noisier the better, too. "Have you heard?"

Her expression was serious, which made me sober up a bit. Eleanore was certainly the Drama Queen of New Kassel, but somehow her expression seemed genuine. "What?" I asked.

"They've put the riverboat casino on the ballot."

"What?" I asked, dumbfounded. This *was* serious.

"Bill wants to bring riverboat gambling to New Kassel."

Bill being Bill Castlereagh, the mayor. Funny, his name had come up quite a bit lately.

"And evidently, he got the go-ahead from the gaming commission and it's going to be voted on," she finished.

"No way," I said. This was a catastrophe. An abomination. It wasn't possible. New Kassel was a historic town. And although I realized that New Kassel was a tourist trap—the town is the commodity—a flashy casino was not the type of trap that New Kassel was all about. New Kassel was about going back in time and learning something about the days before Internet and satellite dishes. It was about history, antiques, crafts and good food. A casino would just . . . I don't know, ruin the mood.

Eleanore kissed two fingers on her right hand and stuck them up in the air. "I swear."

"But, that's . . . that's . . ."

Honk. Honk. That's the bad thing about stopping in the middle of the street to gossip. Some jerk always comes along and wants to use the road to drive on.

"Lucrative," she said, disgusted.

"Ludicrous, Eleanore. Ludicrous." I looked in the rearview mirror. It was nobody I could recognize right off the bat. "I've got to go."

"But what are you going to do about it?" Eleanore asked.

"What can I do about it?" I said, although I was already thinking about what I was going to do about it. Bill was my neighbor. I was sure he'd put aside his petty grievances about my chicken coop and my chickens long enough to have a sensible conversation about how a casino would change the town. Right? I would talk to him this evening when I got home.

"Torie, you have to do something" I heard her say as I drove away.

Four

The Finch estate was technically in New Kassel, but not within the city limits. It was off a two-lane road winding south between New Kassel and Greenwich. In between the two towns were farms, a few of those pop-up subdivisions in the middle of a field, thanks to low interest rates, and government land that I was hoping the government would forget it had. The front of the estate faced west and the back of it east, overlooking the mighty Mississippi.

The house actually sat in a valley between two large hills. A huge sandstone wall edged around the estate, separating it from the rest of the world as if it were a lonely green island. An elaborate "F" was curved in wrought iron on the gate. I got out and opened the gate, pulled my car in the drive and then shut the gate behind me.

As I drove up the driveway, I noticed that the house was three stories high, made out of what looked like the same sandstone as the wall. It reminded me of a small French château, complete with one turret that curved out from the south wall. This was going to be one of those buildings that had more rooms than I could find uses for.

I got out of the car and put the key in the lock of the front door. It was a red door that was rounded on top with an oblong window in the center. The key didn't work. The door wouldn't open. Great. I was going to be really upset if I had driven all the way down here for no reason. I walked around the building to try and find the back door.

An overgrown flower garden nearly assaulted me as I rounded the corner. The grounds had been kept mowed, so it surprised me that the garden had been left to Mother Nature. Who would have done that? A few bumblebees settled on the hollyhocks that were as tall as I was, and a butterfly floated somewhere above the black-eyed Susans. Unfortunately, there were as many weeds in the garden as flowers, and it took me a second before I could find the small red-bricked path that would lead to the back door.

The key worked on the back door and I was happy. I don't know what I was expecting on the inside of the house, but what I found wasn't it. Everything had been left just as it had been five years ago when she died. There was a five-year-old newspaper on the kitchen table, unopened mail scattered on the counter, dish towels hanging on the oven door. I held my nose and peeked in the refrigerator, which had been emptied. So, I assumed that somebody had come in just long enough to clean out the perishables and then locked the place up. I opened the dishwasher and inside were clean dishes.

Suddenly the thought of going through every item in this house seemed unfathomable. I made a mental note to make sure that when I got old I should just start giving stuff away so that nobody would have to come along after I died and do it for me.

To me, it seemed as though the bathroom would be the easiest place to start. Most of the things in the bathroom could be thrown away, especially given the date of most of the items. As if anybody would want or could use five-year-old shampoo. So I found the trash bags under the sink and then went into the great expanse of Catherine Finch's house to find the bathroom.

Finding the bathroom took a long time. I had to make it through a lot of house first. The great room was . . . well, great. A large cathedral ceiling with dark wooden beams was the canopy above a rather rustic room with a bearskin rug and a stuffed jaguar. On either side of the fireplace were two shelves of books. Cool. Books were good. A gorgeous stained-glass window lined the entire east wall. The stained-glass window depicted several fairies in different positions of flight, hovering above flowers or dancing amid the trees. It truly was one of the most gorgeous things I'd ever seen. I was awestruck, trying to imagine that it was actually made out of little pieces of painted glass.

Eventually, I found three bathrooms, two downstairs and one on the second floor. I started with the one downstairs closest to the kitchen. I opened the medicine-cabinet doors and just threw everything away. Under the vanities I did the same thing, except for a hair dryer and hot rollers that I found in the upstairs bathroom. Colin might be able to sell those. The washcloths I put in a bucket to use as rags and the towels I put in a pile on one of the beds. In no time at all, I had the bathrooms finished, with only a small pile of things to keep. Obviously, I pitched the personal-hygiene items. The woman loved Coral Mist lipstick and blue eye shadow. Her favorite perfume was Windsong, because the five bottles of it I found in the house were all half empty, whereas all the other perfumes were still mostly full. Funny that she was wealthy beyond my comprehension and her favorite perfume could be bought at Walgreens.

I opened my notebook and dug a pen out of my purse and wrote down a list of things to bring tomorrow: radio with batteries, fifty-to-sixty boxes, notebooks, packing peanuts/bubble wrap, travel playpen, crayons and coloring books for the girls.

I did not go up to the third floor, nor did I go into the basement, but I did take a quick glance through the rest of the first and second floors. There were no less than six bedrooms, a dining room, kitchen, great room, family room, den and, sure enough, three unidentifiable rooms. If pressed, I'd say that they were living rooms one, two and three. I couldn't imagine what was on the third floor, or what could possibly be in the attic.

In living room number two, on the second floor, was a black baby grand piano, and hanging above the fireplace was an oil portrait of a woman I assumed was Catherine Finch. In the portrait, she stood next to a fireplace in one of those long-waisted flapper dresses; her blond hair was bobbed short and curved under her ears. She wore bracelets on each wrist and a large necklace. Her smile was composed but, somehow, seemed all-knowing.

In the middle of the room a crystal chandelier hung too low, I thought, but what did I know about decorating big fancy houses? All along the mantel and the piano were silver and bronze frames filled with pictures taken in the twenties and thirties.

Yes, it all seemed quite daunting.

And the most daunting thing of all was the thought creeping in my mind about confronting the mayor about the gambling boats. But I loved New Kassel and I was not going to let the mayor bring in the casino. No way. I thought about that a second standing in the middle of living room number two. Even though I had this job to do for the sheriff and a job for Sylvia, my thoughts had meandered back to the threat of a casino. It was too important to me not to do something, but I wasn't sure what to do. I supposed it would depend on what the mayor had to say to me.

I made sure I had my list for tomorrow, picked up my purse and headed downstairs to return to New Kassel.

THE NEW KASSEL GAZETTE

The News You Might Miss
by
Eleanore Murdoch

My fellow residents of New Kassel! May I just say that the wedding of Ms. Jalena Keith and Sheriff Colin Brooke was the social event of the decade! Anybody who is anybody was in attendance. The cake was scrumptious, the party favors simply melted in your mouth. (Thank you, Helen.) Can everybody tell what my favorite part of the whole day was? Oh, the bride was lovely in a handmade crocheted dress from our very own Wilma Pershing, and the sheriff made hearts flip all over Granite County. The attendants were Jalena's daughter, Torie O'Shea, and her husband, Rudy. In other news, Father Bingham wants to thank whomever made the unusually large donation this past Sunday in the basket.

And now for the serious news. We as residents must not allow gambling into our home, which is our sanctuary. Vote No on Proposition 7. No riverboat casino!

Until next time,

Eleanore

Five

Velasco's Pizza is probably my favorite casual hang-out place in New Kassel. Chuck had decorated it in 1950s memorabilia, which he'd done way before the movie *Pulp Fiction* came out, so he liked to tell people that Quentin Tarantino had ripped him off. I tried explaining to him that somewhere in the world somebody else had probably thought of it before Tarantino did, that sometimes good ideas will be thought of simultaneously, but he resisted that notion.

It was later on Sunday evening, and Rudy, Rachel, Mary and I were all seated in a booth. Matthew was sound asleep in his pumpkin seat, which was cradled in one of the high chairs that we had turned upside down. Who would have thought that one of those straight wooden high chairs, turned upside down, was the perfect pumpkin seat holder? I thought about things like that and things like baby monitors, car seats, bottle warmers, bottle carriers that keep milk cold, and thermometers built into pacifiers, just to name a few. How did anybody ever raise a child without those things? It seems like the sixties were the Dark Ages. I don't think my mother even owned a diaper bag when I was a baby.

We were halfway through a half veggie deluxe and half pepperoni pizza when none other than the mayor walked into Chuck's. "There's Bill," Rudy said. He didn't really mean anything by that declaration. If Elmer or Wilma had walked through the door, he would have looked at me and said, "There's Elmer. There's Wilma." It was something to say.

"Yeah," I acknowledged, giving the mayor a dirty look.

"Don't talk to him about the casino thing right now, okay?" Rudy asked. "Let us eat dinner in peace, without making a scene."

"When do you suggest I talk to him about it? When it's too late?"

"No, now, Torie, quit being so touchy over everything," he said. He took a bite of pizza and made that slurp sound that means he nearly burned the roof of his mouth.

Rudy telling me not to talk to the mayor right now about the casino just made me want to waltz right over there and talk to the mayor about the casino. I wouldn't, though, because I didn't plan on holding anything back if Bill was unreasonable about it, and I really didn't want everybody else in the restaurant to witness it.

I wanted to be able to say to Bill that he was a complete money-hungry idiot, if the situation called for it, and how could I do that with an entire restaurant watching? No, I would refrain.

"Mom," Rachel said, "when are we going to get our school supplies?"

"This week, probably," I said to her.

"Cool!" she said and made a fist.

"I want a Backstreet Boys lunchbox," Mary said.

"You will get no such thing," I said. "You're six years old and you will get something befitting a six-year-old. Like Tigger or Pokémon."

Mary's expression dropped.

"What's a Backstreet Boy?" Rudy asked.

"Only the coolest band in the world," Rachel said.

"No, they are not," I said. "None of them play instruments, so therefore they cannot be a band. Am I right, Rudy? You have to play instruments to be a band."

"Last time I checked," Rudy agreed, "you must have instruments to be a band."

"Does Rachel get a Backstreet Boys lunchbox?" Mary asked with her lower lip looking impossibly fat and protruded.

"Mary, pick your face up before it gets in your pizza. No, Rachel's not getting one either."

"Mom!" Rachel said. Now her face was all droopy, too.

"They don't even make lunchboxes with them on it, anyway," I said. In truth, I didn't know if they did or didn't, but it seemed like the right thing to say. "So don't worry about it."

"If they did make them, would you let us have one?" Rachel asked.

"Nope."

The mayor sat down in the booth next to us, the vinyl seat making a scrunch sound as he did so. Rudy gave me that look. You know, the one that says, "Keep your mouth shut or I'm going to put my foot in it." He's so cute.

"Rudy," the mayor said and nodded.

"Bill. How ya doin'?" Rudy asked.

"Good, good." The mayor opened his newspaper and began reading.

"Your wife kick you out of the house?" Rudy asked him.

"No. She's visiting her sister," he said. "They're planning a baby shower for their niece."

"Oh," Rudy said.

"So, I'm fending for myself tonight," Bill said. He hadn't looked up from his newspaper. The restaurant lights made his bald head look shinier than it really was. Otherwise, I'd say that he had to buff it to get it that shiny. He was short and cantankerous and loved to bowl. From his backyard I could see into his family room, which was decorated in nothing but bowling trophies and bowling mementos. He even had his bowling shoes bronzed. Not that I ever really studied what was in his family room.

"I was supposed to eat one of those chicken potpie things," he said. "But I only eat those when my wife's watching. To me, pie should be made out of pudding or fruit."

"Won't she get wise to the fact that the chicken potpie is still in the oven?" Rudy asked. "I mean, I can't even throw stuff away, because Torie goes through the trash."

I nudged Rudy's leg under the table. He just smiled at me.

The mayor smiled and looked over at Rudy for the first time. "You think your chickens are getting that fat on the feed you guys give 'em? Hell, no. I give them whatever food my wife cooks that I don't like."

Rudy and I stared at each other across the table. We were both too flabbergasted to say anything: first, that he would actually do such a childish thing; and second, that he would admit it to us. And didn't that mean that our chickens were cannibals now? But that was Bill for you. He thought he was above any sort of code of conduct. In any arena.

"Well, gee," Rudy finally said. "Bill. You might ask next time. Our chickens are going to get hardening of the arteries."

"Ahh, pooh," he said and waved a hand in our direction.

We sat in silence a moment and then the mayor looked over and winked at Mary. She became all goofy and snarfed her pizza and waved back.

"How are you today, little lady?" he asked.

"Fine," Mary said. "Mom won't let us have a Backstreet Boys lunchbox."

When Mary spoke, all of her s's ran together because she was missing so many teeth. It seemed as if every tooth in her head had got loose all in the same month. We teased her that she was missing more teeth than she had teeth. I couldn't help but smile when she smiled because there were no less than four gaps in the front of her mouth.

"Well," Bill said. "Mean old Mom."

"Yeah," Mary said and then looked at me. Suddenly realizing I was sitting right there, she blushed and looked away. She was quiet a minute, and then out of nowhere she spoke like a true six-year-old, without regret or knowledge of what it was she was actually saying. "My daddy told my mommy not to talk to you about that casino thing."

The mayor said nothing. He only looked at Mary, with the color rising slightly in his face.

"He said that he wanted to eat in peace for once," she added.

It was my turn to squirm. My face grew hot.

"We never eat in peace," she added dramatically, with her eyes downcast.

And it didn't look as though this meal was going to be any different. "Mary," I said and tugged on her sleeve.

"You got something you want to say to me, Torie?" the mayor asked.

"Ahh . . . well." I looked to Rudy, who narrowed his eyes and tried to look as evil as he could. "Now that you mention it . . ."

"Oh, Jesus," Rudy said and threw his hands up.

"Well, Rudy, he asked," I defended.

"Yeah . . . but . . ."

"I think you're making a big mistake," I said to the mayor quickly, before Rudy could say anything.

"That's nothing new. You always think I'm making a mistake," he said.

"Well, that's because usually you are."

He didn't get angry as I thought he would. Instead he just laughed. "It's going to be voted on," he said. "The Gaming Commission gave me the go-ahead. If people don't think it's a good idea, they won't vote it in."

"Yes, but it shouldn't even be on the ballot," I said. "People have a habit of voting for things because it seems like a good idea and it's going to bring money and jobs."

"There's certainly nothing wrong with that," he said.

"Except they don't know the consequences of the monster that they create," I said.

"If they don't know the consequences, then how could you?"

I hate it when people ask such logical questions that you can't answer without looking like an idiot. "All I'm saying is people are misled by all the money and the promises. What they don't realize is a casino will compromise the integrity of the town. We don't want people stumbling around our streets at two in the morning after they've just lost a buttload of money and drunk enough to sink a ship. Even though we go to great lengths to 'sell' our town, it is still a community of homes and families. People live right next door to the shops and the restaurants, Bill. You know that."

"You're just afraid of change," he said.

Well, yes, that was true, but it had nothing to do with this. "Didn't you listen to anything I just said? If you came up with some other money-making gimmick that was geared for a historic town, I'd be all for it. A riverboat casino, with its flashy lights and music, and noisy people, does not fit our town. I don't care how much money it makes."

"That's the great thing about a democracy, Torie. The people of this town are going to vote on it, and for once . . . you have no control over it. You can't bully and finagle, wiggle, or talk fast enough to get your way. If the town votes it in, you can't do a blasted thing about it," he said and smiled at me.

Oooh, he looked so unbelievably smug.

"Really," I said. This was a challenge. He meant it as one, and I took it as one. "And just who is going to be out there campaigning for it?"

He smiled.

"And who do you think is going to campaign against it?" I asked.

He just looked at me and so I smiled deliberately back at him. I got up out of my seat then, and motioned for everybody else to get up. We were finished eating. I was ready to leave. As I walked past the mayor's booth, I leaned in toward him. "And who do you think, between the two of us, is the most liked and respected in this town?"

The mayor's face grew pale. "Yeah . . . my thoughts exactly," I said.

Six

"The nerve of him!" I stammered as I threw the car into reverse. The pavement was still wet from the showers that we'd received a little while ago. My tires spun, which actually made me happy. The tires spinning made me feel as if I were actually doing something with my anger. I know, it was juvenile. "Can you believe him?"

"Torie," Rudy said. "When was the last time you had your hormones checked?"

"Don't talk to me about hormones," I said through clenched teeth. I pulled out of the parking lot of Velasco's Pizza and headed for home. "The man is insufferable. What's more, he's turning our chickens into cannibals!"

"What's a cannibal?" Rachel asked.

"You are overreacting," Rudy said. "Don't give me that look, Torie. You know that you're overreacting."

I stewed in silence awhile as I made a turn and drove down River Point Road. I stopped at the stop sign, with Ye Olde Train Depot, which was now a restaurant, on my right and the old abandoned Yates house farther up the road. I sat there for a minute breathing deliberately, trying to cool my jets. Finally, Mary's tiny voice came from the backseat.

"It's a can of vegetables, silly."

"A cannibal is . . . is . . . oh, you tell her," I said to Rudy.

"I'm not telling her," he said. "You're the one who can't hold your temper. Get yourself out of this one."

I sighed heavily and gave the car some gas. The speed limit in town is ten miles per hour, so I had to make myself obey the law. Because I really wanted to gun it and break the sound barrier. Of course, for me that would have probably been about thirty-five miles per hour. We were moving slowly up the road when something caught my eye at the Yates house. I slammed on my brakes without thinking that somebody could have been behind me. Thank goodness it was just us on the street. "Did you see that?"

"See what?" Rudy asked.

Seat belts came undone in the backseat as Mary and Rachel clambered to the window to see what I was talking about. "Get your seat belts back on."

"What?" Rachel asked. "What did you see?"

"I think I saw a light," I said. I rolled Rudy's window down with the push of a button so that I could get a better view. The two-story house was basically a black silhouette with the moonlight sprinkling along the river behind it. The house had been abandoned for years, namely because when the river flooded, the Yates house always ended up with four feet of water in it, no matter how diligent our sandbagging efforts. No grass grew in the yard, and the paint had long ago curled and peeled off.

"There's no light. Nobody's lived in there for years," Rudy said.

"Maybe it's a ghost," Rachel added.

"It's not a ghost," I said. "No, Rudy, I saw something."

"So what? You want me to go in there armed with a supersonic pacifier and a couple of radioactive dirty diapers? Torie, let's get home and we'll call the authorities. Besides, it was probably just the light from a tugboat or a barge coming through the window."

"I don't think so," I said. "Look, there it is again."

"I saw it," Rachel said. "It's a ghost."

"Mom, she's trying to scare me," Mary chimed in.

Just then, blackness in the form of a man glided silently out of the house and along the edge of the river. "I knew it," I said. "There was somebody in there. What is that in his hand?"

I watched as the shadow picked up speed and ran along the river carrying something in his right hand. I could barely make it out in the moonlight but it was long and slender. The harassing sound of a car horn honked behind us, sending us all into adrenaline overtime. I think I actually squealed, and realized that I had once again stopped in the middle of the road. I gave my car some gas and headed for home, all the while trying to watch the person running along the railroad tracks until he disappeared behind the hill our house was on.

"You get Matthew; I'm going to call Deputy Duran," I said and ran for the door.

Ten minutes later Deputy Duran's squad car was stopped in front of the Yates house with its lights on and radio blaring. I drove my car down there to meet him because, quite frankly, I was too afraid to walk. I mean, what if the person came back?

"Deputy," I said. "Sorry to bother you."

"It's okay," he said. Edwin Duran was a few years older than I was and he had been the star quarterback for one of our rival Granite County teams, the Meyersville Lions. He was built like quarterbacks usually are, muscular, but his center of gravity was lower to the ground than with the big defensive players. He was a handsome guy for the most part, but he had huge ears and that always distracted me. "So, you and Rudy saw somebody inside with a flashlight?"

"Well, I didn't see the flashlight, I just saw a light coming from inside. I just assumed he had a flashlight," I said with an odd sense of being watched. I looked around nervously and finally settled back on Edwin's trusting eyes. "Then we saw somebody run out of the house and along the river. I'm not sure, but it looked like he was carrying a shovel or something with a long handle."

"Okay," he said. "I'm gonna go inside and check it out, make sure that there's nobody left in there, and then I'm gonna come back out and talk to you some more."

"Okay," I said.

"Did your mom and the boss make it to Alaska all right?"

"Yes," I said as he headed for the house. "They called this afternoon."

I got back in my station wagon and locked all of the doors and waited for Edwin to finish looking the house over. When he came out, he motioned for me. I fumbled with the lock and then got out of the car. "Well?"

"I want you to come look at this. Tell me what you think," he said.

"Okay," I said and headed inside with him.

As soon as I entered the house, I wished I hadn't. It stank of rotted wood and river sludge. And trust me when I say there's no smell like it in the world. We stepped over a few boards on our way to the main wall in the living room, which faced to the west. The darkness was suffocating, and I just knew that there were more things crawling around with six or more legs than I cared to know about.

"I know there's a lot of damage to the house," he said. "But this is different."

He shone his flashlight on a section of the wall that looked as though somebody had been hacking away at it. The other walls had cracks and peeling paint, but this was a concentrated area of fresh marks. "Could the perp have been carrying an ax?"

"I . . . uh, I suppose so," I said.

"Because this . . . this is looking like somebody just went at it with a sharp object," he said.

"What does it mean?" I asked.

"I don't know," he said in the darkness. He shone his flashlight up on the water-stained ceiling. "Maybe he was trying to get a jump on the demolition."

"Demolition?" I asked as Deputy Duran led me back toward the door. "Are they finally going to tear down this place?"

"Oh, yeah. What with the riverboat and all," he said.

"What do you mean?" I asked.

We emerged from the claustrophobic house to the familiar street. I knew every street, every building, every light and every crack in this town. As a child I had explored it on long summer days until the sun set and I was exhausted. As an adult, I savored it. I didn't wait for Edwin to answer. "What do you mean?" I asked again.

"Well, if the riverboat goes through, this is where they're going to put it," he said.

"What?!" I exclaimed. "But . . . but . . . it's less than a half mile down the road from my house. I will be able to see it from my living room window. And . . . and hear it! My God, where will everybody park?"

"Sorry, Torie. I'm just the messenger. If it means anything to you, I'm against it one hundred percent. We can only hope it won't go through. But I heard from Elmer, who heard it from Sylvia, that Bill wanted to go ahead and have the building torn down so that it will make a good impression on people. You know . . . 'Oh, look at this big empty spot that we have. We can fill it with a riverboat and make lots of money.' I think it's lame, but Bill thinks it's a great idea. They're supposed to tear it down on Friday."

Oh, this was too much. My head was reeling. In fact, it was reeling so much, I felt like just hurling my pizza. What did it say that our beloved mayor was willing to leave an abandoned, dilapidated building sitting in view for ten years? The eyesore of all eyesores in this town. He didn't want to spend the money for demolition because it was a hazard for our children. He didn't want to spend the money to have it torn down because it was a deterrent for tourists. No. But he could tear it down to try and convince people that we needed to fill the space up with a gambling casino.

"Torie?" Deputy Duran said.

"Yeah?" I asked. I had been off on my mayor-hating tangent in my head and missed what the deputy had said to me.

"I asked if you were all right?"

"I'm fine," I said. "So, what are you going to do about tonight?"

"About the prowler?"

"Yeah."

"Nothing much. I mean, I'll sit out here and watch it tonight in case they come back. And I'll make sure we patrol extra until Friday. But after that, I don't have to worry about it, since that's the day it's supposed to be tore down," he said as he put his hat on and headed for his car. "I mean, I am going to fill out a report, Torie. It's not like I'm blowing it off."

"I know, Edwin. I wasn't suggesting that you were," I said.

"Well, that look on your face. You look . . . disgusted."

"Oh, it's not with you, Edwin. Don't worry. It's not with you."

Seven

Monday and Tuesday came and went without incident. I did notice Deputy Duran parked on my street watching the Yates house on a few occasions, which made me feel good, but as far as I could tell, the perpetrator never came back. I busied myself with cleaning out the Finch house, but I had yet to make it to the second floor. On Wednesday I sat down to read the information that I had printed out from the Internet.

Rachel and Mary were in the backyard on the swing set. Matthew was asleep in the Porta crib in the living room, with our dog Fritz lying under the crib snoozing in harmony with him. This wasn't difficult for Fritz because he was a wiener dog, and he could lie under just about anything.

I set my Dr Pepper on the coffee table and then spread the papers out on the sofa. Tucking my feet up under me, I pondered which one to read first. Some of the articles looked like "official" Web page types of things, while others looked more like fan pages. I picked up the article closest to me and began to read:

Catherine Finch was born in September of 1904 in Granite County, Missouri. Her origins were

humble but she married railroad tycoon Walter
Finch in 1922. She embarked on a music career
that came to a grinding halt in 1938 when her
infant son was kidnapped in a scenario that
played out much like the Lindbergh kidnapping.

I put the page down. An uneasy feeling settled on me. I had forgotten about her baby. Actually, I really didn't know that much about the child. I just remembered hearing, as all native New Kassel residents have heard in passing, about the singer in the valley whose baby had been kidnapped. When Sylvia had asked me to write the biography, I hadn't realized that the singer in the valley with the kidnapped baby was Catherine Finch. I knew it, but I didn't *know* it.

I read on:

It was the summer of 1938 when Catherine was
awakened in the middle of the night by a garish
nightmare of her infant son being murdered. She
ran to the nursery to find it empty. The baby's
bracelet and blanket were the only things Mrs.
Finch found missing.

Unfortunately, Catherine Finch, the woman with
the voice of an angel, would never see her son
again. There was no ransom demand. There were no
threats. He had simply disappeared into the
night. For years, Catherine was plagued by young
men claiming to be her beloved Byron. For years,
Catherine believed that one of the impostors was
really her son, only to learn that he was the
child of a gypsy and was indeed trying to scam
her into leaving him her fortune. Catherine
Finch never saw Byron Lee Finch again,

nor did she ever sing in another public
appearance or record any songs. Her career ended
the night her son was stolen from his crib.

I was creeped out beyond belief. I wouldn't look at anything in that house the same way again. I would always look at it as the place where tragedy struck. I read the rest of the articles, which gave most of the same information that I'd just read, all the while instinctively looking up to check on Matthew. One article went into more detail on the type of music that Catherine had recorded and what some of her hit songs were. It seemed she was one of the few white women of the era to gain respect in the predominately black field of jazz.

One article went on to say that she died in 1995 and the reason that she had never moved was so that if the kidnapper ever wanted to find her, he wouldn't have any trouble. However, it also left an open door for all the reporters and impostors down through the years to harass her.

A favorite pet peeve of the press was that Catherine believed in the forest spirits and things of the netherworld. This was something, judging by the articles, that the press would hound her over, trying to get her to give more specific quotes. Evidently, she realized her error and would never speak of it again or answer anything of that line of questioning. In effect, she became a recluse haunted by her missing son, living in a world that looked at her belief in the "netherworld" as something to criticize her for.

I could not imagine what it must have been like to have had a wonderful career, gaining momentum with every record release, and then suddenly one day to find it was over because of an act of sabotage. And according to the articles, it wasn't over necessarily because the public did not want to hear her music anymore; it was over because she simply could not go on.

I heard the back door open and shut and knew the girls had

come in for lunch. I gathered up the articles and put them on the coffee table and went in to make grilled cheese sandwiches with Doritos.

•

I walked into the main-floor great room of the Finch house with that peculiar feeling of being watched. I had felt it Sunday evening when I was talking to Deputy Duran, and I felt it again now. My imagination, I knew, because there was nobody in the house except me, Matthew, Rachel and Mary.

I stared at the big stained-glass window with the fairies at play in the trees and grass, and I thought instantly of the articles that told about Catherine believing in the forest spirits. That was a politically correct way of saying that she believed in fairies and brownies and gnomes and selkies and a number of other things. If I hadn't read the article, I wouldn't have given this window a second thought. I would have just written it off as an eccentric taste in art. Albeit a beautiful example of an eccentric taste in art. The twenties, when this house was built, were a time of art deco style of furnishing. That era was also a time when people with money were trying something new. Shedding all of that Victorian and Edwardian stuffiness. But now that I had read the article, I realized that this window actually had held some sort of meaning for Catherine.

It also made me look at the books on the shelves a little more closely. They, too, revealed a passion for material on the subjects of the hereafter, ghosts and fairies. There was even a book on different winged creatures. Everything from angels to gargoyles.

I was deliberately saving her office to clean out for last. I figured that would be where I would find the most important information on her personal life: diaries, photo albums, that sort of thing. Right now, I was trying to get the bulk out of the way, things like lamps, statues, rugs, end tables.

Not everything in this house was old. In fact, living room number one on the second floor had all new furniture with two matching recliners and a nice big television. I made a note to ask Colin if he could give me a good deal on the television. It had a remote control. Something we still didn't have in my house.

I had just begun wrapping a bronze horse about two feet high when I noticed that Mary was missing. Mary missing is a bad thing. Rachel I could trust to find her way back without destroying anything; Mary, I could not. My youngest daughter was the type of child who just walked by things and they broke.

Rachel was seated on the big wingback mauve chair reading a book. Her hair was pulled back in a ponytail, which I always thought made her face look so innocent. It reminded me that she was still just a little girl, no matter how grown-up she acted sometimes.

"Rachel, where's Mary?" I asked.

"It's not my day to watch her," she snapped. She gave a big sigh and looked up from her book. "Tomorrow's not looking too good either."

It was at times like this that I had to remember never to let her innocent childlike demeanor fool me. She was really just a pimply-faced, hormone-laden teenager waiting to pop through the innocent outside shell. She was headed for teenagehood in all its glory. "You just lost bike-riding privileges for today and tomorrow."

"Aw, Mom. I'm reading; how am I supposed to know where she is?"

At that moment Mary came flittering down the stairs, spinning and dancing as if she didn't have a care in the world. Well, that would be because she didn't have a care in the world. That was my territory. At her age, it was her mother's job to do all the worrying.

"Where have you been?" I asked.

"Upstairs."

"You know you're not supposed to be up there without me."

"I was up-upstairs. All the way up."

"You went to the attic?"

"No, the third upstairs," she said. "And I found this!"

She walked over and handed me a sterling-silver hairbrush. A sterling silver *baby* hairbrush. Goose bumps broke out along my back and arms. I rubbed my arms self-consciously.

"I thought Matthew could have it. Maybe Grandpa Sheriff would let us buy it for him," she said with her slurred s's.

"W-where did you get this?"

"In the baby's room," she said. "Silly. Where'd you think I'd get it?"

"Rachel, stay down here with Matthew. Mary, take me to the baby's room," I said.

She knew what she was talking about because she led me up the stairs straight to the third floor, talking incessantly all the way about what fun she could have in this house. I had not gone this far up before. We walked down a broad hallway with a lavender runner down the middle of it. To my amazement, there were more bedrooms along this hall and a room that looked like Walter Finch's study. At the end of the hall, on the left, was the room that Mary had walked into, obliviously. I heard her as she went in. "In here, Mommy."

I entered the room and gasped, feeling the hair rise on the back of my neck and tears stand in my eyes. It was an old-fashioned nursery. I would venture to guess it had been kept exactly as it had been for over sixty years. Dust and cobwebs clung to the antique furniture and baby decorations. A redwork quilt, so popular in the thirties, had yellowed with age. I would lay money that this was little Byron Finch's room and that Catherine had never changed a thing.

In fact, stacked in a wicker holder there were folded cloth diapers, each with a scrolled "BLF" in blue embroidery. Stuffed animals lined the crib, and two pairs of shoes sat on the dresser. I opened the dresser, and it was full of baby clothes from an era gone by. Most were a faded blue or white. A few things in yellow. Almost all of them were cotton or linen.

The window through which Byron had been stolen away seemed larger than it should be, as if it were a portal to an evil world. An empty, lonely rocking chair sat next to it.

"Isn't this cool?" Mary asked.

I couldn't speak. I don't know what came over me. Maybe it was because I'd just had a baby boy less than two months ago and I could identify with Catherine Finch's anguish. Maybe it was because it was eerie standing in the room where a baby had been stolen and never seen again. Maybe it was because I knew that, other than Catherine and maybe Walter Finch, I was probably the only person to step into this room in sixty years. Well, and Mary. Whatever it was, I couldn't answer my daughter. I thought if I opened my mouth to speak I would cry.

I motioned for her to come out of the room and then I shut the door.

As we walked down the hallway I found my voice and chastised her. "Don't you ever come up here again," I said. "Do you hear me?"

As we descended the bazillion steps to the bottom floor, I was hit with the fact that I would have to go up there eventually and catalog everything in that room. I would have to catalog Catherine Finch's nightmare.

Eight

"They found a body!" Rudy said to me as I ate my Apple Cinnamon Cheerios.

"What?" I asked.

"Down at the Yates house," he said. My husband was breathless and his eyes were wide, and it wasn't from looking at me in my frumpy housecoat with my hair piled on top of my head.

I swallowed hard and realized that I hadn't actually chewed that last bite very well. I took a drink of orange juice to try and wash down a stuck Cheerio. "What do you mean, they found a body? Rudy, are you feeling all right?"

"Deputy Duran wants you ASAP."

"Why?"

"He wants to know if you can identify it," he said.

I suppose that's the downfall to knowing everybody in the town and everybody's business. "You mean, I have to go look at it?"

"Stop eating," he said and dragged me out of the chair. "He wants you down at the Yates house now. The coroner is waiting on you."

He was serious. He was totally and completely serious. I ran upstairs and threw on a pair of jeans and a faded pumpkin-colored T-shirt, slid my feet into my tennis shoes and headed down the steps. I finished the last of my juice and blinked at Rudy. "It would save us all a lot of trouble if it were the mayor."

"Torie! I can't believe you said that," Rudy scolded.

In truth, I couldn't believe I had said it either. I mean, we all have nasty little thoughts that we never vocalize. Sometimes I don't realize that I'm on loudspeaker. "I didn't mean that I wish he was dead. It's just that since there's already a body . . ."

"You're digging yourself in deeper," Rudy said. "You really need to get your hormones checked."

"Oh, pooh," I said and walked through the living room.

"This is exactly what I mean when I tell you that you don't have to verbalize every single thought that goes through your pretty little head," Rudy called out after me as I went out the door.

I looked down the street and saw the coroner, the sheriff's car, the wrecking company and, of course, the onlookers. As well as some tourists. Even though it was before eight on a Friday morning, people were out in droves.

A lead-colored haze hung in the air. The weatherman had said that it would be a "yellow-air day." Can I just say for the record that having to categorize our air quality is just plain old depressing?

I walked down the street as quickly as I could without running, and immediately I saw the mayor standing next to Deputy Duran. After what I'd just said about him, I was actually relieved to see that he was okay. Now if something bad happened to him, I'd swear it was I who caused it.

"Bill," I said and then looked to Duran. "Deputy. What's going on?"

"We were about to tear down the building," Bill cut in.

"One of the wrecking crew guys went into the house, just to make sure that there weren't any homeless people or hobos inside. Since we're so close to the railroad and the river, they thought there was a good chance that somebody might be in there," Duran said. "Seems that hobos in particular will travel the rail, jump off and stay in old abandoned buildings for a while."

"Uh-huh. And?" I asked.

"There's a dead person inside," the mayor said in a whisper.

"They found a body," Duran said as if the mayor had said nothing. "I know it was dark the night you saw somebody coming out of there, but I just want to see if you recognize him."

"Oh, Edwin," I said. "It was very dark. All I saw was a silhouette, really."

"Yes, but you might be able to determine if he was the right body type at least," he said.

"All right," I said. "Is he . . . I mean, what kinda shape is it in?"

"Come on," he said and started leading me into the house. "He just looks like he's sleeping. Of course, we'll do a complete autopsy."

As I walked into the Yates house, I saw Eleanore standing in the crowd. When she realized that I'd seen her she waved. God help me, I waved back. Maybe there *was* something wrong with my hormones.

"Until we get autopsy results back," Edwin said as we walked through the dark and dank living room, "I can't really say what killed him. I swear, though, he looks like he just came in here and went to sleep."

Even though it was daylight, we still needed Edwin's flashlight to get a really good look at the body. He flashed it on the man, and I would agree with Edwin that it looked as if the man had just curled up in the sludge and gone to sleep. Except that he was wearing a nice sport coat and shiny black shoes. Anybody who could afford decent clothes like this could afford a place to sleep other than a dilapidated building.

"He doesn't look like a hobo," I said.

"No, I didn't think so, either. Because of the nice clothes and good shoes," Duran said.

"Yeah, that and the fact that I know him," I said, taking the flashlight from Edwin. I shone it directly on the dead man's peaceful face.

Surprise registered on Duran's face. "You know him?"

"Well, not personally. I just know who he is."

"Who is he?"

"Patrick Ward," I said.

"Who?"

"He has a sister—oh, what is her name?" I said more to myself than to Edwin. "Patrick was an upstanding citizen of New Kassel until about twelve years ago, when he moved to Chicago."

"Chicago," Edwin said back to me. "Why in hell would a man who lives in Chicago come back here and end up in this building dead?"

"That would be the sixty-four-thousand-dollar question," I said with a shiver.

"How do you know all this?" he asked.

"I work for the Historical Society, and one of the things that Sylvia had me do when I first started working there was to compile genealogical charts of the citizens of New Kassel."

"Huh?" the deputy asked.

"See, people fill out the charts, as much as they can remember, including their siblings' names, et cetera. Then I put them on file. Then later, if somebody wants to research their family tree, we have a lot of it done on file already for them. Plus Sylvia just likes to know everybody's roots, for some reason. I remember the Wards because they were related to a few of the other families in the area and they were *Mayflower* descendants."

"I'm lost," he said.

"The Wards are descended from one of the original *Mayflower* passengers, and if there is one thing I never forget, Deputy, it's a person's family history," I said. "There's a picture of Patrick Ward in the historical society archives from about 1970. He donated a spinning wheel that had belonged to one of his ancestors in about 1780."

"You know," Deputy Duran said, "I really didn't think that you could identify the body when I had Rudy send you down here. I just thought you could tell me if he was the same build as the prowler we had the other night. I never expected this."

"It's a curse," I said. "And so far as comparing him to the prowler, I can't. It was too dark. But if it was him, what was he doing in here? What was he looking for? I mean, I don't know for sure, but I think he was pretty well off up there in Chicago. What was he doing here?"

"Why did he come back?"

"I don't know," I said. "Can we get out of here now?"

"Yeah," he said and led me back through the living room. Before we could make it to the door, something with lots of legs crawled across my foot and I jumped, screamed, and all but climbed on Deputy Duran's back.

"What?" Duran asked and whirled around with his hand on his gun.

"Nothing," I said, regaining my composure. "Something . . . with lots of legs."

"Oh," he said. "Sorry, I'm a little freaked out from all of this."

"Yeah, me too," I said, looking back over my shoulder at the dead man lying in the sludge.

"Hey, about those charts," Duran said as we emerged into the light of the hazy day. "Can you give them a look for me?"

"What for?"

"Find out who his sister is. The one whose name you can't remember. See if any of his family still lives here. He looks close to seventy, so he may not have any family left. But you never know. Maybe he was just visiting, got drunk and then got lost. Who knows, maybe he was an Alzheimer's victim and wandered away from his family."

"That's true. There may be no malicious intent here at all. Sure will," I said. "I'll get right on it."

I started to walk up the hill toward my house and then remembered something. "Hey, Edwin. Are they still going to tear down the building today? I mean, since it's a crime scene and all?"

"Of course we are," the mayor interjected from next to the squad car.

"Maybe," Duran said, throwing the mayor an evil look. "I'll let you know."

"What do you have to let *her* know for?" Bill asked as I walked away.

Nine

I felt like a mother duck walking down the street with my children trailing behind me, with Matthew in one of those backpack baby carriers. I wondered if there was any order to the ducklings when they followed their mother or if they just fell into place however they happened to leave the nest, as my girls did.

The heat rose off the brick of the Gaheimer house and I knew it was going to be a scorcher today. August is usually pretty hot in Missouri, though the first half of this month had been the exception to the rule. But even the heat was bearable; it was when the humidity settled in on the land like a warm wet blanket that you would lose your blooming mind and your air-conditioning bill would be in the triple digits. It felt as if it was going to be one of those days.

We walked into the Gaheimer house and immediately Sylvia was in the parlor like an ancient vulture ready to pounce on my children if they even looked as though they were going to touch anything. "Don't touch anything," I said to the girls, and then looked up and smiled at Sylvia. "Good morning, Sylvia."

"To what do I owe this visit?" she asked, her head shaking from age.

"I've come to look at the charts. I'm still looking at software, you know. I think it would be easier to put the information on the computer," I said as I headed back to my dinky office. My gaggle of ducks and I walked through the long parlor, everybody's shoes clicking on the floor. Sylvia had had the pine floors waxed recently. The sunlight coming in through the long windows took on a blinding effect once it hit the floors. I passed the soda machine in the hallway and then silently counted to five.

"Can I have a soda?" Mary asked. Like clockwork. I love being able to predict my children.

"Nope."

"Please?"

"Nope. You'll just have to go to the bathroom then. You can split one with Rachel on the way out," I said. "Sit down and don't touch anything."

Wilma Pershing appeared at the door. She was about two years younger than her sister Sylvia. Just recently she had started using a walker to get around. It broke my heart to see her have to use the walker because the Pershing sisters had always represented the independence that I hoped I would have at their age. Seeing Wilma with the walker just reminded me that eventually time gets everybody, and that was just depressing. I admit that it bothered me much more than it seemed to bother her.

She was pudgy, the epitome of the joyous old woman. She stood in the doorway and twirled the end of her hair around one finger.

"Children, children. All the children." It was also a very sad, well-known fact that she was becoming senile. More and more she made no sense and seemed to revert to childlike rhymes and repetitions.

"Yes, Wilma. All of the children are with me today."

"Hi, Wilma," Rachel said. Wilma just waved to her. Her expression changed as she realized that her sister Sylvia was coming down the hall and headed in her direction.

"Bye, children," she said and turned around and left. I had to wonder how much of her senility was real and how much of it was just to irritate her sister. Was this what I had to look forward to? Would Rachel and Mary try to irritate each other their whole lives? Would they never become best friends, as I'd hoped?

"So, it was Patrick Ward, was it?" Sylvia asked as she came into the office.

"Yeah," I said as I headed for the file cabinet. "How did you find out so quickly?"

"Elmer's son is the coroner."

"Oh, yeah. I forgot." Small town. News travels fast.

"What's Mr. Ward doing down here?"

"I don't know," I said. "That's why I'm here. Deputy Duran asked me to look up Patrick Ward's chart."

Sylvia left and never said a word. I brought the "W" file over to my desk and stopped when I saw a Norman Rockwell tin sitting on the edge. I opened it and inside were chocolate chip cookies. Another token from my mother. I couldn't decide if she was doing this because she felt so guilty for leaving or just because she loved me. I think it was a little of the first and a lot of the second. "Grandma left us cookies," I said to the girls with a smile on my face. "You want one?"

Both girls clambered to my desk and reached in to get a cookie. Mary took about seven until she saw the evil eye that I was giving her and then she graciously put two back. "Pig," Rachel spat at her.

Mary made an oinking sound. Maybe someday they'll be friends, I thought hopefully.

"How do you know the cookies are from Grandma?" Rachel asked.

I smiled. "Who else would they be from?"

"We have the greatest grandma," Mary said as she shoved another cookie in her mouth.

"Yes, you do," I said.

I sat down without leaning back so as not to squish Matthew, and opened the "W" file until I came to the chart that said "Ward."

Lanna, that was his sister's name. Lanna Ward. Patrick and Lanna Ward were the children of Louis Ward and Anna Smoots. Nobody had penciled in any death dates for Lanna, and Sylvia was usually pretty good about that. In fact, after I left today she would probably come in behind me and pencil in poor Patrick's date. So I assumed that Lanna was still alive. Spouses were listed. Lanna Ward was now Lanna Petrovic. I ruffled through the pages and found the chart on Louis Ward, and it said he had been born in 1901 and had died in 1978. His sisters' names were Tamara, who married Sheldon Danvers, and Catherine, who married . . . Walter Finch.

Catherine Finch.

Patrick Ward was Catherine Finch's nephew.

So what? People are related to people all the time. Right? This was just a coincidence. Catherine Finch hadn't been murdered. There was no ongoing investigation of anything, so what difference did it make if her nephew had just been found dead under mysterious circumstances? None. None whatsoever. Then why did I feel so weird about it?

Sylvia walked by the office and I called out to her. She stopped.

"Did you know that Patrick Ward was the nephew of Catherine Finch?" I asked.

"Yes."

"Sylvia, why didn't you say something to me about it when I first came in?"

"What difference does it make?"

"Well . . . none. I suppose. I don't know, I'm working on her biography; I just thought you'd mention it."

Sylvia simply shrugged and walked on. I picked up the phone and called Deputy Duran. He answered on the second ring. "Edwin, it's Torie."

"Yeah? Whatcha got?"

"Um, Patrick Ward's sister's name is Lanna Petrovic."

"Is she still in the area?"

"Well, the last address I have for her is not in New Kassel, but she's in Granite County. She's out your way, in Wisteria."

"Thank you so much. You really saved me a lot of time."

"No problem," I said and thought to myself: That is how a sheriff should react when you do something to help him. Unlike my stepfather, who resented any help that I gave.

"I'll let you know what the autopsy says. It's going to be about three or four days, though."

"Okay," I said. I wondered why in the world he was going to let me know what the autopsy results were unless it was just a courtesy, since I had identified the body for him. "I'll talk to you later, then. If you need anything else, let me know."

"Sure will."

I hung up the phone and looked back at the papers sitting on my desk. I couldn't help but take a closer look at the family chart for Catherine Finch. She and Walter had had three children: Cecily Finch, Aurora Finch and Byron Lee Finch. This stopped me because I hadn't really come across a reference to the two girls before. If Catherine and Walter Finch had had other children, then why were Catherine's personal belongings and house being sold to strangers? Why weren't any of the personal items in that house going to her daughters?

"Mom, can I have a soda now?"

"No," I said, without even looking up.

"Why?"

"You know why. There is too much sugar and caffeine. You don't need all of that stuff."

"Then why do you drink it?" Mary asked.

"Just shush for ten seconds," I said and tried to continue studying the charts. Catherine Ward Finch had had a sister named Tamara and a brother named Louis. I wasn't sure what else about that information sounded alarm bells, but something did. No matter how much I studied it, whatever it was that I was supposed to see didn't come to fruition, so I put it away.

I thought maybe it was time to start doing some firsthand interviews of Catherine's family. For the biography, of course.

Ten

Aurora Finch Guelders lived just across the river in Belleville, Illinois. On the west side of the Mississippi we tend to forget that Illinois is just a ten- or twenty-minute drive away, because we have no real need to go over there, save for the horse racing. Unless one is attending college at Parks, Belleville or SIU Edwardsville. Pretty much everything we need we can get right here on this side of the river. But the people on the Illinois side usually make trips to the Missouri side on a fairly regular basis. The reason? St. Louis is the largest metropolitan area closest to them. They come over for jobs and shopping, even for the excellent medical care.

I dropped the kids off at my Aunt Emily's for the two hours it was going to take me to visit Aurora Guelders. After making my way north on Highway 55, I swung a right and crossed the JB Bridge. That's local for Jefferson Barracks Bridge. Nobody ever calls it anything but the JB Bridge. The Mississippi seems wider up here than down by New Kassel. I'm not sure if it is or not. Maybe it's because down where I live there are high hills and cliffs, whereas this part of the Mississippi is surrounded by flat land.

Once in Illinois, I headed north on 255, where it would eventually connect with I-64. I know there is another way to get to

Belleville, but I don't know my way around if I take that way. It's amazing how, as soon as you cross the river, the landscape changes almost immediately to flat open land with highways that seem wide, uncluttered and clean.

Passing through East St. Louis always depresses me, so I tried to keep my eyes on the road, rather than have them wander over the dilapidated houses and junk piles.

The last time I had been in Illinois was to visit Cahokia Mounds. I love it there. They are what's left of Indian burial mounds built there hundreds of years ago. Of course, many of them have been bulldozed down through the years by farmers, who had no clue what they were destroying. All they knew was that they didn't want to put a cornfield on top of that unusually steep hill over yonder.

Now there are a museum and a slide show at Cahokia, and the last time I visited they even had Indian powwow dancing. Climbing the tallest mound is not something for those with weak cardiovascular systems, though. I was huffing and puffing by the time I made it to the top, but it was worth it. I could see for miles around, and off in the distance I could hear the haunting sound of an Indian drum. It is one of my favorite local excursions. Well, that and the horse racing at Fairmount Park. But I haven't been there in years.

I finally got off on I–64 and then took 159 south to Belleville. Aurora Guelders lived on the other side of the fountain in the middle of the town square. Every time I go through Belleville, I always end up following the fountain all the way around and going back the way I came. I hate that thing, and I am glad that New Kassel doesn't have one, or I would have gathered signatures by now to get rid of it.

I was paying extra attention this time to make sure I did not go full circle around the fountain. A few streets later I turned left, made a few more turns and pulled into the driveway of a red brick house with a large white wraparound porch. The street invaded the yard, giving an overall claustrophobic feel to the front of the house.

I parked in the street and then walked up the wide steps to the front door, scraping my pant leg on a yellow rosebush that was much in need of pruning. A warm breeze ruffled the flag that hung from the porch, and the smell of roses punctuated the air. I knocked and looked around, waiting for somebody to answer the door. A climbing rosebush was sprawling up the trellis like a wild pink blanket.

A white lace curtain moved in the door and then a face peered out. Finally, the door opened. The woman who stood there said nothing, but waited for me to give her whatever excuse I had for interrupting her day.

"Mrs. Guelders?" I said.

"You are?" she asked.

I knew from the records at the Gaheimer house that Aurora Finch had been born in 1931, but the woman who answered the door didn't look a day over fifty. She was slender, and a few inches taller than I was, making her average height. She had short salt-and-pepper hair and vivid green eyes. I extended my hand. "My name is Victory O'Shea. I live in New Kassel, Missouri. Maybe you've heard of it?"

That was dumb. Of course she'd heard of it. She had grown up there. Stupid, stupid, stupid.

"Yes," she said.

"It's not unlike Arthur and Arcola, Illinois," I said, thinking that I would get brownie points for knowing the names of some tourist towns in Illinois. So far, I looked pretty dumb.

"I doubt that you have Amish living in New Kassel," she said, and she was right. I just smiled. "What is it you want?"

At that moment I thought I could play both lead parts in the movie *Dumb and Dumber*. "Actually, I . . . uh . . . I work for the Historical Society, and, well, the president—"

"Sylvia Pershing?"

"Yes," I said, smiling and still on the porch.

"She's immortal."

"Possibly. Anyway, she has asked me to pen a few biographies on Granite County's more notable personalities. One of them is your mother," I said.

Her expression dropped all the way to her knees in two seconds flat. "I have nothing to say," she said and started to shut the door.

"Oh, please wait," I said and put my foot inside her door. I know that was really pushy and if somebody had done it to me, I would have been outraged. But I didn't know how else to get her to listen. "I'm also handling her estate."

Her green eyes narrowed on me and, if it was possible, turned a shade darker. I counted to five while she fought the internal struggle, whatever it was. "What do you mean, you're *handling* the estate?"

"Please, can I come in? You're losing all of your air-conditioning," I said.

She raised her chin and pulled herself up ramrod-straight. "Of course," she said.

The inside of her house looked as I'd imagined it would, rich colors and with lots of intricate lampshades and lace. Her house was what I call modern Victorian. It was Victorian, but not necessarily old-fashioned. I waited for her to tell me to sit down, because after what had just transpired on the porch, I didn't want to push my luck.

"Come to the kitchen," she said and motioned me through the house. We passed through the dining room, with a table that was set in full china display. Down the hallway hung photographs of what I assumed were her children. Pictures of a boy and a girl taken in the 1950s—that would be about right. And at the end of the hall were newer pictures of children taken in the seventies and eighties. Grandchildren, I thought. Catherine Finch's great-grandchildren.

We reached her kitchen and she motioned for me to take a stool around a breakfast bar. "All I have to drink is tea."

"That's fine," I said.

She poured us each a glass of tea and sat down opposite me. "Now, what is this all about?"

"My stepfather, who is also the sheriff, has won the bid on your mother's estate. He is away on vacation and asked me if I would catalog your mother's . . . things," I said. "And Sylvia also asked me to write a biography about her. It would be very difficult to write a biography about somebody without any personal interviews with the family and friends."

She said nothing.

"Mrs. Guelders?"

She suddenly fixed her gaze on me and then opened her mouth and spoke. "My mother grew into a very bitter woman who trusted nobody. Not even her own children."

"But—"

"Do you know that a woman is supposed to be closer to her daughters than anybody else in her life? After her husband and her own mother, her daughters are the closest things she has. I talk to my own daughter almost every day on the phone. How often do you talk to your mother?" she asked.

I looked down at the ice cubes floating in my tea. "Until two weeks ago, my mother lived with me," I said. "We are very close."

"And her mother?"

"My grandmother lives in the next town. I see her every week, I talk to her a couple of times a week. My mother talks to her every day," I said.

"I don't know who my mother was," she said. "I know who she was before 1938. And for about twenty years after that we had an amiable relationship, but never close. She could not get close to anybody because . . . I'm assuming you know about my brother."

"Yes."

"Because after that she couldn't move on. She couldn't get out of the old world long enough to see that there was a new one going on right in front of her. Our graduations, our weddings. She couldn't be happy about any of it because Byron was gone. After he disappeared, she held herself at a distance. Instead of becoming closer to us because of what happened, the separation increased. Then one day, she just turned her back on all of us. My own daughter never saw her grandmother after her sixth birthday," she said. "My mother lived alone. She died alone. You die by how you live, you know."

I hesitated a moment, letting that last part sink in. You die by how you live. "What made her change?"

"I'm not sure exactly. I have theories, none of which I need to share with you," she said and took a drink of tea.

I looked around, nervous. Her house was modest in the grand scheme of things. Especially compared to her mother's. But I had the feeling that she had money. Her wedding ring sported at least two diamonds that were about a carat each. The earrings she wore were real gold. The china in the dining room looked German, late 1800s. The furniture was good quality. In fact, there was nothing in this house that looked cheap or just thrown together.

"Well, you certainly have that right," I said.

"I don't need your absolution, Mrs. O'Shea."

I was feeling more and more ill at ease. My normal charms were failing horribly with this woman. I could always get people to talk, basically I think people ended up talking just so they could get me to shut up, but at least they talked. This woman, it seemed, had said all she was going to say, and I couldn't charm her for anything. I knew if I got tougher with her she would just clam up and probably throw me out of her house. So, I tried a different approach. I tried sympathy.

"Your brother . . ."

"You can read it all in the sheriff's files. Before it became an FBI case, the sheriff took all of our statements."

"All of whose statements?" I asked. I sipped my tea. Peppermint.

"Everybody who was there that night. I don't wish to talk about this."

"Okay, okay," I said. "I just wanted to let you know that his room—"

"The last time I was in my mother's home, it had been undisturbed. It was the same as it had been in 1938."

"When were you in her home last?"

"In 1957."

"It is still undisturbed."

I let that hang there in the air for a moment, wondering if she was going to let it dissolve or if she was going to grab it and expand on it. She let it dissolve.

"What is it you want?" she asked, irritated.

"I was . . . well, I was wondering if you or your sister would like a few personal items from the house before . . . well—"

"You don't seem to know what it is you want, Mrs. O'Shea," she said with a smile. "Are you suggesting that I pay for my own history? I will not. And neither will Cecily."

"No, no, that's not what I meant," I said. Man, this woman was tough. "What I meant was . . . if there is something in particular that you want. Maybe something of your father's. I can, well . . . I can either ask my stepfather if you can have it or I can just give it to you before I catalog it."

She looked a little surprised. "That's dishonest, Mrs. O'Shea."

"I would tell him later that a few items had been given to family. I just think that . . . I don't know what I think, Mrs. Guelders. It all seems terribly sad, such a waste. I mean, there is an entire house out there full of your family heirlooms and your history. It doesn't seem right that all of it is to be sold in an antique shop to tourists from other states and countries. You and your sister should have something, photographs, maybe."

The whole time I spoke, her expression never changed. She looked at me with the intensity of a bobcat. Yup. She was a bobcat, and I was going to be lunch if I didn't get out of there quickly.

I stood up. "I guess I'll be going. I've taken enough of your time."

I reached into my purse and set my card on the butcher block. "I still have to write her biography. If there is anything at all that you would like to add, please call me." Then I added lamely. "Or if there is anything else I can do for you."

She picked up my card with a well-manicured hand and smiled at me. She walked back through the hallway, leading me out, and then finally to the living room. "Have a nice day, Mrs. O'Shea."

"Oh, one more thing," I said.

"What's that?" she asked.

"When was the last time you saw your cousin, Patrick?"

"Patrick Ward?" Her eyes narrowed and her lips grew taut. It was clear she was irritated with me and probably wondering how I knew they were cousins.

"Yes, Patrick Ward."

"It's been years. Why do you ask?"

"He was found dead, Friday morning. In the old Yates house."

She blanched, but said nothing. Instead, she turned the door knob and ushered me out in pensive silence.

The door shutting behind me sounded deafening, but it wasn't really. She'd shut it normally. She wouldn't have breached any sort of etiquette in showing me out. It was my imagination. I imagined what she really wanted to do was slam the door after me.

I had never felt so thoroughly rejected. I had made no impact on her whatsoever. How could that be?

Eleven

The heat rose to 102 degrees on Saturday. I didn't feel like doing a darn thing, and so I didn't. Rudy barbecued, I read a novel, then watched a movie starring Ed Harris, which is always a treat, and relaxed. I was grateful not to have to go outside in this mess. Whatever I'd wear outside I'd have to peel off when I came back in, and I didn't feel like changing clothes. In a rare moment for Torie O'Shea, certified busy bee, I just wanted to veg out.

I was just getting ready to plunk around on the piano when the phone rang. I answered it on the second ring. "Hello?"

"Victory?"

"Mom! How are you?" I asked, delighted to hear her voice.

"Very good, how are you?"

"Hot. What's the temperature in Alaska?" I asked.

"About seventy."

"Aaargh. It's a hundred and two in the shade here and dripping with humidity."

"How is everybody?" she asked.

"Good. They're tearing down the Yates house. Hey, did you know that they are tearing down the Yates house so that the mayor

67

can put the riverboat casino in there? Did you know that riverboat gambling was even on the ballot?"

"Slow down," she said. "I'd heard through Colin that the riverboat gambling casinos could very well be an issue we were going to have to deal with in the not-so-distant future."

"Yeah, well, the future is here and it stinks," I said, looking out the kitchen window and watching Mary in her swimming suit play on the swing set. How come kids don't seem to be as affected by the weather as adults? When we visited my aunt in Minnesota, the kids lived outside in fifteen-degree weather, while Rudy and I huddled in the house, dressed in four layers of clothing.

"Take a deep breath," Mom said. "Colin wants to know how the estate is going."

"I've got all the rooms downstairs cataloged. I start on the second floor on Monday. I'm taking the weekend off, it's too hot to do anything. Hey, did you know that Bill bought the Finch house?"

She was quiet a moment. "Yes."

Even though I had posed it as a question, I really hadn't expected her to answer yes. I had expected her to say no and then I could go into my big speech informing her about everything. It sort of took the wind out of my sails. "You did? How come I didn't know it?"

"There are some things in this town, Torie, that you don't know. And believe it or not, it is not a sin," she said. I could tell she was smiling across the phone lines.

"But I work so hard at knowing everything," I said, whining. "Oh my God, I really am just a young version of Eleanore, aren't I?"

Laughter erupted on her end of the phone and we shared the laugh for a moment, even though I really was thinking to myself that I was becoming Eleanore. My mother took it as much more of a joke than I had intended.

"How's Matthew?"

"Good," I said. "He's smiling and cooing."

"Oh . . . I can't wait to see him. Well, I just wanted to call and check on the estate for Colin and tell you that we are having a wonderful time."

"I'm glad."

"Oh, wait, Colin wants to talk to you."

"Oh, wonderful. I mean, all right," I said. I winced as Mary dived off the swing into the yard, scaring the chickens in the coop to squawking and flapping their wings. Her face lit up with laughter. She obviously thought that was funny and so climbed back onto the swing to do it again.

"Torie," Colin said.

"Yeah?"

"I talked to Duran."

"Yes?"

"Is he . . . Do you think he can handle this?"

I knew he was referring to the death of Patrick Ward. "What are you asking me for?"

"Because I only know what Duran told me. You were there. Does it seem like this is a really bad one? Should I call in help from someplace else?"

"No, it looks pretty run-of-the-mill. I mean, we were wondering what he was doing in the house in the first place. He obviously wasn't a hobo or anything, but Duran is going to check it out with his family and see if maybe he was ill or drunk or whatever else would cause him to wander into the house," I said.

"All right," he said. "Duran has a way of not telling me the real seriousness of a situation when I'm out of town."

"Well, don't get your panties in a wad. It's not like he's lying to you. I think he just tries so hard to keep things under control when you're not around. He wants to impress you. I'm sure he doesn't want to disturb your honeymoon, either," I said.

"Okay," he said. "We'll be home in a week."

We said our good-byes and, God help me, I had the most horrible thought. I wanted to read the sheriff's files on the Finch kidnapping. Once Colin was home, there would be no way I could get access to them. So, if I was going to read them, I had to do it now.

I hung up the phone feeling really guilty. Might as well feel guilty now and get it over with.

THE NEW KASSEL GAZETTE

The News You Might Miss
by
Eleanore Murdoch

Yeeehaw! Everybody get ready for the Pickin' and Grinnin' festival coming up in September! We hope to invite back several of the same bands from last year's Blue Grass Festival, and add some new ones. Tobias Thorley is the man to speak to if you want to volunteer. Sign up at Fraulein Krista's Speisehaus and he'll call you. We need volunteers to make this run smoothly.

Everybody look out! Our dubious mayor has finally decided to tear down that eyesore known as the Yates house. Good riddance.

Oh, and Chuck Velasco is wanting to put together a winning bowling team this year. So, if you can bowl above 100, he wants to see you by September 1st.

And everybody, since school will be starting in a little over a week, please remember to look out for New Kassel's children as they make their way to school.

Until next time,
Eleanore

Twelve

Sunday broke like sludge. It seemed as if the sun were actually having to work at rising in the sky, fighting the haze trying to pull it down with invisible tentacles. It was going to be hot. I made a big breakfast for the family, took a shower, and slipped on the lightest shift dress that I owned. It was olive-green and all cotton and zipped up the back. I could not dress any cooler without getting arrested.

I drove out to Wisteria by way of the Outer Road, passing my Aunt Emily's farm. I honked at my Uncle Ben, who was out in one of the fields; he waved back. The air-conditioning dried the sweat on my face, and if I could have figured out a way to drive in the seat backward, just so my back could get dry, I would have.

As I drove along the two-lane blacktop, I passed the intersection for Highway P and thought how beautiful the sky looked. The sun was still in the lower half of the firmament, but little prisms of light scattered out from it because of the haze. How's this for optimism? Even though it was an ecological disaster in the making, it was beautiful.

New Kassel Outer Road became Main Street, Wisteria. At the first intersection, after two blocks of fast food heaven, I made a left and pulled up in front of the sheriff's department. Both Deputy Duran and Deputy Miller were working. Deputy Newsome would come in later, which meant that one of the first two would be working a double shift today.

Just for the record, I had no game plan for this. I was going to wing it.

I walked in and saw Deputy Duran sitting with his feet up on the desk, eating an Egg McMuffin. He jumped as soon as he saw me, bringing his feet off the desk and choking on his McMuffin. He coughed, clearing his throat, and then said, "Torie. Nice surprise."

"Hey, Edwin. How are you?"

"Good," he said.

I had thought about bringing some of my mother's apricot bars to segue into asking for the Finch kidnapping records, but that would have seemed like too much of a bribe, which was exactly what it would have been. But it didn't really matter, there weren't any left to bring. Yes, we had eaten them all.

"What brings you out on this Sunday morning?"

Oh, just the thought that your boss will be back this Friday and I want to coerce you into letting me see something I'm not supposed to see. What I said instead was a rather unbelievable "Nothing."

That was a dumb answer. "Oh, uh . . . I have to return something to Wal-Mart, actually, and just thought I'd stop by and see what Patrick Ward's family had to say."

"The damnedest thing," he said. "His sister said that he had no history of Alzheimer's, senility, seizures, blackouts, nothing. But the really funny part is that she didn't even know he was in town."

I just stared at him. "You mean he comes all the way down here to New Kassel to fall asleep and die in an abandoned building? That makes absolutely no sense whatsoever, Edwin. You know that, don't you?"

"I know, I know," he said, waving a hand at me. "Want some coffee?"

"No, thank you."

"I'm just gonna have to wait for the autopsy results, which should be tomorrow. I told the coroner I had to have a fast autopsy because the building is slated for destruction."

"So, you're thinking . . . foul play?" I asked.

"I don't know what else to think at this point. Like I said, I just have to wait."

"Hey, Edwin. If somebody was going to request an old file, how would they do it?"

"An old file where? Whose old file?" he asked, confused at the switch in subject matter.

"What if another sheriff's department, or the FBI or somebody like that wanted to request one of your files from like, pre–World War Two, how would they do it? I mean, where do you keep them?" I asked and hoped that he wouldn't ask me why I wanted to know.

"Why do you want to know?" he asked.

There was a long pause, too long, I thought. "I know somebody that lives in . . . Kansas City and they were just asking me."

"Oh, you mean like maybe for some genealogical thing?" he asked. He knew I was a genealogist and that I was always exhausting every new possible way to find information on my ancestors. I just refused to believe that there were some ancestors that I would never find.

"Sure, yeah."

"There's not really any genealogical information in old sheriff's files." He was deadpan.

"I know, but it helps to round out the ancestor."

"Well, about the most a civilian can hope to get at is the Civil Court records," he said.

"At the courthouse," I said.

"Yeah."

"But that's not going to give details of an investigation."

"You're right. Only if it goes to trial, and then there's the trial records, but I don't know if you can ever get access to those or not.

Not my expertise, Torie. Sorry." He finished off his McMuffin and my frustration grew.

"Yes, but what if somebody wanted to find out the details of an ancestor's investigation?"

"You can't."

"But . . . if somebody could, if you were in law enforcement. Where would you look?" This was harder than pulling teeth. Was I losing my touch? I was seriously beginning to worry.

"Well, we personally keep everything older than fifty years old downstairs in the vault. Just because of space. I don't know if the sheriff makes copies or anything like that. I really don't know. I just know that at the end of the year, he makes us take a big stack down to the vault. We have to keep them, because you never know when somebody is going to make a request for them," Deputy Duran said.

"And they're just in a vault? Like under lock and key?"

"Oh, no. That's just the nickname for it. It's just the basement, Torie." He laughed at my misinterpretation and I could have strangled him right then and there.

I talked small talk for a few more minutes and then I left. I went to Wal-Mart and killed a few hours and then went back to the sheriff's station. Only this time, I parked up the street and waited. I knew it was going to be a hot wait, but it would be worth it. Eventually, Deputy Edwin Duran would go to lunch.

Thirteen

Duran left for lunch at five minutes past twelve. He walked out, looked up at the sky as if in disbelief of the heat, got in his squad car and left. I had to be quick because I couldn't be sure if he was going to dine in or just go through a drive-through somewhere.

As soon as his car was out of sight, I got out of my car, leaving it parked where it was. I entered the sheriff's office; Deputy Miller was now behind the front desk. He was shorter than Duran and heavier, but about the same age as we were. He was not a native New Kasselonian. He was from out west, by Union, Missouri.

"Hey, Deputy. Don't get up. I need to speak to Vada about the Blue Grass Festival we're going to have in a few weeks," I said, walking toward the back where the basement door was. Vada forwarded a call to him and he picked it up. I just kept on talking, headed in the direction of Vada's office, who was the switchboard operator and receptionist rolled into one. "So I'm just going to go back there right now and talk to her. Okay? Don't get up. I know my way around."

I smiled sweetly. Miller looked at me as if I had just dropped in from Mars. Whatever. As long as he didn't follow me. Of course, the way my luck had been going lately, he would follow me. I listened intently for his footsteps to fall behind mine. The phone call kept his attention, though, and so, instead of going to Vada's office, I yanked the basement door open quickly and reached around for the light switch. I finally found it to my left, flipped it up, and I was in business.

I tried not to be negative, but there was no way I was going to get by with this. And if I did get away with it, I was thinking seriously about ratting on myself to the sheriff anyway just so he would fire Deputy Miller.

I descended the steps and stopped in my tracks. Duran wasn't joking. There were boxes piled everywhere. As far as I could tell, there wasn't any method to the madness, either. Somebody had had the insight to put the boxes up on pallets, so even if the basement got wet, the boxes wouldn't. That seemed to be the end of the engineering genius involved in storing the files of the Granite County Sheriff's Department.

Great.

Where to begin? Eventually, I noticed the dates on the fronts of the boxes gave way to dates from the 1950s, and they gradually got smaller the closer I got to the back corner of the basement. The boxes were stacked six or seven high, making them almost taller than me, and several deep.

It was cool in the basement, but humid. I felt soggy and itchy. I always feel itchy in attics and basements. Dust makes me hallucinate.

1940. 1939. 1938 had to be behind 1939. I moved the boxes out and, sure enough, found 1938. There were three boxes marked 1938. I'd thought for a minute that it must have been a record-high crime year, but then realized as soon as I opened a box that at least one box had been devoted just to the kidnapping of little Byron Lee Finch. How could I stand down here and read all of it in the remaining five minutes I probably had until either Duran returned or Miller finally got suspicious? I couldn't. Okay, *reading* something I wasn't supposed to read was one thing. Taking it off the premises was another.

I thought about it a minute. I guessed I could take the box up the steps and set it in the alley behind the station, leave through the front, and then go around and get the box. God, that sounded like . . . like I was doing something illegal. I had to find a way to do this that didn't make me come out looking like a criminal. Otherwise, my conscience would bother me so much that I wouldn't be able to go through with it. Blast my mother anyway, for teaching me right from wrong.

Okay . . . think. I guess I could just take the box out past Miller and tell him that Vada gave it to me. It was . . . a list of bluegrass bands. What were the chances that Colin would find out? Okay, don't answer that. What were the chances that Colin would find out before I could get it read? That seemed much less likely.

Okay. I picked up the file box and headed for the steps. I opened the door slowly with my foot, just in time to see Deputy Miller heading out the door. The phone call must have been an emergency. That meant that the only person in the building besides Vada was . . . me. I headed quickly for the door, knowing that Vada couldn't see me from her office where she answered the phone.

And then . . . I hesitated. Somewhere in the depths of my mind, my mother said, "Victory! You're not really going to do this. Are you?" I looked back at the basement, over to the hall where Vada's office was. Back to the basement. I looked over at Colin's football poster and felt the biggest twinge of guilt in my life.

I couldn't do it.

Besides, if I got the information that I wanted this way, it would just cheapen what I was doing. I would tilt the delicate balance between the *Jerry Springer Show* and *60 Minutes*. I would be on the Jerry Springer end of the journalistic spectrum, and I didn't want that. I never wanted to be on the Jerry Springer end of anything.

I was about to take the box back to the basement when Deputy Duran pulled up in his car. As he got out of his car, I saw him through the glass in the door as he rounded the front of the squad car carrying a bag from Kentucky Fried Chicken. He whistled, tossing his keys up in the air, and I thought, *I'm caught. That's it. It's the end of my career as an award-winning biographer before I even get the first page written.* Not to mention that Sylvia would probably fire me.

And I would never get to see what was in this file.

Edwin was on the sidewalk now.

I had a momentary lapse, thinking, could it really hurt anything that bad? I mean, what could it hurt to take this file box?

Jerry Springer?

60 Minutes?

Victory!

Or my mother?

Edwin's hand reached for the door.

Don't ever think that your children don't listen to you, because I just proved that somewhere, on some level, they do. I put the file box down next to his desk and smiled at him as he came in. He looked a little taken aback, like . . . well, the way my stepfather looks when he's seen me more than once in a week. It's as if he's hoping the building doesn't fall down or something.

"Torie," Edwin said.

"I have a huge favor to ask of you, Edwin."

"No," he said and put the KFC bag down on the front desk.

"What do you mean, no? I haven't asked for anything yet."

"Yes, but the boss told me that whatever you asked for I was to say no."

"What if I was asking for an ambulance?"

He thought about that a minute. "You wouldn't ask me for an ambulance. You'd call 911."

"Okay—"

"No. His exact words were, 'No matter what my stepdaughter asks for, and she'll probably ask for something, tell her no.'"

78

My ears grew hot. I was grateful I hadn't yet cut my hair so it was long enough to cover them. "But, this is—"

"No."

I needed to change my tactic. "But, he already said yes."

Edwin stopped and looked at me strangely.

"He already told me yes," I repeated.

"Then why do you need me to do the favor?"

Good question.

"See, you know that I'm cataloging the estate of Catherine Finch, right? Well, Sylvia asked me to write a biography on her as well. And Colin said that I could . . . that whatever I needed, I could have for the job."

Those had been his exact words. He just hadn't been talking about the same job that I was referring to.

"What?"

"Plus, you could call Sylvia and ask her if I'm on the up-and-up."

"What? What do you want?"

I cleared my throat and reached for an earring to twist. "I need to read the stuff in this box." I pointed to the box at my feet, which had been hidden by the desk leg. Duran looked down and realized that I had one of the files that I had been asking him about earlier.

"No."

"Come on," I said.

"No."

"Colin said that whatever I needed to do this job, I could have. I just need to read it. I'll sit over there," I said, pointing to an unoccupied desk. The brown paneling would drive me loony, but I could suffer through it for half a day to get to read this.

"No."

"What if I got permission?" I asked.

"Permission from who?" he asked, and took his red-and-white box of chicken out of the bag and opened it. He took a deep breath, inhaling the aroma, and then set it down.

"Since Catherine and Walter are both dead, I could get permission from one of their daughters. If I got permission from one of their children, would you let me read it?"

"No."

"Ugggh," I said and slapped my forehead. I should have just stolen the damn thing when I had the chance.

Fourteen

A rap at our front door sent me into a mild panic. Mostly because it was only eight o'clock in the morning on Monday and Rudy had already left for work. Matthew was on the kitchen table in his pumpkin seat, and the girls were putting on their shoes. Phone calls and knocks at the door at unusual times always made my heart flutter just for a second.

I answered the door with a dish towel thrown over my shoulder and no shoes on. A man of extreme height, with graying hair and severe black eyes, stood on the step. It made me wish that I had at least checked through the peephole before opening the door because now he had the upper hand. But that's living in a small town for you. You never expect the person on the other side of the door to be a stranger.

"Mrs. O'Shea?" he asked.

A stranger who knew who I was, no less.

"You are?" I asked.

He produced a business card from inside the breast pocket of his blue suit. It was at least ninety degrees at eight o'clock in the morning and he was dressed in a suit. Yet I could not see a single trace of sweat. I hate people like that. I sweat big-time. It's so unladylike, but I can't help it.

The card read "David Newton" and included an address, a phone number and an e-mail address. But no title. So, basically, it still didn't tell me anything. Before I could ask the question ready to spill from my lips, Mr. Newton finally spoke up.

"I'm an antique dealer," he said.

"Sure you are," I said and handed him back his card.

He looked taken aback and cleared his throat. I'm sorry, but all of the antique dealers I know are broke. He put out his hand, which I shook cautiously. "I am David Newton and I assure you I am an antique dealer."

"Then why doesn't your card say that?"

"Can I come in?" he asked.

"Nope."

He laughed nervously and stuck his hands in his pant pockets. "I understand that your stepfather is handling the Finch estate?"

"You are mistaken," I said and started to shut the door.

"Norah's Antiques is not owned by your stepfather?"

"Norah's Antiques is owned by my stepfather."

"Then he is handling her estate."

"No, he bought her estate. He owns it. There's no handling it," I said. "What do you want, Mr. Newton?"

"I deal in very rare pieces, Mrs. O'Shea," he said. He looked past me into my house. "Are you sure I couldn't come in for just a moment?"

"Nope," I said. "And next time, please visit me at my office."

"Please," he said. "I'm looking for a piece . . . it is said that the last owner of it was Catherine Finch. I would be willing to pay top dollar to your stepfather if he would consider selling it to me."

Tobias Thorley drove up the street and honked at me. I waved to him. Mr. Newton looked around, confused. I guessed he wasn't used to neighborly people.

"What piece would that be?" I asked.

"Well, there are two, actually."

"What are they, Mr. Newton?"

"There's a necklace, it's a scalloped piece with a rather large pearl in the shape of a teardrop. The necklace itself wouldn't be worth that much on its own, if it weren't for its pedigree. It was owned by Alexandra Romanov. The necklace is worth a *mint*," he said.

I was lost in thought for a moment. It had never occurred to me that Catherine Finch would have had things in her home that would be priceless or have historical significance. It made me wonder a moment if Colin was indeed smart enough to know what he had. If Mr. Newton hadn't shown up here today and brought my attention to the piece, would Colin have sold it to some unknowing tourist for a hundred bucks? Or, worse, would he have sold it for a hundred bucks to some scalping dealer who would have turned around and sold it for thousands? That seemed much worse.

"Mrs. O'Shea?" Mr. Newton asked. "Have you seen the piece of which I speak?"

"No, I haven't." It was the truth. I had not made it to Catherine's bedroom or office. I had only cataloged the first floor.

Mr. Newton handed me back his card. "Would you give this to Mr. Brooke—"

"Sheriff Brooke," I corrected.

"Sheriff Brooke, and tell him that I will pay him the highest price, if he would sell it to me. I specialize in royal pieces," he said.

I took the card and looked into his eyes. "What was the other piece?"

"Hmm?"

"The other piece that you were interested in?"

"Oh, a piece of music. Sheet music. It was a piece written for Catherine by Henry Stoddard, although I don't think she ever recorded it. The music is in Stoddard's handwriting. Stoddard was my uncle, so it has a personal meaning."

That probably didn't mean that he wouldn't be willing to sell it, though. "All right," I said. "I'll tell him."

"I appreciate that, Mrs. O'Shea," he said. He nodded his head and sort of clicked his heels together. I guess that was his way of saying good-bye to me, but it reminded me of Hitler or Colonel Klink, so I chuckled. I sort of waved as he walked down my steps to his car. As he got to the edge of the sidewalk I remembered something I had wanted to ask him.

"Mr. Newton," I said.

"Yes?"

"How did you find me?" I asked. He looked at me as if he didn't know what I meant. "How did you know that I was cataloging the estate for Sheriff Brooke?"

"I didn't," he said. "When I went by Norah's Antiques, the young woman working there, Bridget's her name, said that he was on holiday and that his stepdaughter was the only person in town who would have contact with Mr. . . . I mean Sheriff Brooke before he got back. She told me where you lived."

Another drawback of a small town. Everybody thinks that everybody else has friendly intentions. Mr. Newton probably did have friendly intentions. He probably did just want to buy a necklace. But he could have been a serial killer, for all Bridget knew. I turned back into my house, shut the door and set Mr. Newton's card on the top of the piano.

The phone rang. First a knock and now a ring. I answered the phone in the kitchen on the second ring. It was Deputy Duran, sounding chipper and wide awake. He probably started his shift at six in the morning.

"Torie," he said.

"Yes?"

"The autopsy is back."

I was a little surprised to see Deputy Duran calling me over the autopsy after yesterday's fiasco. "And?"

"It was murder."

Shock kept me from forming any coherent sentence. I was sure that I had misunderstood what he'd said. How could it have been murder? Why would it have been murder? "What . . . I uh . . . How?"

"Evidently, whomever he had seen earlier in the day poisoned his clam chowder."

"I still don't understand."

"Sometime on Thursday, Mr. Ward ate a bowl of clam chowder and it was poisoned. A slow-working poison," Duran said.

"So, then do you think he just wandered into the Yates house because he was starting to feel bad, or hallucinating? Or do you think he was headed there for a purpose and just happened to die in there rather than somewhere else, like behind the wheel of his car?" I asked.

"Your guess is as good as mine. We're going to go over the crime scene one more time and then demolition is going to go ahead before Mayor Castlereagh has a stroke," he said. "So, I just wanted to let you know that the house is coming down sometime today."

"All right," I said.

"Oh, and Torie?"

"Yeah."

"About yesterday. I hope that you understand. About the Finch file."

"Yes, I understand. In fact, after sleeping on it, I've come to the conclusion that you've probably saved me from doing something that would have caused me great humiliation." My cheeks grew hot just from the thought of it.

He laughed and that made me feel good.

"Can I ask a favor, though?" I asked.

"Sure," he said.

"Can you not tell Colin? Please?"

"Sure thing."

"I plan on asking him if I can read the file when he gets back."

"Okay, well, I'll talk to you later then," Duran said.

"See ya, Edwin."

Fifteen

ictory?"

V I looked up from my desk to see Sylvia standing in my office doorway. She looked pale today, in a beige double-knit pantsuit that was probably made when I was in the first grade. "Yes?"

"Have you gotten any work done on the biography?"

"Well," I said, looking toward my children playing Pictionary in the corner. I didn't want to lie with them in the room. "I haven't actually written anything, but I'm making tons of notes and I have done an outline."

"Good," she said. A tremor caused by age had taken hold of Sylvia in the past few years. She always looked as if she was shivering. She gazed at me just a minute too long and I knew that there was something wrong. Sylvia usually barked her orders or reprimanded me and moved on. If she lingered there was something that she wasn't saying.

"Sylvia? Is there something you want to tell me?"

"I'm sure it's nothing."

"What?"

"It's Wilma. She's in the hospital."

"What?" I exclaimed. "Why? Is she all right?"

"She thought the kitchen chair was the toilet," she said. "This morning, she mistook the kitchen chair for the toilet."

That was hardly something to put somebody in the hospital for. When I was eight years old, my parents were having a dinner party. I was fast asleep and got up and peed in the kitchen trash can. They didn't put me in the hospital for that. "What else, Sylvia? Surely there is more to it."

"Then she couldn't remember who I was," she said. Her voice cracked, giving away more emotion than I would guess she wanted to. "And she didn't know who she was . . . so I called the doctor. He said to take her to the hospital."

For the life of me I couldn't figure out why she hadn't told me this right away. But that's Sylvia for you. If she had told me as soon as she saw me, she would probably have been too emotional. Asking me about the biography gave her a chance to even out her emotions.

"I was wondering if you could go by and see her. We have no family. Except for each other," Sylvia said.

And that pretty much said it all. Sylvia was all Wilma had, but, more important at the moment, Wilma was all Sylvia had.

"I don't want her to get too lonely. I can't stay there all the time, you know. Could you go by with the kids this afternoon? She's at Wisteria General. She loves your children," she said.

"Well, of course. My gosh, Sylvia. You don't even have to ask. Have you called Father Bingham? I'm sure he'll send the nuns over to visit as well. Everybody in New Kassel loves Wilma. She won't be alone."

"Would you call him for me?"

"Sure," I said.

With that Sylvia walked away. She and Wilma were all that was left of their family. They had had an older brother who was long dead, and he had had two children who were both dead now too. I suppose he had had grandchildren, but I didn't think that they lived anywhere in Missouri, much less New Kassel.

I wasted no time in phoning Father Bingham, who in turn was as surprised as I was and said he'd be right over. I rounded up my kids and headed out to Wisteria General.

•

Hospitals can be places of great joy but also so depressing that you feel your spirit sink to your toes as soon as you enter the building. It just depends on your reason for being there. A birth or a surgery that saves a life, and you think the hospital is the greatest place ever. But that same building can turn into a dark vortex, sucking the life right out of you if you're not there for a happy event.

Wilma lay in a hospital bed with one of those generic blue-mint gowns on, looking totally out of place and devoid of identity. I knew it was Wilma but it wasn't Wilma. I left Rachel in charge of Mary and Matthew in the waiting room, something I shouldn't have done because Mary will push her older sister to the limit of adolescent patience, but what else was I to do? They wouldn't let the kids come back to the room. It wasn't officially visiting hours.

I reached out to touch Wilma's arm and she jumped before I even made contact. She opened her eyes and looked around the room, finally resting her questioning gaze on to me. Her hair was down, long and silver, wrapping itself around oxygen tubes and IV lines.

"Wilma?" I asked.

"Did you bring me something to drink?" she asked.

She thought I was a nurse.

"Wilma, do you know who I am?"

Her blank stare answered the question for me. Tears welled up in my eyes and a lump instantly grew in the back of my throat. She was afraid, I could tell. She wasn't afraid because she didn't know me. She was afraid because somehow she knew she should have known me and didn't.

"It's Torie," I said.

"Torie," she repeated in a voice so quiet I had to strain to hear it.

Just then the nurse came in, bringing her one of those combination plastic-Styrofoam pitchers of water and a cup. She smiled at me and I tried to smile back, but I'm sure the tears glistened in my eyes. "Has the doctor talked to Sylvia yet?" I asked the nurse.

"Sylvia?" she asked.

"Her sister."

"I believe so," she said.

"And? What's the prognosis?"

"Are you family?" she asked.

I looked to Wilma, whose skin was so paper-thin that her purple veins looked as if there were no skin to cover them. Her hands were folded on her stomach. She always had her hands folded. "Yes," I said. I had known her my entire life. My mother has a photograph of me sitting on her lap during the bicentennial celebration in New Kassel. And I still have the first embroidered potholder that I made when I was six, the result of Wilma's kind and loving determination to try to find a trace of girl in me. Yes, she was family.

"I'll send the doctor in," she said.

"Thank you," I said.

After about ten minutes of watching Wilma doze in and out of consciousness, the doctor finally came in. He looked at me and smiled, his teeth extremely white against his dark Indian skin. He extended a hand and told me his name, which I couldn't have spelled, let alone pronounced.

"I'm Torie O'Shea," I said.

"Wilma, unfortunately, doesn't have a whole lot of time left," he said.

My heart sank. The news shocked me more than if somebody had told me that John Wayne had been a Communist. Why? Lord, the woman was in her nineties. How much time *could* she possibly have?

A vision flashed in front of me of Sylvia all alone in that big house. *Older people have a tendency to give up once they lose their closest relations.* I had read that somewhere.

"She is very weak and her heart is old and tired. I'm afraid that the heart is not getting a proper supply of blood to her brain."

"Has she had a stroke?" I asked.

"No, no. She simply isn't getting enough oxygen. She can't remember things very well and she is a danger to herself. However, most often at times like these, the patients will start to experience ministrokes and heart attacks until they pass away."

Pass away. Wilma? No way. My eyes filled with tears, I looked away from him to Wilma, lying there oblivious to the fact that two people were discussing her death right in front of her. "But . . ."

"She is very old, ma'am. She has lived a long and good life."

"Yes, but . . ." I couldn't speak. What did I expect? Did I expect her to live to be a hundred? What then? A hundred and ten? A hundred and twenty? I looked back to the doctor and tried to smile. "Thank you, Doctor."

I walked swiftly by him out to the waiting room, where I gave a whistle and Rachel and Mary stood up to meet me. Rachel took one look at me and the color drained from her face. "Mom, are you okay?"

"Why are you crying, Mommy?" Mary asked.

"Wilma is very sick," I said to them as I unlocked Matthew's stroller.

"Where are we going?" Rachel asked.

"Home," I said. "We need to go home and make some phone calls. I need to find a baby-sitter for you so that I can come back. I . . . I need to talk to Sylvia."

"Is Wilma gonna die?" Mary asked.

"She's very sick" was all I could say.

Sixteen

Traffic wound up River Point Road and was at a complete standstill. Traffic. In New Kassel. What the heck was going on? I thought about it a minute; it was just too hot to make my car wait very long with the air-conditioner grinding and God knows what in the middle of the road. So I turned around in Charity's driveway and decided to go the back way. I'd go up Hermann Road and come down over the hill. It took me a few extra minutes, which in my current state probably took a week off my life. I wanted to get home and I wanted to get home quickly.

As I came down over the hill, the river was on my left and the swell of houses on my right had all the trappings of suburbia. Roses, marigolds, manicured lawns and my next-door neighbor's prized magnolia tree, which isn't native to Missouri. I could also see past my house and my neighbors' houses to where the Yates house stood. Or at least used to stand. The demolition crew was there, along with the emergency vehicles, the sheriff's cars, the neighbors and the coroner.

The coroner?

"Mom, what's going on?" Rachel asked.

A heavy sigh escaped me and I gripped the steering wheel

tighter. My hands were sweaty, the result of too much anxiety. "I don't know," I said and passed my house up.

At the foot of the hill, where the river started to curve just slightly, I pulled in behind Deputy Duran's squad car and got out. "You guys stay in the car," I ordered. "And don't touch anything."

The faces greeting me were long and grim. Especially the mayor's. The building had indeed been torn down and some of the rubble had been stacked off in what was the Yates house backyard. Deputy Duran, having made eye contact with me from across the piles of garbage and the crowd of people, headed straight for me with his head hung low.

"What? What is it, Edwin?" I asked.

"You're not going to believe this," he said.

"Another body?" I asked.

"Sort of."

"Sort of? Is there or isn't there?" I asked, searching his eyes for whatever it was that he wasn't telling me.

"When they started clearing away the rubble, one of the demolition crew found a skeleton."

"A skeleton."

"An infant skeleton," he said. "In the wall."

"A wall baby," I said, dumbfounded.

"A what?" he asked.

"It seems as though putting a baby in a wall was a good way to hide an unwanted child."

"Huh?"

"I know, hard to believe, but it has happened. Young girls who could hide their pregnancies would dispose of their babies that way when they were born," I said.

"That's awful," he said. "I wonder if that's what happened here."

"It's either that or . . ."

"Or what?"

"Or somebody wanted to cover up the death of an infant."

No sooner had the words left my mouth than the world began to spin, and goose bumps danced down my arms and spine. Edwin seemed to be in a vacuum somewhere, because I could barely hear what he was saying. Something about how they almost missed it, but then a piece of drywall broke. And on and on he went.

"Byron Lee Finch," I said. My own voice sounded faint and far away from myself.

"What?" he asked.

"I'll lay you dollars to doughnuts that the body is Byron Lee Finch."

Edwin looked totally confused for a minute. Then the clouds cleared in his mind and some recognition flashed in his baby blues. "Wait a minute . . . isn't that—?"

"Catherine Finch's baby that was kidnapped sixty-something years ago," I said.

"Well . . . you don't know that for sure, Torie."

"Well, no, but jeez, Edwin. A baby is kidnapped less than two miles from here and a body never found—no ransom note, no nothing—and now there's a baby skeleton in the wall! I'll betcha it's Byron Finch." I shivered at my own hypothesis.

"The files you wanted," Edwin said. "That's the case you wanted to read, isn't it?"

I nodded and looked past him to the mayor, who was wiping the sweat off his brow as he leaned against a wrecker. Poor Bill. This whole demolition thing was wearing him down. He just couldn't get that house torn down smoothly for anything. Inwardly, I smiled.

"And guess what?" I said.

"What?" he asked. Bless his heart, he was beginning to sound just like the sheriff when he was exasperated.

"Patrick Ward was Byron Finch's cousin. How much of a coincidence is that? Patrick Ward ending up dead in the building where his cousin was put in a wall back in 1938?"

"Whoa, whoa, whoa. Torie, you don't know that the baby in the wall is Byron Finch. This is just pure speculation," he chastised me.

"Yeah, but it feels right," I said.

"Well, you can't go around paying attention to your feelings, for crying out loud. Who knows what kind of catastrophe will strike," he said.

"Torie! Torie!" I heard a voice from the crowd. I turned and found Eleanore standing there in an orange tank top and shorts and a bright green hat. She looked like a giant pumpkin. She waved me to her. I held up a finger.

"God, I wish Sheriff Brooke was here," Edwin said. "He's gone three weeks and all bloody hell breaks loose."

Indeed, Edwin looked severely concerned about his new predicament, as he should be. The sweat trickled down between my shoulder blades as the silence fell between Edwin and me, as disconcerting as it was thick. "Can I see it?" I asked.

"See what?"

"The bod—skeleton."

Edwin looked at me long and hard. I knew what he was thinking. He was hearing the voice of my stepfather, his boss, telling him to say no to me no matter what I asked. But at the same time, Edwin needed some grounding, and I knew if there was anybody present who could make him feel better, it was I. It was just a matter of whether his insecurity would win out over his boss's orders.

"All right," he said.

I would say that I was almost gleeful, but as soon as I got over the fact that I had won, it hit me that I was going to have to look at a baby skeleton. I told him just a minute and ran back to the car to make sure the kids were okay. The car was running and the air-conditioning blowing enough to make Rachel's hair fly back from her face.

"You guys all right?" I asked as I stuck my head in the door.

"Yeah, we're fine," Rachel said. "What's going on?"

"Nothing. Edwin wants me to look at something. Okay? Be good and don't touch anything," I said.

"Can we turn on the radio?" Mary asked.

"Sure, just don't turn it up too loud," I said. "Matthew is sleeping."

My gaze lingered on Matthew for a second. He was finally starting to fill out with baby fat beneath all of that loose-fitting skin that infants are born with. I took a deep breath and walked back to Duran with more determination than I really thought I had. Since I'd asked for this, I couldn't act queasy now.

He led me over to a pile in the middle of what was the Yates house. Lying there beside a piece of drywall was the skeleton of a baby about twenty-four inches long. I have no idea if this was the position it had been found in since the drywall had fallen all around it. But it was lying on its side, with one hand up by its head. The skull looked abnormally large compared to the rest of the body, as baby's bodies are out of proportion.

Something caught my eye. "What's that? Next to the body?"

Edwin knelt down and moved away debris. He took out a handkerchief and picked it up. "A diaper pin," he said.

My stomach lurched and I felt instantly dizzy. If it was at all possible, my face grew hotter than it already was. Somehow a diaper pin made it more personal. It wasn't just a skeleton in a wall. It had once been a baby. A real-live baby, with fat feet and pink cheeks. Like the one in my car. And it had either been put in this wall dead or put in there alive and left to die. It was gruesome either way.

"Oh my God, Edwin," I said. "Let me see that."

He handed the handkerchief to me in the palm of my hand, with the diaper pin lying face-up. I didn't want to smudge any of the dirt away, because it was evidence. But from what I could make out, it was either silver or silver-plated and had what looked like a fairy etched in it.

"Are you okay?" he asked. "Please, don't get sick on me."

"No, no, I'm not going to get sick. It's just that . . . How do you stay removed?" I asked.

He looked up at me with moist eyes. "I don't."

Seventeen

Before I could make it to my car, Eleanore grabbed my arm. "Is it him?"

"Is who what?" I asked.

"The skeleton. The baby. Is it Byron Finch?"

Seems I wasn't the only one jumping to the logical conclusion. "How do you know there was a baby skeleton found?" I asked, looking around the crowd of gatherers.

"One of the wrecking crew yelled out, 'Hey, Sheriff, looks like a baby skeleton in here!' We all sort of abducted that to mean that there was a baby skeleton found," she said.

"Deducted. Not abducted."

"So it's true?"

"Eleanore, don't go around spreading gossip," I said. What was I thinking? That was like asking a dog not to hike its leg. "We don't know anything yet."

Just then I saw Rudy walking down the street. He, too, had gone in the back way and parked in our drive. I forgot Eleanore was there as I jogged up to him and threw my arms around his neck. "God, am I glad to see you."

"What's going on?" he asked.

"The sky is falling," I said, still clinging to him. Oxytocin is powerful stuff. All I had to do was feel his arms around me and I started to calm down.

"What do you mean?" he asked.

"When they went to tear down the Yates house, they found a skeleton in the wall." I looked into his eyes for dramatic effect. "An infant."

"What?" he asked, confused.

"I think it's Catherine Finch's baby," I said.

"No," he said. "I'm sure it is some other baby."

I wasn't sure if Rudy was trying to convince me it was some other baby so that I would feel better because I was sort of involved with the Finch family, or if he was just hoping it wasn't Byron so I wouldn't be more involved. Really, it could go either way.

I let it go for now. I had more disturbing news to tell him. "And Wilma is in the hospital. Her heart is failing."

Rudy didn't look shocked when I told him. He looked unbelieving. As if what I had just said was so preposterous that he wasn't even going to bother reacting to it. Finally he closed his eyes, and when he opened them, he believed me. "Oh, no."

"We have to make some calls," I said. "My mom will want to know."

"No," Rudy said. "Don't interrupt her honeymoon."

"Rudy . . . if Wilma dies and my mother wasn't told, she is going to be fuming. She'll leave tire tracks on your backside."

"You're right," he said. "I'll meet you at the house."

I just stood my ground watching the coroner's gurney being pulled out of the wagon. This was the first time a child of any age had ever been found dead in New Kassel. At least in the last fifty years. Before that I'm sure nineteenth-century disease took its toll on the children here as it did everywhere.

"Torie. It could be another baby," he said again.

"How many babies disappear in New Kassel, Rudy?" I asked.

"That baby could have been there for hundreds of years," he said.

"No."

"How do you know?"

"Because the Yates house hasn't been there for hundreds of years." Just then it dawned on me.

"Torie?" Rudy said in his best parental voice.

"I've got to go to the office. Drive the kids home for me, okay?"

"Torie!"

"I'll be home in half an hour."

As if he believed that. I took off at a brisk pace toward the Gaheimer house. I cut through Charity's backyard, careful not to step in any flowers or dog doo. Running wasn't something that I indulged in when I was perfectly healthy, much less only eight weeks postpartum. One should only run when being chased. But I did cover the ground to the Gaheimer house at a pace a little quicker than a walk.

When I made it to the Gaheimer house, it was locked. It stopped me for a minute, because it was never locked. Not until Sylvia went home for the evening. Then I remembered that Sylvia had probably left early and gone out to Wisteria General. Not a problem, I had a key.

I had a key on my key ring in the ignition of my car.

I hate it when I do stupid things. As I was about to go back to the house to get my key, I remembered that Sylvia kept a key in the back. I went around back and remembered that the thing I loved about summer was its long days. The sun was up when I awoke and nearly up when I went to bed. If it had been any other season, I'd be fumbling around in the dark back there. But it was about six in the evening and the sun was still cooking. I found the key on the inside of the wooden flower box, hanging in front of one of the back windows.

I let myself in through the kitchen and went straight to the basement where we kept the files. Even if we put everything on computer, any self-respecting historian would still keep the original documents, so this basement would always be in use. Unless I could talk Sylvia into moving the files upstairs to the den or something.

I pulled on the chain and the basement was awash in amber light. I went to the filing cabinets and found the one I needed. In the third drawer down was the housing developments file, and the history of buildings in New Kassel. I was thinking of compiling a "Then and Now" type of book on the town, but Sylvia was convinced it would be too expensive to make.

And there it was. The ground was broken for what we now call the Yates house in 1938, and the house was finished in late 1938, early 1939. It was built by Roy Thurman. The Thurmans lived in the house for a while and then, when the flood happened in the forties, they decided to move to higher ground. The house went through several owners in the forties and fifties, until finally Lyle Yates bought it in 1961. He and his family lived in it until they too got tired of fighting the floodwaters of the Mississippi and moved out in the nineties. I was there when he said he was too old to sandbag. FEMA was willing to pay him for his flood damages, so he took the money and moved out of Granite County to Festus.

Bill had never been willing to pay the wreckers to tear down the house. Until now.

I cannot tell you how disturbing it was to think that the Yates family had lived there for thirty years with a dead baby in their wall. I was convinced that the baby was Byron. I would have bet that whoever kidnapped him had dropped him in the unfinished wall of the Thurmans' home. When the contractors came along, they did not know the baby was there, and they finished the house. It would work if there were open sections that hadn't been dry-walled at the time.

I shivered as I thought of something more sinister. What if one of the Thurmans had kidnapped Byron and then closed him up in their own wall? Why? Why kidnap a baby and then never ask for a ransom? Unless they were a childless couple and just wanted their own child. But then that wouldn't work, because the townspeople would have noticed that overnight they had acquired a nine-month-old baby. A nine-month-old baby that remarkably resembled Byron Finch. His picture graced the cover of every newspaper for weeks. The Thurmans would have had to move. But they hadn't.

The only reason I could come up with at the time would have been that they kidnapped Byron and, for some unforeseen reason, he died. Then they were forced to dispose of the body.

I suppose the question tickling at the back of my mind was whether or not the Thurmans knew the Finches.

Of course, I suppose I should wait to see if it really was Byron they had taken out of that wall. And then, there was always the possibility that there would be no positive identification. With only a skeleton left, there wouldn't be much to go on, except the things found in the wall.

The diaper pin.

I shut the drawer, headed up the steps and went to retrieve my car. I was going out to the Finch estate.

Eighteen

I agreed to meet Rudy and the kids at Wisteria General as soon as I was finished at the Finch house. I left him to make ravioli and phone calls. There are days when I think that I am the most terrible wife and mother in the universe. But then I think about all the psychotic people who come out of perfectly structured homes and I figure my kids will turn out all right.

I have to admit that when I pulled into the driveway of the Finch estate, I expected thunder overhead and Vincent Price music to play. I also hated getting out of my car to open the heavy wrought-iron gate. I shoved and it squeaked. I hopped back in my car and noticed that there were clouds forming on the horizon, the setting sun turning them crimson and orange underneath. It had been a pretty dry summer, the farmers would welcome rain.

I drove up the driveway, anticipating and dreading what I might discover in Byron's nursery. I got out, unlocked the back door and went in. There were boxes and covered furniture everywhere on the bottom floor, due to my half-finished cataloging job.

I went first to the second floor, where Catherine's office was, partly because it was on the way to the third floor and partly because I was putting off going up to the nursery until the last possible moment.

Her office was done in blond wood and lavender fabrics. The desk was a monstrosity of turn-of-the-century woodworking at its best. A large oil painting hung on one wall, featuring what I assumed were Catherine's three children. Cherubic faces stared out at the artist with nearly textbook innocence. They each wore a gauzy outfit of pastels and were situated perfectly in front of one of the house's many fireplaces.

Catherine's desk was covered with old photographs in antique frames; most of the photos were of her with other people. One of the faces I recognized was Benny Goodman. The type of music she sang wasn't Big Band or swing, so I assumed that she and Goodman had just been friends.

I opened the drawers one by one, looking for an address book or a party list, something that might tell me if the Finches knew the Thurmans. I found an address book. Names had been crossed off, I was assuming as the people died or moved. There was no listing for anybody with the name of Thurman. I did find a list for a caterer, musicians, maids, housecleaners, you name it. Everything Catherine would need to throw a party for the rich and famous.

In the closet I found boxes on top of boxes of letters, tied in bundles about three inches deep with purple crochet string. A sofa by the window held pillows with a cross-stitch design of some sort, and the light fixtures in the wall were antiques that had been wired for electricity. This was a room well used and well loved.

I went back downstairs and found one of the small boxes I had brought in earlier last week. I took it back upstairs and put the address book, the lists, a few of the bundles of letters and a journal of some sort in the box. I looked around the room one last time to see if there was anything else that might be of importance.

On a shelf in the corner I spotted three photo albums. I opened them and they were the old kind with black pages and corner tabs on sepia photographs. Beneath the albums I found two old tins, also full of photographs. I put them in the box.

Then I went upstairs to Byron Finch's nursery. I tried not to look around too much. I went straight to the changing table and found a silver tray. Silver boxes with carved lids sat on top of it, and I opened each one, looking for diaper pins. In the third one, I found eight or so diaper pins. They looked exactly like the one Deputy Duran had shown me at the Yates house. One side of the large sterling pins was flat. A fairy with her wings spread wide was etched into the silver. Just as on the one Duran had found.

I shivered from the inside out.

Nineteen

Rudy and I were awakened by a pounding at the door. After we had come home from the hospital last night, I had stayed up until midnight reading Catherine's journal, so the sleep did not clear from my eyes very easily. At first we just lay there, waiting to hear if the noise would come again, because when one's sleep is interrupted this early, in this manner, it's as if your mind is playing a trick on you. Did I really hear that knock on the door?

Bang, bang, bang.

Yes, I really did.

Rudy and I both jumped at the same time. I glanced at the clock. 7:02 A.M. I couldn't imagine who it could be. I threw on a robe, tripped over Fritz snoring on the floor beside the bed, and took the steps two at a time. Rudy followed close on my heels.

We gave each other a worried glance as Rudy turned the knob and opened the door.

Somebody snapped our picture, the flash momentarily blinding me. At that point it was as if the world gained speed. A small microphone was shoved in my face and a wiry man with sandy-blond hair began speaking so fast, it hurt my head to keep up. All

I understood was something about Somebody from Somewhere News, wanting to know about Byron Lee Finch.

"Uh . . ." That came from both Rudy and me.

He went on firing questions at us until finally I held up my hand and screamed, "Stop!"

He looked at me oddly. He was perfectly still; the only sign that he was alive was the blink of his eyes.

"Who the hell are you?" I asked.

"I'm Colby Stevens from the *Newsworthy*. I understand that the body of Byron Lee Finch has been found and that you have intimate knowledge of the case," he said and put the microphone back in my face.

"No comment," Rudy said.

"Nobody knows whose body was found," I said.

"My source says that it's the body of the kidnapped baby of one of the most famous singers of the jazz era," he said.

"Your *source* is jumping the gun," I said.

"No comment," said Rudy.

"Is it true that you have intimate knowledge of the case?" he asked.

"No comment," Rudy said.

"No," I managed.

"Is it true that you're writing a biography of Catherine Finch and that you have access to all of her personal papers?"

"No comment!" Rudy yelled and slammed the door in Colby Stevens's face. Then he turned to me. "What the *hell* was that?"

"I have no idea," I said. It was obvious that Rudy didn't believe me. "Don't look at me like that; I really don't know."

"Deputy Duran isn't spreading it around that the body found was Byron Finch. So, who is?" he asked.

"Rudy, I'm not the only person who thought instantly that it was Byron Finch. I mean, a kidnapped baby makes a national sensation—almost as big as the Lindbergh kidnapping—and sixty-something years later a baby skeleton is found in a wall less than two miles from the scene of the crime. I mean, it doesn't take Einstein to jump to those conclusions," I said.

"My head hurts," he said. "I need coffee."

He headed for the kitchen and I followed. "But in case you're interested, I'm positive it is Byron."

"Oh, of course you are," he said, reaching for the coffee in the canister.

"The diaper pin that Edwin found is identical to the ones I found in Byron Finch's nursery. It's him, Rudy."

"So, it's him."

"I'm just saying, I'm not going to be the only person to put two and two together and get four."

He held his hand up. "Just don't talk to me until the coffee at least starts to perk."

"All right," I said and ran my hand through my hair. I was walking over to the cabinet to get out my Cheerios when the phone rang. I immediately thought of Wilma. Phone calls at unusual hours are usually bad news. I grabbed it on the first ring.

"Hello?"

"Is this Torie O'Shea?"

"Yes, it is."

"This is Amanda Hauer and I'm with the *Post*. I've been informed that you are Catherine Finch's biographer. What is your comment on the wall baby found yesterday in your small town?"

"What is going on?" I asked, dumbfounded.

"Ma'am. Do you deny having knowledge of the wall baby?"

"No comment," I said and hung up.

Rudy shook his head. "Don't speak until I've had at least one sip."

I leaned up against the counter and ate Cheerios right out of the box. I watched Rudy as he watched the coffee perk. He wore blue-and-green-plaid boxers and a Ramones T-shirt. His hair stood up on end and his mouth was wide in a yawn. Finally the coffee was done and he poured himself a cup. As he took a drink, his eyes rolled back in his head and an exhausting sigh escaped over the rim of his cup.

"Now, what is going on?" he asked.

"I don't know. Somebody must have leaked that there was a baby found in a wall and people have jumped to conclusions," I said.

"Why are they calling you?"

"I guess somebody has let it out that I'm cataloging the estate or writing a biography or both," I said.

"And who would that be?" he asked.

I thought a minute. Bright orange shorts stretched tight across a top-heavy body appeared in my mind's eye. "Eleanore. She's the only one."

The phone rang again.

"Don't answer that," Rudy said.

"I can't go all day and not answer the phone."

"Don't answer the phone until we get Caller ID."

"Rudy, that's preposterous," I said and answered the phone. It was my mother. "Mom! Am I glad it's you."

"We're coming home," she said.

"What? Why?"

"Wilma is sick and Deputy Duran called and told us about the baby skeleton," she said.

"Mom, isn't it like three in the morning there? Why are you guys up so early?" I asked, popping a handful of Cheerios into my mouth. Rudy slurped down more coffee.

"Our flight is at five, so we had to get up this early," she said.

"So Duran called you?" I asked.

"Yes. And we actually heard it on the late news," she said.

"You're kidding."

"No. Dead babies are headline news, I suppose. Not that many of them. Plus, I think most people are thinking that it's the Finch baby. Imagine if somebody had the chance to solve the Lindbergh case today. It would be all over the news," she said. "I suppose this is about the same."

"Unbelievable," I said.

"Bill will be happy. Free publicity for the town."

"Oh, great," I said and shook my head. Rudy never took his eyes off his coffee cup.

"How's the casino issue going?"

"It's been really quiet. There's a lot else going on. I think Bill was focusing on the Yates demolition. Thank goodness," I said.

"All right, well, we'll talk more when we get home. Can you or Rudy come and pick us up at the airport?"

"Certainly," I said.

She gave me the flight number and time of arrival and said good-bye. I hung up the phone and the kitchen was perfectly quiet. The only noise in the room was the coffeepot sizzling every time water bubbled onto the surface. Finally Rudy put his cup down on the table and looked straight ahead.

"So, Colin's coming home early," he said.

"On his white horse," I said snidely.

Finally Rudy looked at me, circles beneath his eyes. "It must be the Finch baby if Colin is leaving Alaska early."

"Yeah, that's what I thought."

Twenty

I picked up my mom and Colin at Lambert Field later that afternoon. To somebody born and raised south of St. Louis, North County can seem like a completely foreign country. So I made sure I watched the signs carefully, exited where I was supposed to and crossed my fingers a lot. To me, Lambert Field is far enough away to be a day trip.

I knew my mother would get irritated if I talked while trying to load everything in the car, so I waited until we were away from the airport and safely southbound on I–270. Even with all the clouds that had formed yesterday, only a few drops of rain had actually fallen, which just made it stickier outside. I threw the AC on high.

"How was your trip?" I asked.

"Splendid," my mother said. "Colin got sneezed on by a moose."

I looked in the rearview mirror at my stepdad blushing all the way to his shirt collar.

"I would have paid good money to see that," I said.

"Very funny," he said.

"It was very funny," Mom said. "He was totally covered in moose snot, he had to go back to the hotel and take a shower."

It was quiet a second and then my mother burst out laughing and, begrudgingly, Colin followed from the backseat. I, of course, chimed in because it was a joke at my stepfather's expense. Sheriff Brooke covered in moose snot. The fact that I had not been there to see it just shows you how completely unfair life is.

"Did you miss me?" I asked.

"Yes," my mother said.

"No," said Colin.

We chatted a few more minutes about how beautiful Alaska was and how relaxing their trip was. I was hoping Colin would be the first to bring up Byron Finch and the strange goings-on in New Kassel as of late. If I had done it, my mother would have probably berated me for it, whereas if he did it, it was his job. A few minutes later, I got my wish.

"So, what's the scoop, Torie? And don't even try and tell me that you don't know anything about what's going on, because you would be lying," Colin said.

Instantly he went from stepdad to sheriff. I even felt different talking about the whole Finch mess than I had talking about him and the moose snot.

"Okay, here's what's happened as far as I know." I took a big breath and then let it rip. "Bill tells me they are going to introduce riverboat gambling for the next election. So, I find out he wants to tear down the Yates house, because that's where he wants to put the casino. Of all places. So, sometime last Thursday night, Patrick Ward has a bowl of poisoned clam chowder and he wanders into the Yates building and dies."

I put on my blinker and got over in the right-hand lane. "Then, Friday, they go to tear down the building and they find a baby skeleton in the wall. But the bizarre thing is that Patrick Ward, although he's originally from New Kassel, has lived in Chicago for the last twelve years or more. He has a sister who lives in Wisteria but she didn't even know he was in town. Which makes no sense whatsoever. So then, I go to the Finch house and find that the diaper pins there match the diaper pin that Duran has found with the wall baby, so I'm almost positive the body is Byron Finch."

Gravois passed and I knew the next exit was Telegraph, then finally Highway 55, which would lead us home. I had to be careful not to miss it in my excitement of telling the story. "Now the really weird part is this. Patrick Ward and Byron Finch were first cousins," I said, looking in my rearview mirror at Colin. "Is there anybody on the planet who is going to believe that was a coincidence? I'm betting he knew that Byron was in the wall."

"Wait, wait, wait," Colin said, undoing his seat belt and leaning forward. "Let's just say for one minute that the baby is Byron. And let's just say that Patrick knew that Byron was in the wall. Why would he go there? Why would he come all the way from Chicago to be in the Yates house that night?"

"I don't know, but you need to put your seat belt on. You're going to get me a ticket," I said. "And we wouldn't want that to happen, now would we?"

He let out an exasperated sigh and put his seat belt back on.

"I think that somehow, Patrick Ward found out that Bill was going to tear down the Yates house, and I think that he was trying to get the skeleton out before the wrecking crew found it and the whole world did like we did—assumed it was Byron. Thus bringing the story back to the front-page."

"Which would mean he had something to hide," Colin said.

"That would be my guess."

I let the silence hang in the air for a minute. "Which brings me to the next bit of news."

"Oh, no," he said.

"The media has gotten a hold of it. I had two reporters this morning try to get me to comment on what is going on," I said.

"How did they find out?"

"This particular time, I think it was Eleanore. But you know, Colin, it really was just a matter of time until they found out by other means," I said.

"True. But it could have bought us some time to at least get something together. The FBI will probably be visiting, too."

"Which brings me to the next bit of news."

"Can it get worse?" he asked. He held his hand up. "No. No, don't answer that."

"I tried to convince Duran to let me read the original sheriff's file on the Finch kidnapping," I said. Out with it. If he heard it from me, he wouldn't be as angry as if he heard it from Duran. "Which he refused to do."

"Remind me to give him a raise," Colin said.

I ignored the little remark. "No, now listen. I'm doing her biography, and if her children don't care if I see the file, why should you? The FBI came in and took over the investigation, but still, there should be preliminary stuff in there. You know, like who all was present and accounted for at the house that night. Maybe Patrick Ward was there. If so . . ."

"I see what you're getting at."

"What are you getting at?" my mother asked.

"If Patrick was there the night Byron disappeared, and then he's found dead in the abandoned house, chances are he had something to do with the kidnapping."

"But there are two things that you're forgetting," Mom added.

"What's that?"

"Number one, who killed Patrick? I mean, you said he was poisoned. Which means that there is somebody else out there who would have to know that Byron was in that wall all these years, too."

Colin and I let that settle on us like a lead weight. Only the rhythm of the tires against the highway invaded the moment.

"What's the second thing?" I asked my mother.

"You missed your turnoff," she said.

Twenty-one

Wisteria General Hospital's waiting room was empty save for the collection of New Kasselonians that had gathered there later that evening. Rudy, Colin, my mother, Chuck Velasco, Vada and I were all waiting our turn to visit Wilma Pershing. The room was small and stuffy, its walls and floors graced with that characteristic tan color that was so popular in 1970, when the hospital was built. Even the furniture was just a shade darker than the walls, vinyl and sticky. It didn't matter how much the air-conditioning pumped, it always seemed as if my legs stuck to vinyl furniture.

All in all, a very boring and depressing room.

Vada came over and sat next to me. "Deputy Miller said that you wanted to talk to me about the Blues Festival," she said.

"I did? Oh, yes, I did," I said. I had forgotten that I had told Deputy Miller that the day I was trying to read the Finch file. See, my mother always says that if you lie, you have to tell twice as many lies to cover up the first lie, and then, before you know it, everything you say is a lie and you can't remember to whom you told what. And then you get caught. My mother is a smart person. "I just wanted to tell you that my grandmother had a request that you ask that one band back from last year."

"Which band is that?" Vada asked. She was about fifty-five, a heavy smoker who was thin as a rail. She was one of those women who never changed. Her hair was still teased every morning and worn in that hairdo Tammy Wynette had made famous.

"The one that went last."

"The Tennessee Trio," she said. "Oh, yeah. Got my eye on that lead singer, I do."

"That's sort of what my grandmother said, too," I answered. And in truth, she had said something to that effect. Only more crude.

"Don't worry, honey," Vada said. "They've already agreed. Don't forget, though, it's the second weekend of September this year."

"I won't forget," I said. How could I? My town would be overrun with music lovers, which actually are better tourists than just your average tourist. They buy more in the way of food and souvenirs and always come back.

"But we may have it on the church grounds this year, instead of the civic center."

"Why?"

"Because Ruthie at the civic center said that all those people did too much damage to the grass," she said.

"Oh," I said. I was about to tell Vada that I would put a good word in for her with the nuns and Father Bingham when a nurse came to the doorway and called my name. She held a clipboard in her left hand and wore an expressionless look on her face. It must have taken years of practice to master that look.

"Victory?"

"Yes," I said.

"Sylvia wants to see you," she said.

The words sent shivers down my spine. I looked over at my mother, who gave me the chin-up sign and nodded. My mind raced with all the worst-possible scenarios that I could face once I got to the end of the hall. And they all came back to one. Wilma was dead. That was the worst-case scenario.

I followed the nurse down the hall, where she pointed to

Wilma's room. Once she had shown me to the room, she walked over to the nurse's station to go back to work. I paused a moment, peeking in Wilma's room through the doorway. The only things I could see were her feet covered with a sheet, and Sylvia standing at the foot of the bed.

As I had feared, it was the worst-case scenario. I entered the room quietly and stood beside Sylvia. She was so little and so frail. And she stood at the feet of her dead sister.

Wilma lay peacefully in the hospital bed, her plump hands lying at her sides on top of the sheet. I remembered those hands twirling her hair around her fingers. Those same fingers and hands had made my mother's wedding dress. Her eyes were closed, her long white hair brushed over one shoulder.

"You must deliver her memorial," Sylvia said.

"Oh, Sylvia," I muttered. I managed to stifle the sob that threatened to burst forth. I breathed deeply, the tears spilling down my cheeks. I wiped at them, succeeding in smearing the tears all over my face. "I can't."

Sylvia instantly turned on me. "Don't tell me what you can't do, Victory. You must."

My hand reached out and touched Wilma's arm, caressing it for only a moment. "Father Bingham will do a wonderful memorial. You know he will."

There were no tears on Sylvia's face, no hint that she had cried or grieved in any way. Her demeanor was silent and grim. My guess was that she was waiting until she was alone to grieve. Ever the businesswoman, Sylvia knew there was business to attend to in a death. There were casket colors and sizes, plots to pick out, flowers to send, a tombstone to order. Even the wording on the little memorial cards would be left to Sylvia. There was nobody to share the burden with. It was all hers. And it had to be done. It had to be done before any grieving could take place.

"It would be better coming from . . . a friend," she said.

"I think you should have somebody more removed give the memorial, Sylvia. Wilma's character will suffer at the hands of my blubbering," I said.

"She loved you, Victory. Do not insult her love."

Why did this woman succeed in manipulating me? What was it about her? Was it what she said as much as the way she said it? Did I give in and do as she bid out of respect? Fear? Sometimes I thought it was because I saw in Sylvia what I did not want to be. A lonely and bitter old woman, afraid of emotion. Afraid of showing or feeling emotion. Was that it? Was I humoring her? Was I pitying her? I don't know, but with Sylvia it almost always worked.

"Of course," I said, against my better judgment. "I'll do it."

"Thank you. Now you must go and tell everybody," Sylvia said.

Just like that, she dismissed me. Still, no emotion from her. No hint of grief. As I walked out of the room, I looked back over my shoulder and saw Sylvia lay a hand upon Wilma's foot. A brief gesture from the woman who had shared nearly every moment of her life with Wilma. And that was it.

Now I had to go and tell the waiting room full of people that Wilma Pershing was dead.

Twenty-two

At seven the next morning I was once again awakened by a knock at the door. Only this time Rudy was in the shower, so I had to answer the door all by myself. I was practicing how to say "No comment" as loudly and with as much venom as I could when I opened the door to Sheriff Brooke.

He stood in full uniform with a large box in his hand. Sheriff Colin Brooke had become such a part of our personal lives, whether I liked it or not, that seeing him in full uniform was a little disturbing. He was a large man to begin with, a decade younger than my mother, but it was clear that my mother's cooking was already beginning to settle in places it shouldn't. His uniform was taut around his middle. I couldn't even take pleasure in the fact that he was getting soft, because I knew he was having the time of his life being pampered by my mother.

"What do you want?" I asked. I took a moment to look down at myself to make sure that I was dressed decently. Sometimes, when it's hot, I'll sleep in just a slip. Luckily this time, I had slept in a pair of lime-green shorts and a T-shirt with a large dragon on the front. "Do you have any idea what time it is? Of course you do.

You had to get up, get dressed, and drive over here. Couldn't you have used the phone?"

He just stared at me.

"Is there something wrong with my mother?" I asked, suddenly concerned.

"No, no. She's fine, Torie."

"Then to what do I owe this before-the-birds-start-singing visit?"

"I brought you something," he said. "But if you're going to be such a brat, I'll just take it back."

"Oh, brat, huh? You think because now you're my stepfather that you can start talking to me like you're my stepfather? Just who do you—" I stopped mid-sentence. "What did you bring me?"

"Are you gonna ask me in? What are you trying to do? Cool the whole neighborhood? You're letting all the air-conditioning out." He smiled from ear to ear. "Did that sound enough like a parent?"

"Not too shabby, Mr. Sheriff. Not too shabby," I said and gestured for him to come in. "But you have to sound as if you're irate over the fact that I'm air-conditioning the whole neighborhood. Put some oomph into it."

"I'll remember that next time," he said. He walked straight into the kitchen. I mean, it's not like he was a stranger here or anything. He knew where every room was, where we kept the extra toilet paper and where Rudy's favorite fishing lures were. Come to think of it, that was pretty creepy.

He put the box on my table, careful not to knock over the juice that Mary had left in her Togepi glass the night before. She never puts anything away. One time she had an apple for a snack. I found the core in between the cushions on the couch.

"What's that?" I asked.

"It's a box inside a box," he said.

"Okay, it's too early for riddles. You can leave now."

He laughed and took the lid off of the box. Inside was indeed another box that he took out and I recognized right away. It was the box that I had tried to remove from the basement of the sheriff's office the other day. It was the file on the Finch kidnapping.

"Is this a trick?" I asked.

He shook his head no.

"All right. What do you want?" I asked.

"Coffee," he said.

"Coffee I can make, although I don't drink it, so I have no idea if it's any good," I said, heading to the coffeemaker and the canister. "But, if Rudy is any indication, as long as you can't see the bottom of the cup it's good."

"That'll be fine by me."

As I made the coffee, I also pulled a glass down out of the cabinet for me. Then I got out a can of Dr Pepper, popped the lid and poured the soda into my glass. My caffeine. I sat down at the table.

"Okay, what gives?" I asked.

"I want you to tell me everything that has happened, starting with the night Jalena and I left for Alaska. Then I want you to tell me everything that you've taken from the Finch estate," he said.

I started to protest that I had done no such thing when I realized that I had taken a journal, some photo albums, and that sort of thing. To my credit, I blushed. "All I took were things that I'm using for research for the biography. It will all be returned," I said.

He nodded.

"Actually, if it's all right with you, I was wanting to know if we couldn't give a few of the really personal items to her children," I said.

The sheriff looked at me oddly.

"You didn't know she had any living descendants?"

"I thought it was just nieces and nephews," he said.

"No, she has two daughters. And I'm not sure how many grand-kids," I answered.

He studied me a minute. "All right, we can do that. We'll ask them what they want," he said. "When this is all over."

"Of course."

Rudy walked downstairs then, tucking his blue oxford shirt into the waist of his pants. He didn't seem too surprised to see Colin. But then, Colin had nearly become part of our furniture in the months before the wedding. But when Rudy saw the coffeepot perking, he stopped in his tracks. "Jesus, Mary and Joseph. How did you get Torie to make coffee?" he asked.

"A bribe," Colin said.

"Oh, I figured it had to be something like that."

I just sat there for a moment letting them have their fun. "Okay, sophomores, you finished?"

Rudy got out two mugs, filled them and handed one to Colin. Spying the box on the table, he said, "What are you getting my wife into now?"

"Well, since your wife does such a good job at knowing everybody's business, I thought she could help me. I mean, I've never seen *anybody* as nosy as she is. She is the knower of arcane things."

Yup, twenty years from now I'd be wearing big plastic jewelry and big neon clothes, after I'd gained forty pounds, of course. I was becoming Eleanore. When I thought about it, though, I actually liked the way I was. Did I care that I was becoming Eleanore? Not really. Because I was going to be a better Eleanore than Eleanore was. And I just couldn't wait to irritate some young whippersnapper who thought she was The Knower of Arcane Things.

I let them laugh a few minutes. Then I told Colin about the person we had seen running out of the Yates house and how it had appeared that he had been hacking away at the wall. The very wall behind which we would later find the skeleton of Byron Lee Finch. Then I told him about identifying Patrick Ward and so on. He sat and listened to everything I said, slurping occasionally from his coffee mug.

"Then we've had reporters calling," Rudy added.

"Yeah," I said. "Oh, and a man came by . . . an antique dealer.

I can't remember his name. Newton, that's it. He wanted to know if you would sell him a piece of jewelry from the Finch estate, exclusively. You know, he didn't want anybody else to have a chance at it. The necklace had supposedly once belonged to the Romanovs."

"Really?" Colin said, raising his eyebrows.

His reaction told me two things. First, as I suspected, he had never dreamed that Catherine Finch would have anything of that caliber in her estate; and second, he was seeing dollar signs dance in front of his eyeballs. It was like watching an old Warner Brothers cartoon.

"Otherwise, the cataloging of the estate is going well. I hope you've got a storage facility lined up, because there is no way you can fit even the one floor of her stuff into your shop. I am finished with the ground floor, by the way. But I swear, this house is just like it was in 1938. I mean, Byron's nursery is exactly like it was," I said.

"How do you know? I mean, how can you compare it? You weren't there in 1938," the sheriff asked.

"Well, his clothes are still folded in the drawers, clean diapers in the changing table. Everything is dust-covered, but otherwise it looks like a fully functional nursery. The whole house is like that," I said.

"Huh" was all the sheriff said.

"So . . . do I get to read what's in the box?"

"You have as long as it takes me to make myself some breakfast and finish that pot of coffee. Oh, and of course, as usual, you have to tell me the minute you find out anything. If I'm sharing with you, you're sharing with me," he said.

"But you inhale your food," I protested. Dare I say, I even sounded a little whiny.

He looked at the clock.

"Look, Wilma is being laid out at three P.M. I have to start getting ready at two. Why don't you give me until then," I said.

"I'll give you until lunchtime."

"Are you going to be here the whole time?" I asked.

"Yes," he said. Ooh, he was smug.

"Good, then you can watch the kids while I read." I picked up the box and grabbed my soda with the other hand. I have to admit that I live for moments like these.

"Where are you going?" he asked.

"To my office," I said. "Matthew has a bottle in the refrigerator, and Rudy can show you where the diapers are."

"Diapers?" Colin asked with a fearful expression.

"Grandpas have to learn to change diapers." I smiled all the way up the steps to my office.

Twenty-three

I cleared the piles off my desk, which took at least fifteen minutes, and then sat down in my chair to read. Between my feet sat the box containing the original sheriff's investigation reports. I pulled the stack out, sat it on my desk and began to read.

On the night of September 6, 1938, Byron Lee Finch was put to bed at seven-thirty in the evening. His mother rocked him to sleep, laid him in the crib and went back downstairs to attend to her company. At about ten-forty she checked on him and the other children and went to bed. She woke at about four in the morning after having a nightmare that Byron had been murdered, went to his bedroom and found him gone.

The people present and accounted for that night were Catherine, her husband Walter, and their other two children, Cecily and Aurora. Catherine's sister Tamara Danvers and her two children, Hope and Hugh, had been over for dinner, along with Catherine's brother, Louis Ward, his wife, Anna, and their two children, Patrick and Lanna. The ages of the children ranged from six to twelve.

So, Patrick Ward had been there the night that Byron disappeared, and now he had turned up dead in the rubble of the house where Byron was found more than half a century later.

There were two servants who were live-ins, and two business associates of Walter's, who left before 8 P.M. on that night. So Byron was still in his bed when the business associates left for the night. Louis and Anna said that they left about nine-thirty. Tamara Danvers left at 10 P.M. However, the four cousins—Hope Danvers, Hugh Danvers, Patrick Ward and Lanna Ward—stayed for a sleepover.

So, that meant that during the time between ten-forty, when Catherine last checked on Byron, and four in the morning, when she awoke from her nightmare to find him gone, the only people in the house were the two servants, the four cousins, Catherine, Walter, Cecily and Aurora.

The only other person with a key to the house was Sylvia Pershing.

Sylvia Pershing?

I read the report again. "Sylvia Pershing had a key to the house because she was Catherine Finch's best friend. In case of an emergency, Sylvia was the one allowed into the house." Those were the words written by Sheriff Kolbe.

I couldn't quite wrap my mind around that. Sylvia knew all of this, obviously. Why hadn't she said anything to me when she asked me to write the biography? Maybe she was waiting to see if I was a good enough researcher to find out on my own. The report went on to say that when Miss Pershing was interviewed, she stated that she was the first person to arrive at the Finch estate when it was discovered that the baby was missing.

My head hurt.

The report continued in the sort of stilted prose used in official forms that other people will read. It stated that the items Catherine found missing were the clothes Byron was wearing when he went to bed. A diaper, a cotton nightgown and booties. A blanket was also missing, as well as his baby bracelet, which she had forgotten to take off him when she put him to bed.

There was no forced entry. The windows were all locked from

the inside because there was a terrible storm that night. Nobody knew how the perp got in or got out. There were no tire prints or marks made on the house by a ladder. No broken foliage around the windows. Nothing. It made Sheriff Roger Kolbe note that most likely the baby had been kidnapped by somebody in the house.

I remembered Sheriff Kolbe. He had been an old man when I was a little girl. He was the father of our current fire chief, Elmer Kolbe. I made a mental note to go and speak with Elmer about this. Maybe his father had suspected things that he never put down in the report. Maybe he had talked about it with his family. Especially once the FBI came in and took over; then Roger Kolbe might have felt more comfortable talking about it with people. You never knew.

It was also Sheriff Kolbe's opinion that the baby was simply carried out the front door, down the sidewalk and the driveway, and then into the night. It was the only explanation he could come up with. After the kidnapping the family waited by the phone for days. The days turned into weeks. There was never any ransom request for little Byron. Sheriff Kolbe also made a note that he thought Byron was dead already. He wrote that Byron either died for some unforeseen reason and the kidnappers had no baby to ransom, or that the kidnapping was a crime far more devious than that.

Sheriff Kolbe, like me, had thought maybe Byron had been taken by somebody who just wanted a baby and couldn't have one of her own. Which could only be one of the two house servants. Or Sylvia, I reminded myself, since she had a key.

He had a second theory: Cecily or Aurora had killed the baby brother out of jealousy and disposed of the body, since it was no secret that the boy was the favorite child of both Walter and Catherine.

Oh, I did not want to go there. I didn't even want to think about it.

The two associates of Walter Finch were interviewed several

times. Both said that it was an uneventful evening. There were no arguments, no tension among the visitors. They had a nice dinner and talked business with Walter for half an hour while Catherine and her siblings talked in the downstairs living room. The children played, running through the house. Everybody had a relaxed evening. Both associates basically had similar accounts. It was an uneventful but pleasant evening. One of the associates said he decided not to stay for drinks because there was a storm coming and he didn't want to drive home under the influence during a storm. The other associate left right away because his wife was pregnant and due to give birth anytime.

And then the FBI came into the picture, and the investigation was turned over to them. There was an awful lot of paperwork basically to sum up that everybody except the people sleeping in the house had alibis.

It was noon. My time was up.

THE NEW KASSEL GAZETTE

The News You Might Miss
by
Eleanore Murdoch

One of New Kassel's most beloved residents is dead. Wilma Irene Pershing was born in February of 1907 in New Kassel, Missouri. She was the Vice President of the Historical Society and in her younger days headed the Rotary Club, the Quilting Bee and the Foster Care Program of Granite County. She has been a legal secretary and a cook, and was even a nun for two years.

She is preceded in death by her parents, a brother, two nieces and one nephew.

She is survived by her sister Sylvia Pershing, three nephews, one niece, and seventeen great-nieces and

-nephews. This is one of the saddest days in New Kassel history.

And remember to vote NO on Proposition 7, or the second saddest day in New Kassel history will occur.

Until next time,
Eleanore

Twenty-four

The Santa Lucia Catholic Church was located at Jefferson and New Bavaria Boulevard. The exterior was white sandstone with arched stained-glass windows, evenly distributed down both sides of the church, that depicted scenes from the Bible. The wooden benches had been hand-carved by the first German immigrants to this town over two hundred years ago. I've never understood how a German town in predominantly German Missouri had a church with a Spanish name.

New Kassel had remained mostly German until the Irish influx of the mid-1850s. Then New Kassel had been shaken up just a bit. And, of course, the twentieth century brought people from other areas. My parents were some of them. My dad was from southeast Missouri, my mother from West Virginia. They met in St. Louis and somehow ended up in New Kassel in the 1960s. But the town was still largely full of originals, people whose families had been in the New Kassel area since before 1900.

In St. Louis, it was the other way around. The French had settled it, but by the middle of the 1800s scarcely a French name could be found. It had been taken over by German and Irish immigrants. Later came the Italians. Even now, it's one of the leading destinations for the newest immigrant, the Bosnians.

But New Kassel, except for the Irish invasion, seemed to be lost in a vortex somewhere. Nothing ever changed much. Which is part of its charm. The whole riverboat casino thing seemed just too tasteless and tacky to me.

I was deep in my thoughts about the tackiness of a casino when somebody sat next to me in the back pew. I like sitting back there because then I can see the whole church. Santa Lucia is very soothing. Even with Wilma's casket sitting directly under the giant crucifix, it was still comforting and warming. I looked over to see who had sat down next to me. It was Sylvia.

I had just given my memorial speech at the funeral home. It wasn't as difficult as I had thought it would be to get through it. I just sort of focused on odd things: Eleanore's big yellow hat, the spokes in my mother's wheelchair, Helen Wickland's tapping foot in the front row. And before I knew it, I was finished.

"Where's Rudy?" she asked.

"Parking the car," I said.

"You're early," she declared.

"I walked straight over here after the wake," I said. "I wanted to walk. Besides, everybody else stood and milled around."

"The things you said about Wilma," Sylvia said. "They . . . they were perfect."

A compliment. From Sylvia. I braced myself for an earthquake.

I guess I shouldn't be so snotty. She was allowed to be sentimental at her sister's funeral. It was just so out of character. Chuck Velasco entered to our right, dressed in his best suit and tie. He genuflected and sat in a pew about ten rows in front of us. Chuck cleans up well.

"The things I said about Wilma were all true," I said.

More people came in. The mayor and his wife sat up front. Tobias Thorley sat way over to the right. I saw his son come in a few seconds later, with his latest "woman," and sit next to Tobias.

There had been so many people over at the funeral home that I had to wonder who was working the shops.

Finally, I scooted over closer to Sylvia. "You know, you never mentioned that you were good friends with Catherine Finch," I said.

Sylvia didn't even turn her head toward me. She gave me a sideways glance. Had I impressed her or ticked her off? With Sylvia it was hard to tell.

"How did you find out?" she asked.

"Why didn't you tell me? I mean, you asked me to write a biography of one of Granite County's most interesting characters, and who but one of her best friends could give me the kind of inside information I need? Her children can't. As you must obviously know. Because they haven't interacted with her since the mid 1950s. Who else could tell me?"

She said nothing.

"Or was this a test? Did you just want to see if I was good enough to find out on my own?" I asked.

Still nothing. I shifted in the pew.

"I can't tell you very much about the later Catherine, either. I hadn't spoken to her in nearly thirty years," Sylvia said at last.

"Why?"

She was quiet a moment, fiddling with the seam in her black pant leg. "Hector Castanza" was all she said.

"What?" I asked. "Who's that?"

"An impostor."

"What do you mean, an impostor?"

"Sometime in the late fifties, Hector Castanza was one of many young men who came to Catherine claiming he was her son Byron. He claimed he had been raised by a gypsy woman who 'bought' him from somebody in exchange for a gypsy cure," she said. "It was preposterous. Everybody knew that he wasn't Byron."

"Everybody except Catherine," I said.

Sylvia nodded her head. "Hector Castanza, as luck would have it, bore a striking resemblance to Catherine's brother, Louis. He'd done his homework on the kidnapping and on Catherine in general. He convinced her he was her son."

"But you knew differently," I coaxed.

"I tried for years to convince her he wasn't Byron. For years their relationship grew. She invited him to all of the family functions, bought him a new car. Showered him with gifts. And if her daughters didn't accept him as their brother, she was prepared to write them off," Sylvia said.

The church was beginning to fill up and I knew that there were only a few minutes left to our conversation. Soon there would be too many people for us to talk comfortably, and Father Bingham would begin the funeral mass.

"So that's why her children became estranged? Because they didn't believe Hector was their brother?"

"It wasn't quite that simple," Sylvia said with her head down. Boy, that seam in her pants must have been exceptionally fascinating.

"What do you mean?"

"Catherine and I had many arguments over this. Many. Finally, after about three years, I had Hector investigated," she said.

I winced. That was a pretty bold step.

"You don't understand. He had infiltrated every part of their life. The girls were beginning to feel alienated. Catherine tried to make up for all the birthdays and Christmases he missed. It was a pitiful sight," she said. "So, I had him investigated. It turned out that he was a used car salesman from Atlanta, Georgia, named Mario Finkleman. His mother was a retired prostitute who had orchestrated the whole thing. His mother had been the benefactor of many of the expensive gifts that Catherine had bestowed upon him."

"Oh my gosh," I said. "How awful."

"Yes," she said.

"So . . . I don't understand. Did Catherine never forgive you because you had him investigated?" I asked.

"I think it was two things, really. What she never forgave me for was destroying her fantasy. In Hector, she had found her son. But I think what drove us apart more was that she suspected I knew what really happened to Byron," Sylvia said.

I sat there a minute, unsure if I should say what I really wanted to say. Finally, I just decided, what the heck? Sylvia was always blunt with me. Turnabout was fair play. "Well, did you?"

She smiled a wry and wrinkled smile, but did not answer me. So I tried a different approach. "What happened with her children? Why did she detach herself from them?"

"The exact same reason. In Catherine's mind, since she was so thoroughly convinced that Hector was Byron, she believed that the only way Cecily and Aurora could be as thoroughly convinced that he wasn't Byron was if they knew what really happened to him," Sylvia said.

"Everybody became a suspect," I said.

"No," Sylvia said. "Catherine knew what the investigators were saying. Byron's disappearance was linked to somebody in that house that night. Or me. Since I had a key. So here were three suspects who were sure that Hector wasn't Byron. She couldn't understand how we could be that positive about something unless we knew what had really happened."

"Do you think the girls knew what happened to Byron?" I asked.

She didn't answer.

"Is that why she left them nothing in her will?"

"Yes."

"Sylvia. Did you know what really happened to Byron?"

"I knew without a doubt that Hector was not Byron. Of nothing else could I be sure," she said. Her body seemed to fold up and say that was it. She was finished discussing this.

Father Bingham made his entrance into the church and we all stood. Rudy and the kids sneaked in just as the whole congregation was rising. He waved to me from the back door. I don't think there was a place for them to sit.

Sylvia took this last moment to add something. She turned to me, eyes milky with age. "How did you find out that I was Catherine's best friend?"

"I'm the best genealogist west of the Mississippi," I said with a smile.

"I think that goes beyond genealogy," she answered.

Father Bingham made the motion for all of us to sit and we did. He started by saying, "Today we bury one of New Kassel's most loved residents. I think I can safely say that she probably saw ninety percent of us grow up from childhood. I can only imagine the secrets about this town that she knew. I find that the saddest part when somebody dies. The fact that the rest of us left alive will never know all that they knew."

I fished for my Kleenex in my purse as the tears rolled down my cheeks.

Twenty-five

Fraulein Krista's Speisehaus was a big building with exposed wood beams and a stuffed bear at the end of the bar. It was my favorite restaurant in town, not only because the food was fabulous, but because it just had a cool feel to it. Where else could one find adults running around in green velvet knickers and dresses? Sometimes I thought if I stayed in here long enough that, when I left, New Kassel would have turned into Bavaria.

I sat at a booth eating sauerkraut and wieners, relishing every moment that I had to myself. My mom and Colin had been home almost a week now. The kids were with their grandma in her new house in Wisteria and happy that things were back to seminormal. School would start in a few days and then, except for dealing with Matthew, I would have more time to myself. I had brought some of the journals and such to the restaurant to read.

Krista Dougherty, the owner of this fine establishment, walked up to my table, her smile bringing out her dimples. Ocean-blue eyes peered from beneath blond lashes. Her hair was equally blond, and there were freckles across her nose. She had to be the tallest woman in town. "Torie, how are you?"

"I'm doing good," I said.

She sat down opposite me and folded her hands. She was used to me coming in here. She knew this was my retreat. Rudy and I went to most places in New Kassel together, but Krista's was the place where I went alone.

"I can't believe Wilma is dead," she said. In the past week most of the town's small talk had centered around Wilma's death. It was as if nobody could accept it.

"She had become a permanent fixture, had she not?" I asked.

"I think I thought she was going to stay an old woman forever, and still be an old woman when I got to be an old woman," she said.

"I know exactly what you mean."

She was quiet a moment. "You want a raspberry tart?" she asked.

"Need you ask?"

"I'll be right back," she said and disappeared into the kitchen.

I went back to reading the journals, which really were more of a glorified calendar. Catherine would write things like: *Performance 7:00 P.M. Philadelphia, Penn.* Then under that she would write a few sentences summing up the performance. *Cold audience, had to work for every applause.* Or *Brought the house down. Saxophone player was on tonight!* Sometimes she would make a note of special guests. Famous people who would come to hear her and come backstage, that sort of thing. But, to my disappointment, nothing very personal.

I thought Krista had come back and sat in the booth across from me, but when I looked up it was my stepdad, the sheriff. I still have trouble deciding how to describe him. Was he the sheriff, my stepdad? Or my stepdad, the sheriff? Very confusing, and darn him anyway for making my life more complicated than it already was.

"Hi," I said. "To what do I owe this visit?"

"We got the autopsy report back on the skeleton," he said.

"Oh, yeah?" I asked. "Wait a minute. That was fast, wasn't it?"

"It's been a week. Not a lot of autopsies in Granite County," he said.

"Why is that? Is it because our crime rate is so low?"

"Most of the people who die in Granite County are little old ladies or fat men who die of heart attacks," he said. I looked surprised by his answer. "I'm serious. We're rural with a small population. And most people don't want to cut up Grandma or Grandpa unless there was foul play involved. Not that many mysterious deaths, regardless of what *you* think."

"All right, all right. Don't get your shorts in a knot," I said. "Sorry I asked."

Krista came back with a raspberry tart for me and a big mug of black coffee for the sheriff. I have never understood how people can drink coffee in the summer. We both thanked her and she went back to work.

"Do you want to hear this or not?" he said.

"Yes," I said. "I do."

"Some of the bones showed what they call vitrification," he said.

"What's that?"

"Glassification."

"Well, why didn't you just say that, smarty pants," I said. I paused a second. "What is glassification?"

"It's when the bones are exposed to a significant amount of heat so that they sort of glassify. Like sand becomes glass when exposed to intense heat," he said.

"Oh." That explained nothing to me.

"The skull was expanded."

"Expanded."

"Yes," he said.

"From the inside out?"

"Yes."

"So, his brain was enlarged?"

"Yes."

None of this made any sense.

"Also, on his wrist and his pelvic bone were what they think are burn marks. Where the baby was wearing something metal, which heated up and scarred the bone."

"Like a baby bracelet and a diaper pin," I said.

"Exactly."

"So, what—did he die in a fire?"

"No," Sheriff Brooke said. "It looks as though he was hit by lightning."

I just sat there with my fork halfway up to my mouth. I blinked and blinked again. The nerve endings in my brain must not have been functioning or something, because I just wasn't getting what he said.

"When bodies are hit by lightning, they are exposed to intense heat. Heat you just can't imagine," he said. "The brain literally heats up so quickly that it expands and forces itself out of the skull. If they are wearing metal, it will imprint itself on the bone. And glassification or vitrification will occur in the bones. I can think of nothing else that would do all of these things. The baby in the wall was hit by lightning."

"But that makes no sense," I said.

"Sure it does."

"How did it get hit by lightning?" I think I had expected such a sinister fate to have befallen Byron that when the sheriff said it was a natural disaster it just took me by surprise.

"Think about it, Torie. It was storming that night. So severely that one of the guests wouldn't stay to have a drink and left early."

"Oh my God," I said. "That's right."

"You said that you read somewhere that Byron was wearing a baby bracelet," he said.

"Yeah."

"I think it is Byron. In fact, I am so sure of it that I'm ready to announce it," he said.

"Whoa, whoa, wait. Before you go announcing anything, just wait."

"Why?" he asked, with a surprised look on his face.

"Because, whether that baby was hit by lightning or not, somebody still put him in that wall. Somebody still kidnapped him. And somebody killed Patrick Ward. I just wonder if it's a good idea to tip your hand just yet. You know, hitting people with that bit of news in an interview can get you a million-dollar reaction. If they already know that he's been found, they'll be prepared for it."

"I agree, but there's one thing."

"What?"

"The reporters already know that there's been a baby found. Whoever our suspects are, the culprit, if he or she is still alive, already knows he's been found," Colin said.

I thought about that. "Yeah, you're right. But what did you mean if they're still alive?"

"It happened a long time ago. People do die, you know," he said.

"Well, yeah. There's that."

"Whatsa matter with you?" he asked. "You're a little slow today, Torie."

"I think I was just so expecting Byron to have been intentionally murdered that I just can't get my brain to wrap around what you're saying. You've thrown me for a loop," I said.

"Excuses, excuses," he said and smiled.

"I can hit you now, can't I? You're related."

He just gave me that look that said, oh, yeah, let's see you try it. I let it go. He could beat me up and I knew it.

"Wow," I said and shook my head. "I don't know what to say."

"Well, at least we know why there was never any demand for ransom. The baby died before they got a chance to ransom it," he said.

"You know, people ransom children and still end up killing them. I mean, nobody knew that Byron was dead," I said.

"So?"

"So, what was to keep the kidnappers from ransoming him anyway, and then delivering a dead baby?" I asked.

"Hmmm," he said and took a sip of coffee. "What are you driving at?"

"I think, based on who the suspects were, that there was never any intention of ransoming Byron," I said.

Twenty-six

Cecily Finch Todd lived in a big beautiful house on Butler Hill Road in south St. Louis County. Butler Hill was just about as far south as one could get and still be in St. Louis County. About a mile or two later you cross the Meramec River and travel into Jefferson County.

I made a left onto the Butler Hill exit from Highway 55, crossed back over the highway and headed west. Passing the Schnucks Supermarket, the Burger King and the Taco Bell, I was immediately in a cozy neighborhood of one nice house after another. Within a minute I pulled into Cecily's driveway. I sat there for a moment thinking about what to say. Like her sister Aurora, she did not know I was coming and I hadn't a clue as to what to say to her. But I was banking on the fact that Aurora had probably phoned her to tell her about me. So, that might be a little chip in the ice that I was certain would greet me.

She answered the door wearing a pair of tweed pants and a blouse with pastel seashells printed on it. She was taller and older than her sister. There was a resemblance between them, but only a slight one. It was one of those resemblances where if you put the two together you'd see it, but otherwise nobody would have reason to suspect that they were siblings. It made me wonder what Byron would have looked like if he had made it to adulthood.

"If you're with the *National Enquirer*, *The Star*, or any of those other trashy grocery-store tabloids," she said with much venom, "no comment!"

I was stunned at first, but then I had to giggle. "I don't mean to laugh, but I've said nearly those same words several times in the last week."

Her eyes narrowed on me. "Why? Who are you?"

"I'm Torie O'Shea. I work for the Historical Society in New Kassel, and my mother's husband bought your mother's estate."

"Oh," she said. "My sister told me about you."

"I was hoping she would."

"The same goes for you. No comment," she said and slammed the door.

Hmmm. Ever the optimist, I knocked on the door again. "Please, Mrs. Todd!" I banged on the door and hoped with all my heart that she wouldn't call the police and have me arrested. "Mrs. Todd. We've found your brother."

After a moment she opened the door. She stared at me through the glass of her storm door, eyes meeting mine and sizing me up. She opened the storm door and held it open for me, signaling for me to enter.

Which I did, but not without my share of trepidation. People were crazy nowadays, you know. Big, heavy maroon drapes hung above the big picture window in the living room. On one end of the room hung a large gold mirror, with maroon and navy-blue flowers arranged above it. The carpet was the same navy blue. She did not offer me a seat.

"What do you mean, 'We've' found your brother. Who's 'we'?"

"My stepfather is also the sheriff of Granite County," I said.

"Colin married your mother?" she asked.

"Yes," I said. "You know him?"

"He went to school with my son. He spent many days in my basement and my backyard," she said.

I just blinked at her. A side to the sheriff I didn't know. It seemed there were many, many sides. He was going to be the world's first octagon person.

"We lived in Wisteria until about 1960. Then we moved to St. Louis. Ten years later, we moved here," she said.

"I did not know that he knew you that well. He never mentioned it," I said.

"No. He probably wouldn't. It wouldn't be professional," she said. "Colin was always like that. I knew he'd be in law enforcement, because he was always bugging the friends that he hung out with about obeying the rules and doing what was right."

"Yeah, sounds like Colin," I said.

"I read what the papers are saying about Byron, heard it on the news, and obviously had my share of reporters here hounding me. Phone calls at all hours. They haven't really come out and officially said that the baby was Byron," she informed me.

"Oh," I said. "I guess I sort of jumped the gun." I wondered just how believable that actually sounded.

Her hand went to her throat, where she reached for a necklace that wasn't there. It was my bet that she normally wore a necklace of some sort that she fiddled with when she was nervous. "How do you know it's him?"

"Things in the autopsy," I said, deliberately vague. "But, what I'm really here to talk to you about is your mother."

"Why?"

"Because Sylvia Pershing has hired me to write a biography of her," I said. "It will be issued by the Historical Society, published by one of the colleges. It's her goal to have a set of biographies on notable people of Granite County."

"How is Sylvia?" she asked.

"Good," I said.

"I was sad to hear the news about Wilma. She was a great lady. I can't tell you how many times she's baby-sat me or my sister," she said.

"Yes," I said. "I think Wilma baby-sat every child in New Kassel at one time or another."

"What is it you want to know?"

She still hadn't offered me a place to sit, nor had she made any motion to sit herself. I tried to remember some of the things I had mulled over in my mind to ask her. "Aurora mentioned that your mother became estranged from you sometime in the 1950s. That eventually you two had nothing more to do with her. What would make her behave that way?"

"She'd spent fifteen or more of her adult years trapped in a nightmare. She'd forgotten how to live in the real world. Or to take joy in the things that were here," she said. "Only disappointment in the things that were not."

"So Hector Castanza had nothing to do with it?"

"Who?" she asked. She turned a little white around the mouth, but otherwise she did a great job of pretending she didn't know who he was. But of course she didn't know that Sylvia had told me all about him, so she couldn't know that I knew that she knew darn good and well who Hector Castanza was. And to pretend that she didn't just made it all the more obvious.

"The man who tried to convince your mother he was Byron," I said.

"There were so many of them," she said.

"Yes, but your mother showered this one with gifts."

"Oh," she said. "It's been so long ago. I really don't want to talk about this."

She put her hand on the doorknob and somehow I got the feeling that I wasn't going to get much more out of her. Something caught my eye behind her, and I tried to peer over her shoulder without looking as if I was being nosy. It was a curio cabinet filled with porcelain and crystal fairies. There was part of her mother with her after all.

"I'm sorry to bother you," I said. "I am curious about one thing, Mrs. Todd."

"What's that?"

"You haven't asked what the autopsy results were."

"You already told me it was Byron."

"Yes, but you didn't even ask what happened to him. Or how he was killed," I said.

"Does it matter?" she asked. "He was taken from us a long time ago and it changed our lives. For the worse. I don't mean to sound cold, but I'm not sure that I really care after all this time. I mean, I wish he wasn't dead. I wish he had never been kidnapped. But I can't say that I want to know what happened to him."

"Oh," I said. I'm so brilliant with my elaborate ability to speak that I surprise even myself. Oh. What kind of reaction was that?

Cecily opened the door then and I knew if I didn't have something intelligent to say to her that I would never get the chance again. "How did you know he was dead? You don't seem surprised that he was found dead. It's just hard to understand how you wouldn't ask these questions."

"My sister and I, and our father, realized a long time ago what our mother never realized," she said. "That more than likely Byron was dead."

"Why? It never occurred to you that somebody who wanted a child could have kidnapped him for their own?"

"No, it didn't."

"Oh," I said again.

"And after all these years, Mrs. O'Shea, I don't really think they'll ever be able to tell what happened to him. I don't even understand how they can say it's him without a doubt. I think the whole thing is preposterous. How can you identify a baby skeleton?"

"It's a matter of proximity, for one thing. He was found less than two miles from his home. The house that he was found in was under construction on the night of his disappearance. A diaper pin was found with him that matches the ones in his nursery," I said.

"His nursery? I don't understand," she said, reaching for that imaginary necklace again.

"The nursery is intact. I'm cataloging your mother's belongings for Colin. The diaper pins were in the third silver box from the left, on the silver tray," I said. "And the one found with the skeleton matched."

She said nothing.

"A fairy," I said and pointed behind her to her own collection. "That is what was on each diaper pin."

She swallowed.

"Your mother stated that she forgot to take off his bracelet, and there was a burn mark on his wrist bone that indicated he was wearing a bracelet when it happened," I said.

"When what happened?" she asked.

"When he was struck by lightning," I said.

"White as a ghost" were the perfect words to describe Cecily Finch Todd. White and pasty and visibly disturbed. "Good day, Mrs. O'Shea."

"Good day, Mrs. Todd," I said. "Don't hesitate to call me if there's something you need."

Twenty-seven

I let Cecily Finch Todd's reaction to our conversation settle on me for a few days. I wasn't exactly sure what to do about it. It almost seemed to me as if she had known Byron was hit by lightning—as if she knew, but never in a million years thought anybody would find out. Of course, that was just my opinion from watching her reaction. Maybe she had turned so white because it made her sick to think of her baby brother being hit by lightning. Really, it could go either way. And I had no reason to think that she knew other than that she had been in the house the night her brother disappeared.

"In Catherine's mind, since she was so thoroughly convinced that Hector was Byron, she believed that the only way Cecily and Aurora could be as thoroughly convinced that he wasn't Byron was if they knew what really happened to him." Sylvia's words made sense in an odd sort of way.

I was once again at the Finch estate, and I was now cataloging the second floor. I tagged the piano and documented it in the spiral notebook that I was keeping for Colin. There were quite a few pieces of large furniture that I made no attempt to move. I just tagged them and recorded them. It was late in the evening and I didn't want to stop what I was doing because I had a great momentum going. As I got ready to leave what I had now dubbed as the piano room, I glanced at the photographs on the mantel of the fireplace. I picked up one of the empty boxes by the door and put all the photographs in it, intending to take them to Aurora Guelders as a sort of peace offering. It would also be an excuse to go there and see if I could get any sort of reaction to the lightning theory from her.

I suppose it really was cruel of me. It was her brother, after all. But there was a part of me that believed that the sisters knew something. They knew *something*, I just couldn't be sure of what.

I was deep in thought and passing from room to room with the box with my hand when I heard a crash upstairs. I shrieked and nearly dropped the box of photographs. I stopped and listened for footsteps or any other indication of another human being in the house. I heard nothing.

Then I remembered that Mary and Rachel had been here with me yesterday, and I just knew that Mary had gone back upstairs and probably left a window open. She seemed to be drawn to the nursery. I could hardly keep her out of it without threatening to take away all of her stuffed Tiggers. Which usually worked, but not until after she'd already gotten into something in the first place.

I set the box down and went upstairs to the third floor. I headed straight to the nursery because I just knew that was where Mary had been. Sure enough, the window was standing wide open and the wind flew in at a furious gust. It had knocked over a picture frame on the dresser. I picked it up and saw a clean crack running down the glass across the face of what I assumed to be Byron Lee Finch as a newborn.

Lightning struck somewhere in the distance as a brief flash lit up the Illinois side of the Mississippi. The storm must have reached certain parts of Illinois before hitting us. Almost all our storms came from the southwest. Even so, long reaching arms of a curving storm could reach Illinois before certain parts of Missouri. The trees bent in the wind and the thunder boomed in the distance. It was still pretty far away.

I decided to head home. Hopefully, I'd beat the storm.

Before I could shut the window, another gust of wind came in and nearly knocked the mirror off the dresser. As it was, something fell and rolled across the floor. I shut the window quickly, cussing myself the whole time that I hadn't shut it faster. Then I got down on all fours to look for whatever it was that the wind had knocked off the dresser.

Funny how things look different from the floor. I noticed that the closet door wasn't shut all the way. I crawled around on my hands and knees a bit longer until I was satisfied that whatever it was that had flown off the dresser had disappeared into that vortex that seems to exist. At least it exists in my house. It's a dark place where somebody in another dimension finds the matches to my socks, the tape and all of my bookmarks that never seem to be in any of my books.

I walked over and opened the closet door, which was actually more a storage area than a closet. It was only a few feet high and had a slanted roof. I realized that it was the entrance to the attic. Well, as much as I wanted to see what was in the attic, I sure as heck wasn't going to do it on a night with a vicious storm brewing. We'd had several near misses with the weather lately. Storms that would brew up on the horizon but never actually hit us. I didn't think we were going to be that lucky this time.

As I turned around to leave, I noticed a panel that was loose on the floor just to the right of the door. Of course, I had to look at it closer. I know, I know. Torie O'Shea, confirmed nosy rosy. I'm sure I have some good qualities somewhere, I promise.

I bent down and moved the panel and inside was a dark square. I wasn't about to put my hand down in the hole without being able to see what was in it. Whatever it was, it didn't go all the way down to the second floor because there was no light coming from it. I ran down to the piano room, where I had noticed candles on the mantel earlier. I picked one up, lit it with one of the umpteen matchbooks in a large fishbowl, and walked back up the steps and down the hall to the hole in the floor.

Silly, I know. I should have been leaving to go home. But, curiosity killed the cat. Someday some wise man will change that to say, curiosity killed Torie O'Shea.

I held the candle over the square in the floor and nothing with lots of legs crawled out. Still . . . I firmly believed that things with more legs than I have also have a high intelligence and live to scare the living daylights out of me. So, as soon as I stuck my hand in that dark recess, something with lots of legs would crawl up my arm and I would have a heart attack and be dead, and nobody would find me for hours, maybe days.

I banged on the floor around the hole, trying to scare whatever was in there to come out. Finally, when the storm was getting louder and I knew I couldn't wait much longer, I just plunged my hand down in there and felt around. I squealed at first, just because I felt something. I would have squealed if it were a rock, just because it was something in the dark. But this was soft. I pulled it out.

I carried it out of the nursery where I could see it in the hallway light.

It was a baby blanket.

A baby blanket with blue embroidered initials, BLF.

A baby blanket with scorched edges.

•

A loud clap of thunder shook the house, and I was plunged into darkness. Thank goodness I had the candle. Rain pelted against the windows and the roof, and I was cussing myself silently for not having left sooner. I headed down the hallway to the steps, walking slowly in part because candlelight does not throw light very far and in part because if I moved too swiftly the candle would go out.

And then I heard it. Footsteps on the stairs.

Don't panic, O'Shea. I ran into one of the bedrooms and looked out into the driveway. There was no car. So whoever it was had come on foot and that was not a good sign.

Maybe it was just a homeless person who wanted shelter from the storm. I could hardly hear anything because of all of the rain and thunder. But as I stood on the balcony I could see a flashlight moving against the walls every now and then, as if someone was ducking in and out of rooms. Maybe it was just lightning.

Just as I was about to panic, I remembered the servants' stairs. I went as quickly as I could down the hallway to the other end, opened the door to the servants' stairs, and descended them like there was no tomorrow. The servants' stairs would come out in the kitchen on the first floor and then I could just jump out the back door and to my car and safety.

When I reached the bottom of the servants' stairs, whoever was in the house reached the bottom of the front stairs because I could see the flashlight. It's at moments like these when your mind just sort of shuts down and goes on automatic pilot, and only in hindsight can you see that what you did was not such a great idea. I grabbed a frying pan out of one of the boxes in the middle of the room, extinguished the candle and set it next to Byron's baby blanket on the table.

I tried to disappear into the wall of the kitchen quickly because I could see the flashlight moving on the walls of the dining area and it was getting closer and closer. I gripped the frying pan, my hands sweating and slippery. As the stranger came into the kitchen area with his flashlight blinding me, I smacked him on the side of his head.

He in turn stepped on my foot, elbowed my chin and conked me on the head with his flashlight. "Ouch!" he cried.

"Ouch!" I screamed.

My fear subsided quickly for two reasons. First, pain will make you forget most things; and second, I recognized the voice. He shone the flashlight into my face and I heard the voice in the dark say, "Torie?"

I tried to shield my eyes against the flashlight, but I was too busy hopping on one foot, rubbing my chin with one hand and rubbing my head with the frying pan all at the same time. "Edwin?"

"What the hell are you doing?" he asked.

"I'm . . . I work here. What the hell are you doing?"

"I came to get you because of the storm."

"What? I don't understand."

"Rudy called me and said that he was worried about you because you were later than usual, and the storm was coming up and he wasn't sure if you'd try to come home in it, or if you'd have your nose stuck in a corner somewhere and not even know it was storming. God, I could have shot you, you idiot!"

Rudy had been right. If the wind hadn't knocked over Byron's picture I probably wouldn't have known that the storm was about to hit, until it actually hit. It's really disturbing to think my husband knows me that well. Funny, I don't seem to mind when he knows me well enough to know what I want for dinner or what my favorite flowers are.

"Oh," I said. "Well, where's your car?"

"I couldn't get in the gate. I left the car at the gate and climbed over it," he said.

"Oh," I said. "Well, why didn't you call out my name?"

"I did when I first came in. I guess you didn't hear me."

"Oh," I said again.

"So, why didn't you just say, 'Who's there'?" he asked. "God, my head hurts."

"Because," I said. "Don't you ever watch movies? If I called out 'Who's there?' then you'd know I was here."

"Yeah, and do you have a point or did you hit my head so hard that I'm not hearing everything that you say?"

"If you were a bad guy then you'd know I was here," I said. "My head hurts, too. And my toes and my chin."

"We should go," he said. "We both are in desperate need of ice. Feel my head."

I reached up and felt his head. A lump the size of an egg had risen almost instantly on the side of it, right above his rather large ear.

"And I'm seeing stars in the dark," he said.

"You want me to drive?" I asked.

"Yeah, I think you better."

"Okay, just let me get something," I said. I ran over to the table and grabbed Byron's blanket. Then I felt around on the kitchen counter for my purse, which had my keys, found it and headed for the door.

Edwin didn't follow. "Deputy? Are you all right?"

"Yeah," he said from somewhere in the dark.

"Where are you?" I asked.

"I think I'm on the floor," he said.

"Do you have a radio in your car?"

Twenty-eight

The emergency room of Wisteria General was no happier a place than the waiting room had been. Still that drab tan color. I was flipping through a very beat-up issue of *Field & Stream* magazine, because the timid high school student waiting for results of her mother's X-rays had the only *People* magazine. Call me shallow, but I'm much more interested in reading about the love lives of the rich and famous than reading about the love life of a fish. I just can't help it.

Sheriff Brooke casually made his way down the hall and to my chair. I put the magazine down. "Well? How's Duran?"

"I just want to know one thing," the sheriff said.

"What?" I asked, exasperated.

"Why aren't you on our bowling team if you've got an arm like that? You gave the poor man a concussion."

I swallowed. "I did?" I asked.

"Yes."

"I think it was more the density of the frying pan than it was my arm."

He just glared at me.

"In fact, I'm sure of it. Because without a frying pan I've never given anything a concussion. Honest."

Again he just stared and never blinked.

"What?" I asked. "What? I thought he was an intruder or something. It was self-defense. You should teach him that if he calls out somebody's name and they don't answer, he should try again. I didn't hear him call out my name. But if he would have kept on calling out my name all the way up the steps, I would have eventually heard him. I'm trying desperately to defend myself here. Give me a break."

"How's your toe?" he asked.

"Purple, thank you very much. Although it's not broken."

"Call your mother. She's worried sick."

"Right," I said. I sat there a minute thinking about the blanket I'd found, and just what the implications were. "I think Aurora and Cecily, and their cousins, know what happened to Byron Lee Finch."

"What do you mean?" he asked and sat down in a brown vinyl chair across from me.

"I found Byron's baby blanket hidden in a panel in the floor. The same blanket that Catherine said was missing with Byron. And it was scorched."

"That makes no sense. Why keep an incriminating piece of evidence like that in the house?"

"I don't know. All I know is that they were kids. The oldest one of the six couldn't have been more than twelve. Maybe they didn't realize they had it with them until they were home, and then they panicked. I don't know," I said. "But I think it seriously lends credibility to the theory that somebody in that house was responsible for what happened to Byron, and somebody in the house knew that he was dead."

"So . . . we're talking Aurora, Cecily, Hugh, Hope, Patrick and

Lanna, the two servants, and then Byron's parents, Catherine and Walter."

"That's who was in the house. But I think it's one or more of the six cousins."

"Byron only had four cousins," he said, confused.

"I meant, the six kids, including Aurora and Cecily. They were cousins to the Danverses and the Wards. That's what I mean. The six cousins."

"Okay," he said and stretched. He put his hands behind his head and stared at the ceiling for a moment. "Why? Why would the six of them kidnap him?"

"Maybe they didn't," I said.

"You just said that they did."

"No, I didn't. I think the cousins know what happened, and might have been responsible, but I never said they kidnapped him."

He tapped his foot and then suddenly stopped. "You think it was an accident."

"Exactly. I think, for whatever reason, the six kids took Byron and went somewhere in the middle of the night. They probably had it planned the whole day. The seven of them would sneak off in the middle of the night, for whatever reason. You know how kids are. Maybe they had a tree house or something. A private, cousins-only club."

"Only they didn't count on the storm."

"That's what I'm thinking. They took Byron out into the night and the storm came up. I can only imagine what happened after that. I mean, obviously, somehow he got hit by lightning. And there's another thing. Sylvia, who was Catherine Finch's best friend, said that impostors plagued Catherine's life forever. People pretending that they were Byron."

"Yeah, and?"

"One in particular seemed to be perfect. He bore a striking resemblance to Catherine's brother, Louis. Catherine was convinced that he was Byron. But Aurora and Cecily knew that he wasn't."

"I don't understand," he said, just as the intercom blared a request for a doctor in room four.

"Catherine felt that the only way Aurora and Cecily could be absolutely sure that this impostor wasn't their brother was because they knew what really happened to Byron," I said.

"And that the knowledge wasn't good. In other words, they knew their brother was dead," the sheriff said.

"Yeah, pretty much," I said. "Obviously, I would be suspicious of anybody who came around twenty-five years later and pretended to be my long-lost son or brother or whatever. And that wouldn't mean that I would have had something to do with his disappearance. But, at the same time, Catherine's deduction does sort of make sense."

"I agree. On both counts," he said.

Marriage made him a much more agreeable sheriff.

"I'm curious," he said.

"What?"

"Do you realize who one of the cousins is?"

"What do you mean?"

"Hope. It's Hope Danvers. Governor Hope Danvers."

"Oh, wow," I said, sitting back in my chair. "You thinking what I'm thinking?"

"It hadn't occurred to me until talking to you just now," he said. "But, let's say the six cousins knew what happened to Byron. So they all know he's in the wall."

"They might have even put him there," I added.

"Right. So, let's say for whatever reason Patrick Ward decides to blow the whistle. One of them finds out."

"And poisons him before he actually gets a chance to expose Byron's whereabouts," I said.

"And they probably didn't count on him actually making it to the Yates house, either. Because obviously somebody might make the connection between him and Byron," he said. "Providing, of course, that it could be proved that it *was* Byron."

"I'm following you," I said.

"So, one of them has a lot to lose. Hope Danvers. She panicked because she's getting ready to run for senator. She doesn't want any marks on her name," he said.

"Yeah, but gosh. They were just kids," I said. "Would that make a difference with voters?"

"It could," he said.

"I could see, if there were evil intentions, how that might deter voters."

"The simple fact that she hid it and never told the truth would sort of cast a shadow on her character in general," he said.

"I suppose. But I'm still not sure that would be enough. I mean, so far there's nothing to indicate the children had any sort of vicious intent when they took Byron. No devil-worshipping or anything."

"So far," the sheriff echoed. "Of course, there is Patrick Ward's murder."

Twenty-nine

The Murdoch Inn was our official anti-casino headquarters. Eleanore, Helen Wickland, Charity Burgermeister and I were attending to our various duties in our effort to stop the riverboat casino from anchoring in our town. I was busy stuffing envelopes with our "Vote No Proposition 7" pamphlets when the mayor came bursting in. He wore black-red-and-white-checked golfing pants, a white polo shirt and polished white shoes. He looked like a dork, but then, the mayor always looked like a dork.

"You can cease and desist," the mayor announced.

"What the heck are you talking about, Bill?" Eleanore asked.

"I'm just here to tell you," he said, rocking up on the balls of his feet, "that the governor is here to back me up on the riverboat gambling issue."

"What?" Helen asked.

"She is having a press conference this afternoon from the proposed site for the casino, and she is going to blow you all out of the water," he said.

"Bill," I said, "I remember your acceptance speech when you became mayor. And I believe that your words were, 'I am mayor of New Kassel second. I am a citizen first.' Have you forgotten that?"

"No," he said.

"Then why are you behaving like a horse's butt? You know the casino will kill this town," I said.

"And what's more," Helen added, "we don't care what Governor Danvers says. She has never, not once, in all her years in public service, offered to help this town. This is where she was born and raised, and she hates it. She's ashamed of it. Why would we care what she thinks?"

The mayor clearly looked perplexed. He had not gotten the reaction from us that he had hoped to achieve. Just then the clamor of cars and tubas could be heard from outside.

"That's the governor," he said and ran outside.

We all followed him out onto the porch of the Murdoch Inn. A procession of cars drove through the bend on the way to River Point Road, and ultimately to where the Yates house once stood. Tobias had managed to get most of the Kassel Players together to welcome the governor with their ensemble of brass parade music.

"How come nobody knew she was coming?" Helen asked.

"I invited her last week," Bill said. "She phoned this morning that she was coming. Tobias was pretty ticked about the short notice. Three trumpet players couldn't get off from work and a trombone player is on vacation."

Helen, Eleanore, Charity and I stood on the porch with our arms folded and wearing scowls. It was a beautiful day, a green-air day. The storm had come in last night, cleaned out all the junk in the air, cooled it off by about ten degrees and sucked up the humidity. It wouldn't last, I knew, but it should make for an ideal weekend for the Pickin' and Grinnin' Festival.

Right behind the governor's car and her entourage, were the television crews. Two of them. As if they hadn't been here enough in the past few weeks, what with the discovery of Byron Lee Finch and the whole gambling issue in general.

The four of us made our way on foot down the road to where the Yates house had once stood. The mayor had arrived before us, and I made a mental note that his short legs could move much faster than I ever thought possible.

The sheriff pulled up in his squad car, barely came to a stop, jumped out and made his way directly to me. He looked mean, and ticked, and the sunglasses only helped to perpetuate that image.

"Hi, Dad," I said.

"Ha, ha," he said. "What the hell is going on?"

"The mayor invited the governor to speak on behalf of the riverboat gambling, and she accepted," I said.

"He didn't call me or anything. He knows I have to get extra security in here," he said. His nostrils flared when he spoke, so I assumed that he was pretty peeved. "Hang on. I'll be right back."

He went over to the squad car, used the radio and came back. He had called in the deputies. When he came back he took his sunglasses off and looked down at me. "What is she? Nuts?"

"Who? Governor Danvers?"

"Yeah, that's who. She's making an appearance right where they found her cousin," he said.

"Both cousins," I corrected.

"Yeah, both cousins."

"Maybe that's her point," I said.

"What do you mean?"

"Maybe she's trying to throw people off. Why would she show up here unless it's just to prove she has nothing to hide?"

"Yeah," he said. "And maybe she really does have nothing to hide."

"I doubt that seriously."

"That woman is the ass part of a jack-ass," Helen said.

"Which is the biggest part," Charity added.

"Do you feel that strongly about her?" I asked. They ignored me.

"The nerve of her," Eleanore said. "She has never cared one aorta about this town."

"That's iota, Eleanore. Iota." If she didn't learn to speak, I was going to kill her.

"Showing up here like she's all sincere about the welfare of New Kassel. The Mississippi could swallow us whole and she wouldn't even blink," Eleanore said.

"Shh, she's getting ready to speak," I said.

"More like bark," Helen said.

Then I remembered something. Hope Danvers's brother, Hugh, had been Helen's Aunt Ivy's second husband. The Danverses had not been cordial to Helen's family. So some of this was personal, although, I imagined, not all of it, because Charity and Eleanore had never had a Danvers as a second husband in their family, and they didn't like the governor much either. Just for the record, Helen's Aunt Ivy had had two more husbands after Hugh.

"Ladies and gentlemen of New Kassel," Mayor Castlereagh said into a microphone, which echoed out of a portable amplifier. "It is my pleasure to introduce Governor Hope Danvers."

A crowd had formed. People had actually just stepped out of their shops, shut the doors and walked on over. In the distance I saw Sylvia making her way toward us as well. She walks all over this town. She never drives anywhere, unless I take her or she takes a cab from Wisteria.

"It is my pleasure to speak here today on this picture-perfect September day," the governor began. Hope Danvers was sixty-nine or seventy years old, with short salt-and-pepper hair and long legs. She wore a pink suit that fit snugly on her nearly curveless body. It was bizarre, but she appeared both feminine and masculine.

Three aides or bodyguards stood next to her, ready to move in if things got ugly. I think this was an ordinary precaution and not just for the benefit of little old New Kassel. All three wore dark sunglasses so that nobody could tell in what direction they were looking. Well, that and it was sunny.

"New Kassel is my hometown," the governor said, with arms open wide. "I grew up in a house on New Bavaria, my brother Hugh

162

and I. This town hasn't changed at all since I left it. And we're going to change all of that. You and I together."

Oh, brother.

"New Kassel is in desperate need of new blood. A shot in the arm. The school building is the same, the Knights of Columbus Hall is the same. There have been no new sidewalks, or new roads paved. But, with the riverboat casino, we can bring much-needed revenue to this town."

"Yeah, and ruin it!" Elmer Kolbe yelled out from somewhere to my left. Elmer was the fire chief and did some security work at the Gaheimer house with me. I've known him all my life, and would recognize his voice anywhere.

"We don't want a bunch of drunks and sinners stumbling through our streets at midnight!" Charity called out.

I leaned over and whispered. "Hey, Charity, when did you get all fire and brimstone on me?"

"Shh," she said and grinned.

"I want to know why the governor would waste her time meddling in the issues of a small town like this?" a pressman asked.

"We realize it is an election year, but come on!" Helen yelled.

To Governor Danvers's credit she smiled, took a deep breath and spoke in a calm and easy manner. "This is my hometown. When Bill called me and told me the situation that he was in, my heart went out to him. Here is a decent and honest, hardworking mayor trying to bring revenue to his stagnant town. The opposition was tough, he said. I felt honor-bound to come to his aid. It's one of the perks of being in a position of power. Being able to help my friends when they need me."

"Ah, pooh!" somebody said.

"Please, voters. Vote yes for Proposition Seven. It will turn this town around in nothing flat. You'll have the money for air-conditioning in your school. Sheila won't have to keep the school bus held together with her bobby pins and rubber bands anymore. How about a big public parking lot for the tourists?" she went on.

"There won't be any tourists when you get finished with this town. Just gamblers," Charity said.

Eleanore got ready to say something and I put my hand on her arm to keep her quiet. So far, the townspeople were winning this showdown, and I didn't want Eleanore to open her mouth and change all that.

"What about the ethics of gambling, Governor?" another pressman asked. "There are moral issues here."

"Riverboat gambling is a completely honest and legal way to bring revenue to a town. What stand do you think the governor of Nevada takes? He wouldn't have a state to govern if it weren't for Las Vegas," she continued. "Already in the years since riverboat gambling has been legalized, Saint Charles and downtown Saint Louis have seen an amazing increase in profits. A revitalization of what made them great to begin with. We can make small-town Missouri a hotbed of activity and profits, too."

My father says that all politicians should be strung by their toes just for good measure.

"No, thank you!" Elmer yelled out. "Do it somewhere else."

"Shh," somebody in the crowd said. "Let the governor speak."

"If you pass up the chance to bring jobs and profits to your hometown, you will regret it. There are people in this town who drive almost an hour one way to their jobs, because there aren't enough jobs in New Kassel, and definitely not jobs that would pay them decent wages. With the riverboat, those people could have jobs right here in their hometown. When Bill opens up his hotel, there will be more jobs to fill, and more visitors who will spend money in our restaurants and our shops. As it stands now, the Murdoch Inn is perpetually half empty."

"It is not!" Eleanore yelled.

I grabbed her arm.

"Well, it's not," she said to me. "I only have two vacant rooms right now."

I knew and Eleanore knew that our town was doing just fine.

And most of us here did. But the governor had now painted a half-empty Murdoch Inn in some of the townspeople's minds, and it would take a lot to make that vision disappear.

Wait a minute. What hotel was the mayor going to build?

"What hotel?" I yelled.

Red creeped across the top of Bill Castlereagh's head. He looked at the ground nervously, and then out at the Mississippi River. I imagined that he wanted to go jump in it right about now. It was obvious that he wasn't prepared to talk about it.

"Tell them about your plans, Bill," Hope Danvers said.

"Well," he stammered. "As some of you know, I've bought the house that once belonged to Catherine Finch. It is my plan to turn it into a grand hotel."

It was also clear that Hope Danvers hadn't known that Bill was going to renovate a building already there. She seemed shocked by the news. Or maybe it was by the mention of Catherine Finch. Or maybe it was the mention of the house where her cousin had disappeared sixty-two years ago. Yeah, that could be it.

The crowd murmured and mumbled. The Finch house would make a perfect hotel. It was large, it had more rooms than any other building within fifty miles, and it was beautiful. As of right now, we couldn't fill it, though. So the mayor was counting on the riverboat to fill up his new hotel.

I knew all along he had a personal stake in all this. I just knew it.

"Speaking of Catherine Finch," a reporter said, "Governor Danvers, what do you make of the authorities' finding the body of your cousin sixty-something years later?"

"I . . . I think it is a wonderful thing that his whereabouts all these years are now known. All of this can now be put to rest. I only wish my Aunt Catherine were alive to see it," she said. Good recovery. Or was it? Certainly she had to have known that the subject of Byron would come up today. She was standing in the very spot where he was found. She had to have known it.

In fact, I'd say she had been banking on it. This way she could play the bereaved cousin and cast off any doubts of her involvement that the public may have had. But the first part of the day didn't seem to have gone the way she and the mayor had intended.

Neither would the second part, if I could help it. The subject had been broached; I couldn't let the ball drop.

I walked through the crowd, leaving the sheriff and the gang to wonder behind me. I walked up to a cameraman and tapped him on the shoulder. I pointed to his badge, which he wore around his neck. "Can I borrow that for a minute?" I asked.

"No," he said, appalled. "You think I'm crazy?"

"I guarantee you great footage," I said. "If you let me use your press badge, I promise you a show you won't regret."

He just stared at me.

"Think about it: only you and one other station are going to have footage that the whole state will want," I said, pointing to the only other cameraman in the crowd. "If you'll just let me borrow that badge. Please?"

He looked around, unsure of what to do. His anchorwoman had her back to us, a few rows up. "I'm not going to do anything bad. It will all be within journalistic rights. Scout's honor," I said and held up three fingers. I had never been a scout, so I don't know if I was supposed to hold up two or three fingers. Evidently, he had never been a scout either.

"All right," he said and took it off and handed it to me. "But it better be good."

I wasn't sure what he was planning on doing to me if I didn't produce quality stuff, but I didn't have the time really to contemplate it at the moment. I put his badge on around my neck and walked right up to the front row. "Governor Danvers," I said. "Victory Keith here, from *New Kassel News*. How do you suppose that little Byron Finch managed to get out in the woods on the night he disappeared?"

"In the woods . . ." was all she said.

"He was hit hit by lightning. He had to be outside, somewhere."

Governor Danvers turned white and her mouth dropped open. Funny, the news seemed to have the same effect on everybody. She tried to speak but nothing came out. She cleared her throat, but she just stood riveted in place. This time when she tried to speak, she had more success. "I'm sure I wouldn't know."

"You were there the night that Byron disappeared."

"I'm not here to discuss this. I'm here to discuss riverboat gambling in New Kassel." Her voice broke and sounded as though she was about to cry. The crowd was now murmuring and restless.

"Governor, it is a known fact that you were there the night he disappeared."

"Along with five other children," she said justly.

"That's it? Just five children? Weren't there any adults in the house?"

"Yes, of course," she said.

"Then why would you only mention the children, Governor?"

She shook from head to toe, with anger or fear, or possibly both. One thing was for certain—her glare never left me. I felt as if I were cooking under the intensity of it.

"Governor, you are aware that one of your other cousins, Patrick Ward, was found dead right here, where you're standing, just a few weeks ago?"

"A most unfortunate accident," she said.

"Oh, a most unfortunate poisoning. A big helping of clam chowder, I believe," I said. The murmur from the crowd grew louder. I had to raise my voice to be heard. "Governor, when was the last time you saw your cousin, Patrick Ward? And don't tell me it was the night of the disappearance of Byron Finch. He was there, too, I'm aware. But surely you've seen him since then."

Hope Danvers stammered and stuttered. Not even the pinkness of her suit could manage to keep any color in her face. I went on. "The authorities now have enough evidence, Governor, that they believe some members of the family may actually have known the fate of poor little Byron all these years. You wouldn't be one of them? Would you?"

With that, Governor Hope Danvers walked off of the stage, ran to her limousine and drove off, leaving her aides in the rubble of what was once the Yates house. The crowd was humming and buzzing with excitement. The mayor was scowling at me, but what else was new?

I turned around and tossed the cameraman his press badge. "Was that good enough for you?" I asked. He just smiled at me and clutched the badge as I walked by him. The jaw of his anchorwoman was close to the ground.

I was feeling quite proud of myself and was happily accepting the greetings of my fellow New Kasselonians when the sheriff grabbed my arm with such fierceness that the pain shot all the way down to my hand. "Ouch! What is the matter with you, you big ogre?"

"That's Sheriff Big Ogre, to you. Get in the car!"

He all but threw me in the car and slammed the door. The whole car shook with the reverberation of it. Then he got in and slammed *his* door, and rattled my teeth all over again.

"What the *hell* was that?" he screamed. His face was as red as a tomato.

"That was journalistic magic," I said, with my hands spread apart the way those cheesy magicians do.

"It has not been publicly released that Patrick Ward was poisoned by clam chowder," he said. "Nor has it been publicly released that Byron Finch was hit by lightning."

"But I thought—"

"No! No, Torie, that's the problem. You weren't thinking. Not one little bit!" he yelled and hit the steering wheel. "Dammit, anyway."

"But . . . you had to have released . . ." I said, feeling my high ebb away from me.

"I don't have to do anything but die and pay taxes, and if you ever make me this angry again, I fear all I'll have left to do is pay taxes!"

"But you said you were going to release the info. It's all over the *National Enquirer*, for Pete's sake," I stammered. "Eleanore gave me a copy."

"No. What is in the papers is that the skeleton of Byron Lee Finch was found in a wall of an abandoned building in a small historic tourist town of eastern Missouri. End of story. That's what the papers say," he said.

"Oh." Well, in truth, I hadn't actually read the article in the *National Enquirer*.

He turned the engine on and rammed it into gear and drove away. He backed into my driveway and then turned back the other direction, toward the outer road. "Where are we going?" I asked, as I saw Eleanore waving to me from the crowd.

"Don't speak to me," he said.

"Well, if you don't want me speaking to you, then let me out of the car."

"Shut up," he said.

I shut up and watched the town disappear behind us as we made our way down the outer road. We were headed for Wisteria. He was taking me to my mother. I just knew it. He was going to take me to Mom and tell on me. Then she'd berate me, make me feel horrible, make me apologize to him and mortify me.

Instead, we pulled in front of the sheriff's station. Okay . . .

He got out, came over and opened my door, and once again grabbed my arm as tight as he could.

"What—"

"Shut up," he said.

"But—"

"Shut up."

I shut up as he led me into the office. I smiled at Newsome as

I went in, tried to say something polite, but the sheriff tugged on me and cut me off in mid-sentence. And then I saw it. At the end of the hall was the jail cell.

"Oh, no, you don't!" I said.

But it was too late. He opened the cell door, threw me in, and locked the door.

"I'm claustrophobic!" I yelled.

He turned and walked away from me.

"Sheriff! Colin. Dad . . ."

Thirty

H ey! Are you gonna arrest me, or what?"

I'd been sitting inside the Wisteria jail cell for close to six hours. It was boring as heck in here, which was the point. The seat was as hard as a rock, and there weren't even any interesting mice to keep me from losing my mind. No, there was nothing. No phone call. No visitors. No food. And no rest room break. I'd been thinking about my slowly filling bladder for the past six hours. "Colin! If you don't let me pee, you're going to have a mess in here!"

I was past angry. I had been angry. Then I was embarrassed. Then I was laughing hysterically for about an hour. Then I started crying. Now I was angry again, only this time I was fuming. He hadn't spoken to me since he threw me in here, and that was against my constitutional rights.

I thought.

Hell, I didn't know. How would I know something like that? Why would I know something like that?

I grabbed ahold of the bars and tried to move them. "I need to peeeeeee!" I screamed at the top of my lungs.

"Are you miserable enough?" Colin asked me. He had just appeared like magic while I had my eyes squeezed shut, shouting to the heavens.

"Yes," I answered through clenched teeth.

"Good," he said. He pulled up a chair and straddled it backward. He hung his hands over the edge and smiled at me. "Now you sit there and squirm while I talk."

I didn't roll my eyes as I wanted to. I barely even breathed. I've never seen him so angry in my life.

"Here are the rules, Torie O'Shea. I like you, really I do. You're spunky, and I admire that. You're my stepdaughter now, and I don't want anything to interfere with my relationship with your mother. I admire all that you do. You're an amazing woman. You're like this hound dog. You attack a project and you don't miss one little detail," he said.

I must admit that this was not the berating I thought I would get.

"But if you ever, and I mean ever again, give away the details of an investigation, I will arrest you for interference. And I will press charges. I don't care whose daughter you are," he said. His eyebrows twitched, hinting at just how angry he really was.

God, I felt so little.

"Do you understand what I am saying? I trust you with information because, Lord help me, you have become an invaluable assistant on certain investigations. But we had an agreement. Remember? I'd let you do your thing as long as you told me what you were doing and as long as you didn't endanger yourself or interfere," he said. "What you did today with the governor was interference. No way around it."

"I didn't know."

"What do you mean?"

"I didn't know that it was still a secret," I said in a small voice. "I would never had done it otherwise. I just wanted to see her squirm. You believe me, don't you? That I would never have intentionally in front of rolling television cameras done something like that?"

"Lord help me, but yes. I do believe you," he said.

I squirmed myself, because quite frankly my bladder was about to explode. "So . . . am I like your official sidekick?"

"Oh, no," he said. "There's nothing official about you. You are unofficially my unofficial sidekick. But I mean it. You ever do anything like that again and I will arrest you and press charges."

"I totally understand," I said.

He sat there for a minute looking at me. Then a big wide smile played across his face. "Oh, man, did you see her squirm?"

"Yeah," I said. "Pretty cool, huh?"

"Don't push me," he said, the smile instantly gone. He held up a finger. "Okay, here's the deal. I went and had a talk with the governor while you were getting to know Bertha a little better."

"Bertha?"

"The jail cell," he said, like I was stupid or something.

"Oh. Well?" I asked.

"Part of the reason I threw you in jail was because I didn't want you begging to come along," he said.

"No fair," I said.

"Shut up," he said and pointed his finger at me. I shut my mouth. "I had to try and come up with a good reason for how a 'journalist' got ahold of that information. It wasn't easy. I told her I had a leak in my department and that the guilty party had already been fired."

"That's good," I said. If he didn't let me use the rest room soon, I was going to scream.

"Let's just hope she doesn't start checking, because I haven't fired anybody in the department in two years," he said.

"Oh."

"But I think it worked. So then, as the investigating officer, I had to officially ask her questions about the night of the kidnapping and Patrick Ward," he said.

"And?"

He stood up then and put his chair back to where he had gotten it. "She can prove that she didn't see him that entire week. Nor was there any clam chowder served at her house that week, either."

"That makes no sense. She has the most to lose," I said.

"Maybe," he said. "What we think is enough for a motive may not be what somebody else thinks is."

"I guess," I said. "But her reaction. She knows something she's not telling us."

"Probably," he said. Colin started to walk away.

"Colin?"

"Yeah?"

"Are you gonna let me out of here?" I asked.

"Oh, yeah. Almost forgot," he said, smiling. Oh, he just thought he was so funny. He pulled the key out and unlocked the jail. "You have to go by and see your mother before you go home. Rudy and the kids already ate dinner."

"Great," I said. "You called everybody and told them?"

"Didn't have to. Eleanore called Rudy and wanted to know where I had taken you," he explained. "So Rudy called here looking for you."

"And you told him what?"

"That you were in jail."

"Uh," I said, stomping my foot. "What did he say?"

"He said, 'Let me know when you cut her loose,' " he said.

"He did not."

"I swear," he said, holding up one hand.

Thirty-one

I arrived home late. Rudy and the kids were already in bed, but he had been a really nice husband and left me a plate of food in the microwave. Meat loaf, which he knew I wouldn't eat because I thought it was the grossest thing on the planet, broccoli, carrots, and yellow rice.

I zapped the food, watching the plate spin round and round, not really wanting to go upstairs and face Rudy. Today's escapade had to go on my list of dumbest things I've ever done. But I had just been so caught up in the moment. I guess that's how activists go a little too far with things sometimes, because they just get so caught up in what's going on that their judgment gets dulled.

On the table sat a small rectangular box, wrapped in silver paper and tied with a big pink bow. I stood there staring at it a minute, with the microwave whirring behind me, wondering what in the world I had done to deserve a present. It wasn't my birthday or anniversary. And I certainly hadn't been a model wife as of late. Well, for that feat I'd have to go back to the first year we were married, when I actually *believed* the part when the priest had said, "Obey your husband." When my first labor pain hit with Rachel, I pretty much figured that from then on out that my days of obeying

Rudy were over. I still honor him and respect him, and, of course, love him. But that obey stuff is sort of Elizabethan.

Eventually I walked over to the table, just as Fritz came running in, dragging his belly. He smelled the meat loaf in the microwave and knew that he was going to get a midnight snack. I looked down at the package, and there was a note under it. It read:

> So that you won't give our deputies any more
> concussions. We don't have that many of them.
> Can't afford to lose any.
>
> Love, Rudy
> P.S. Somebody Newton called for you.

I opened the box and inside was a cellular phone. Wow, the internet and a cellular phone all in one year! And I still didn't have a remote control for the television.

This was a really cool gift, which, of course, made me feel worse about having been in a jail cell all afternoon. When the guys at Rudy's work sit around and talk about their wives tomorrow, he's probably the only one who can say that his wife spent the afternoon before in Bertha. Well, there's no probably about it.

The microwave dinged and I took the plate out. I put the chunk of meat loaf on one of Fritz's plates and set it on the floor. He was a happy dog. His belly seemed to get lower to the ground living with us. And one wouldn't think that his belly could get much lower, considering he's a wiener dog.

I was totally wound up and did not want to go upstairs. Rudy was going to be very upset, and he had every right to be. Of course, on the other hand, the only people in this world who ever get things done are the movers and shakers. The people who will go out on a limb and take a chance. So, I guess my guilt in today's events would have to be determined by which side of the line you are on. Are you a mover and a shaker? Then I made you proud. Are you the type to watch and not make waves? Then I embarrassed you to death. Actually, all of life is sort of like that. Relative. It's all relative. I bet Einstein had no idea that he was defining life with his theory of relativity. He just thought he was defining the movement of a train.

I couldn't stand it one more second. I was thinking entirely too philosophically, which always got me into trouble and usually depressed me to boot. I needed to do something. I supposed I could work on that signature quilt that I had started when I hosted the family reunion last year. But then I'd have to haul it all out, which wasn't a good thing to do since it was so late. Which meant that I wouldn't put it away and then Rudy would find it in the morning and have one more thing to be angry with me over.

I reread the note, and the part about Somebody Newton calling for me sort of stuck out. That poor guy was still waiting for Colin to call him back over that darn necklace. That was what I could do. I could go out to the Finch house and go through her jewelry, so that I could call this guy tomorrow and at least let him know if I even found it.

I had my trusty cellular phone with me now, and it was already charged. I wrote Rudy a note and told him I'd be back around two or three in the morning. The Finch house was only five minutes away. And how long could it take me to go through her jewelry? I'm a night person, anyway. I always work best between 10 P.M. and one in the morning. Of course, it could be that I'd conditioned myself to do that because that was when the kids were in bed. Whatever the reason, it was when I did my best work.

I locked the door behind me and drove out to the Finch house. I will admit, going through all those tall weeds and flowers in the back garden to get to the back door was pretty creepy at midnight. I made it in the house and locked the door behind me. I flipped on a light, then another light in the main great room with the stained-glass window. Then I went upstairs to Catherine's bedroom.

The more I thought about being alone in the house at midnight, the more it bothered me. I'd been there this late before, but I'd stayed all evening. There was something different about coming into the house after the world had gone to sleep, rather than leaving while the world was still awake. It was as if I wasn't supposed to disrupt the house. I know that houses don't have souls or anything like that, but that was the feeling I got.

So I decided I would just dump Catherine's jewelry into a box and take it home to sift through it. I had just set the fourth jewelry box inside a big packing box when I heard it. A crash on the third floor. It was only when I was halfway up the stairs that I realized that Mary hadn't been here since I'd been here last, and there was no way she could have left a window open. Unless she'd opened more than one the last time she was here.

I couldn't find any open windows on the third floor. I checked all of them except the one in Byron's room, because I had shut that one the night before. I remembered doing it.

Just as I was getting ready to head downstairs, I turned back to look at the open doorway at the end of the hall that was Byron's room. The hallway seemed to get longer and narrower even though I hadn't moved.

This was silly. If somebody was going to break into this house, they sure as heck would pick a floor closer to the ground than this one. Colin must have been in here yesterday. I walked down to the end of the hall toward Byron's room.

Yeah, but why would Colin come here yesterday and open the window in Byron's room? That made no sense, either.

The world seemed to slow down. My legs became heavy as lead weights. Every step toward Byron's room was a calculated effort. Until I rounded the door and saw the window in Byron Lee's room wide open. Just as it had been yesterday. I didn't shut it. I didn't even go in the room. I turned and ran down the hall.

It made no sense. None of it. Nobody in his right mind would break in on the third floor when there were two floors below it. I'm not even sure if someone could find a ladder that would go up that high unless he was a professional painter. What were the chances of professional painters breaking into the Finch house? Nil.

Even if they would, why would they keep picking Byron's room? Why not some other room on the third floor? It made absolutely no sense. By the time I'd hit the second floor, something new assaulted my senses.

Music.

Somewhere on the second floor, Catherine Finch's old Victrola was playing "Monday Mornin' Blues." One of Catherine's best-loved songs and biggest hits.

I stopped short on the steps. I had planned on going by and picking up the box of jewelry, but now I was frozen stiff on the stairs. Goose bumps traveled down my arms and legs, reaching all the way to my toes.

"My baby's leavin' on Monday. Goin' back to Caroline. Means come Monday mornin', I be losin' my mind." Catherine's husky and mournful voice echoed down the hallway to me. It seemed to wrap itself around me, embracing me from a place lost in history.

"Monday mornin' got no reason for livin'. Monday mornin' got no reason for carin'. Monday mornin' I be losin' my mind."

I ran down the steps as fast as I could, through the great room, through the kitchen and out the back door, all the while feeling as if somebody was on my heels. I ran as best as I could through the overgrown garden, tripping once on my own shoelace. Finally I made it around to the front of the house where my car was.

I was grateful that I hadn't locked the door. Rudy was always drilling that into me. "Make sure you lock the car doors, Torie." It was just so hard for me to get used to doing that. I grew up in New Kassel, for crying out loud. Nobody locked anything in New Kassel. Well, Tobias Thorley kept his liquor cabinet locked. But other than that . . .

Once I was in my car and my heart rate had come down under a hundred beats a minute, I pulled the cell phone out of my pocket and dialed the sheriff. Well, actually I dialed my mother's house. No matter what, it would be my mother's house and he just lived there. Silly, I know.

"Hello?" Colin answered.

"Colin, it's me, Torie," I said.

"Yeah?"

"I'm out at the Finch house."

"Okay," he said. "Why?"

"I couldn't sleep, so I thought I'd come out and get some work done," I said.

"So why are you calling me?" he said, the sleep evident in his voice.

Just then I noticed something. I got out of the car, with the cell phone held up to my ear. From where the driveway was positioned, I had a perfect view of the stained-glass window in the great room. In my effort to leave the house in record speed, I had left on all the lights. And looking at the stained-glass window from the outside, with the light behind it, I made a startling discovery.

"Torie?" he asked.

"I know why Byron Finch was in the woods that night."

Thirty-two

Y ou wanna run that by me again?" said Colin.

I sat across from him in his kitchen, with my mother seated next to him. The sun was beginning to rise through the window behind them. They lived in a nice ranch house on Weeping Willow Avenue, in the heart of the residential area of Wisteria.

I had made Colin stay on the cell phone line until I arrived at their house. He sent out a deputy to dust the house for prints, but I didn't stay around to greet him.

"What part do you want me to repeat?" I asked.

"None of it makes any sense," my mother said. "Open windows. Music playing. Are you suggesting there's a ghost in the Finch house?"

"No, of course not," I said. Although I believed what I just said, I still got goose bumps thinking about the Victrola playing down the hallway, with me frozen on the steps. "I think somebody is trying to scare me."

"Why?" she asked.

"Obviously, because she knows too much," Colin said. "And she's got complete access to the house."

"I think somebody is afraid of what I'll find."

"The blanket?" my mom asked.

"Could be. Maybe there's something else in the house I haven't found that they don't want me to find. So they're trying to scare me off," I said.

"Like in Scooby Doo." Colin smirked.

"Zoinks, Shaggy!" I answered.

"Shut up, you smart aleck," he said.

"Sorry."

They were both quiet a moment. Mom picked at the design in the wood of the table, trying desperately to stay awake. Finally, Colin spoke. "I think you shouldn't go back out there alone. It's too dangerous."

"They're just trying to scare me."

"How do you know you won't end up like Patrick Ward?" he asked.

"I hate clam chowder."

"Torie," he said in his best fatherly tone.

"All right," I said. "I won't go back out there alone."

"Now what about the other part. The part about Byron and the woods. Why do you think he was in the woods that night?" Colin asked.

My mom's kitchen was done in country red and green, with apples as the accent. She had an apple cookie jar and apple canisters. I had to wonder how Colin really felt about all the apples, and the lace doilies in the living room. It was kind of funny, actually. "Mom, you like apples, don't you?"

"How can you tell?" she asked and smiled.

"Because they're all over your kitchen. When we walk into Elmer Kolbe's house, what do we instantly learn about him?"

She shrugged and then added, "That he's Catholic. There's a crucifix and a picture of Mary in the hallway."

"Exactly. We know that Bill is a bowler by all of his trophies."

"And his bronzed bowling shoes."

"And Tobias is the biggest Cardinals fan west of the Mississippi," I said. "Why else would he have Cardinal T-shirts, pennants and photographs all over his basement wall?"

"What has this got to do with Byron?" Colin asked.

"In the great room of the home of Catherine Finch, there is a large stained-glass window, almost the size of the whole wall. The stained-glass window depicts fairies."

"Fairies," he said.

"Yes. They're all over the window. Some are flying, some are playing, one is sleeping in a tree. And in her library there are books on the existence of fairies and other forest spirits."

"Other forest spirits?" the sheriff asked.

"You know—brownies, gnomes, that sort of thing. Characters from what we would call folklore," I explained.

"Okay," he said. "I'm following, really I am."

"No, you're not. You're as lost as you can be because you dismiss fairies as nothing more than folklore or the stories you tell children at bedtime," I said. "But Catherine believed in them. She believed they were real."

His expression was still blank.

"The changeling," my mother said with horror on her face.

"Exactly," I said.

"What?" Colin asked. "What are you saying?"

"The one thing in the window that I didn't pay too much attention to was the baby. There's a baby, behind a rock. I was so taken with the beauty of the window, and all the fairies dancing around, that I really didn't give the baby much thought. But last night, looking at it from the outside, I understood. It all made sense."

"Well, it's still not making sense to me," Colin said. He looked over at my mother as she shivered.

"Fairy folklore, Colin. The changeling baby. The fairies would take a human baby and replace it with a changeling," I said.

He looked at me a moment and then shook his head. "Are you trying to tell me that a fairy took Byron? I must have left you in the cell too long."

"No, I'm not," I said. "What I'm trying to say is that Cecily and Aurora grew up being taught their mother's religion. Just like you were taught the Catholic way and my old boss was Jewish because he was raised Jewish. Cecily and Aurora were being raised, well . . . I guess it's what you'd call pagan. Anyway, they would have believed what we consider to be folklore."

"I still don't understand what you're saying. So what if they believed it?" Colin said. "A fairy didn't come and take Byron into the woods."

"No," I said. "They did. I think Byron was fairy bait."

Colin just looked at me as if I'd grown an extra head. Then, without finesse, he just threw his head back and laughed as hard as he could. He continued to laugh until I thought he'd pop a blood vessel.

"Don't laugh," I said. "You're going to sprain something."

"That's . . . preposterous," he said.

"Think about it, Colin. If you were ten years old and you believed in fairies and you and your cousins decided you wanted to catch one, how would you go about it?"

He stopped laughing.

"You'd have to have bait. And everybody knows how the fairies love human babies," I said.

"Oh my God," he said and ran his hand through his hair.

"I think that was the plan of the cousins that night. They were going to try and catch a fairy. So they took the only baby they had access to out into the woods, never intending any harm to come to him. They laid him on the ground to wait for the fairies to come . . ."

"And he got struck by lightning," Mom finished.

"It makes perfect sense," I said.

"Oh, yeah. I can just see me basing an investigation on this," Colin said.

"If he wasn't kidnapped, what other reason would there be for him to be in those woods? Somebody took him into the woods, where he was hit by lightning. Once he was dead, that somebody stuffed him in a semi-finished wall."

Colin got up and walked over to the coffeepot, where he poured himself a huge mug of freshly brewed coffee. My mother looked at me across the kitchen table with that look. The one that said that she believed me but she wasn't sure what good it would do.

"You really believe this?" he asked and turned around to face us.

"It sounds exactly like something a group of kids would do. I believe they had absolutely no intention to hurt Byron. I think they panicked and hid him in the wall. I mean, Byron was Walter and Catherine's favorite child. What would life have been like for Cecily and Aurora if their parents found out they were responsible for the death of their favorite child? So they put him in the wall, snuck back in the house and the next morning went along with the kidnapping theory," I said.

"Only, Catherine got wise," my mother added.

"I believe so. I'm not sure how. Maybe it was just a mother's intuition. Maybe she found the blanket, too. Maybe there's something else in the house that I haven't found that Catherine did find, eventually. And then she became estranged even more from her daughters," I said. "Because she knew they had been responsible and had known all along and watched her suffer."

"Incredible," Colin said. "It makes sense, yet at the same time it just seems so far-fetched."

"Not for children. Mary is convinced that if she clicks her heels together three times and says, 'There's no place like the North Pole,' that she'll eventually wake up in Santa's workshop. Kids are very impressionable. And trusting. They believe what their parents tell them."

"So what do you do next?" Mom asked.

"Well, we either try and find more evidence in the house, or we get one of them to confess," Colin said.

"What about Patrick Ward?" Mom asked. "One of the remaining five killed him. You know they did."

"But why? If it wasn't Hope Danvers," I said, "then who would have done it? After all these years?"

"Call it a hunch, but I don't think it was his sister," the sheriff said.

"The sad thing is, if I'm right, there isn't anything anybody could do to the five of them. They were all juveniles. Very young juveniles. It was an accident. The only thing they did wrong was not telling the truth. There really isn't anything anybody could do to them at this point," I said. "Until one cousin had to go and kill another cousin. Now someone has gone beyond the point of no return."

Colin set his coffee cup down on the counter and stretched. A big yawn came out of him, and then he rubbed his eyes. "Well, as soon as I get to work I'm going to conduct some interviews with Hugh Danvers and Lanna Petrovic. Maybe even work my way around to Cecily and Aurora. Then you and I are going to go through the remaining things in that house," he said. "There has to be something."

With that, he kissed my mother and disappeared down the hallway. I assumed he was going back to bed and that he was finished with me. My mother smiled an affectionate smile.

"What?" I asked.

"It's good to see you two working together," she said.

"Well, it's either that or go back to Bertha," I said.

"Oh," she said, laughing. "You deserved that. I only wish I had had a jail cell when you were growing up."

"Uh, you . . . you . . . You're terrible," I said.

Suddenly, she turned very somber on me. "Children do stupid things, Torie. Ice-skating on a pond not totally frozen, playing with their dad's guns. Trying to summon a fairy doesn't sound all that outrageous to me. It's no more far-fetched than kids playing with a Ouija board or trying to conjure up Satan. And we all know that kids have done those things. When you think about how children play, especially before the days of Nintendo and television . . . It's not impossible at all, really."

"I know," I said. "It's one of those things that sound really far-fetched when you say it out loud. But when you think about it, when I was ten years old, I did a lot more stupid things than that. I just never had a baby brother who accidentally got killed while I was doing them."

Thirty-three

It was the morning of the first day of the Pickin' and Grinnin' Festival. This was one of my favorite annual events held in New Kassel. Some of the bands came back every year and so we were on a first-name basis with them.

The Murdoch Inn no longer had any vacancies and, in fact, many of the fans that came to the festival stayed in Wisteria or Meyersville. I sort of liked the idea of the Finch house becoming a hotel. It was certainly big enough and beautiful enough. If only we could fill it year-round and not just when we had a music festival, an Octoberfest or some other event. But riverboat gambling was absolutely not the answer.

I was in the bathroom getting ready for the day when the phone rang.

"Torie, tell me you had nothing to do with the article in this morning's *Post*," the sheriff bellowed.

"Okay, I had nothing to do with the article in this morning's *Post*," I repeated. "Now, you want to tell me what this is all about?"

I carried the cordless phone to my bathroom, which was located on the upper floor, as was my bedroom. I picked up my mascara tube and began applying the dark brown sticky stuff to my poor eyelashes, which certainly had never done anything to warrant such punishment.

"There's an article in this morning's *Post* telling the whole story."

"What whole story?" I asked.

"You honestly haven't seen it?"

"No, I've been trying to get ready for the festival," I said.

"The article in the *Post* cites the finding of Byron's blanket in the Finch home as proof positive that one of the six children present that night kidnapped and murdered him," Colin said.

I dropped the mascara tube into the sink, which left a dark brown trail of sticky stuff all over the white porcelain. "You're kidding. No, you're not kidding." I sat down on the edge of the toilet.

All I could hear was Colin's steady breathing on the other end of the phone line, and Fritz downstairs barking at something. The rest of the world seemed to fade away, while those two sounds seemed to get louder.

"How is this possible?" I asked. My breathing came in forceful spurts. I'm pretty sure I was having a panic attack.

"I'd say somebody leaked the information," he said. I could tell by the tone of his voice that he didn't believe me one bit. He thought that somehow I had leaked the information.

"Colin, I've told nobody about the blanket except you and my mother. And you've told the other deputies. You have the evidence, I don't even have it anymore," I said.

I needed air. I tried to open the tiny bathroom window, but it was stuck as usual. If it didn't get shut just right, it would be in crooked somehow and it couldn't be opened without a crowbar.

"Well, it doesn't matter now, I guess," the sheriff said, disgusted. "I have to haul all the cousins in for questioning."

"Because of the article?" I asked. I walked out into the bedroom and opened the window there. I needed air. Of course, in my state of rapid-breathing-induced confusion, I forgot that the air outside was going to be hotter than the air in the house. I found out real quick, though. Shutting the window, I went to the air vent for the air-conditioning and stuck my face over it, where I took deep breaths and let the cool air flow over my face. I'm told that panic attacks are just all in my head. I didn't much care. Cold air always made me breathe better.

"Well, yes," he said.

"Okay," I said. "Are you not coming to the festival then?"

"No, I'll be there eventually. Although I may have to go wherever Hope Danvers is, rather than have her come to me."

"Okay, I'll see you there," I said.

"Torie?"

"Yeah?"

"You're telling me the truth?"

"I swear to you that I did not tell anybody about the baby blanket," I said. "Except you. And Mom."

"All right," he said. "I'll see you later."

I sat down on the floor next to the air vent wondering just how this story had leaked. It couldn't have come at a worse time.

•

An hour later, I was standing next to Tobias Thorley, who was making kettle popcorn. He was about the scrawniest person in New Kassel. A good wind could knock him over.

Kettle popcorn was the best-smelling stuff in the world. It smelled like popcorn, but it had a more robust country smell. Since it was made in a big iron kettle, the oil and the kettle smell actually mixed with the popcorn smell.

One booth down was Chuck's booth. He was serving beer and pizza by the slice. Obviously, he was running a very popular booth. Across from us was Helen's booth. She was selling four different kinds of fudge from her business, The Lick-A-Pot Candy Shoppe. She was also selling rock candy, cinnamon sticks and pralines, all made by her wonderfully talented staff.

Soda booths, cotton-candy booths and hot dog stands dotted

the landscape, all adding, not just color, but wonderful aromas to the air. Elmer had set up the berry booth. It was filled with our leftover strawberry and blackberry jams, preserves, syrup and pies from earlier festivals of the year. The pies had been frozen, of course.

Mary and Rachel were on the rectory steps handing out maps of New Kassel to the tourists. The maps pointed out where the public rest rooms were, along with historical buildings and all the shops. The girls looked especially cute today. Rachel wore a lime-green dress and Mary a lemon-yellow one. Wilma had made them and Rachel had requested that they wear them today. It was the first festival without Wilma, she had said, and so she and Mary wanted to do something special. Underneath those pre-teen hormones was still a thoughtful little girl, which made me very happy. It made me feel confident that she would survive her teenage years without too much turmoil.

The only thing I didn't like about the Pickin' and Grinnin' Festival was that I only got to sit down and actually listen to a few of the bands. The rest of the time I had to work.

I walked through the crowd of people to find my grandmother sitting in a lawn chair before the stage. She was right smack-dab in the middle of the front row, where she sat for all of our music festivals. I'm not sure who she thought she was, but she definitely thought she was entitled to a front-row center seat. I sat down next to her on a piece of lawn. "Hey, Gert."

"Don't talk too much," she said. "I want to hear the music. Reminds me of home."

As it should. Most of the music that would be played this weekend could be traced back to the Appalachian region that was her home. And her parents' home and their parents' homes. She was of the predominantly Scotch-Irish stock that had come from the British Isles in the eighteenth century and settled in the mountain region of Appalachia. Mostly Virginia, West Virginia, North Carolina and Kentucky.

With the people of the British Isles had come the music. The jauntiness of American fiddle music is really the Scotch-Irish high-land music, just Americanized. It moved west with the settlers in the form of centuries-old folk music. My father's family was just as influenced by this music as was my mother's. My grandpa Keith was a fiddle player whose great-grandfather had come from North Carolina. I used to sit at his feet and listen to him play that fiddle, and I was completely entranced with the speed his fingers would move across the neck. I still am. There are no chord markings on the neck of a violin, as there are on the neck of a guitar. How did he know where to put his fingers?

Maybe that's why this music is so well loved. It reminds people of family, of home. It puts us in touch with days gone by, with people and places that we would never have an opportunity to know. And yet, through this music, they are stretching out across time and mountains to reach us in little old New Kassel.

The Blue Ridgers had just finished a traditional song called "Ragtime Annie." It was one of my favorites and it combined a guitar, bass, banjo and fiddle. "College Hornpipe" was next, and they finished up with "Wildwood Flower." For that final piece a little girl about ten years old came out and played the fiddle part. Her fingers flew across that violin with such familiarity that I knew she could probably play it in her sleep.

We clapped and clapped and then took a break to wait for the next band to come onstage.

"Can you do me a favor?" my grandmother asked. She was a lovely, although grouchy, octogenarian, with beautiful skin and high cheekbones.

"Sure," I said and stood up. I wiped the grass from my backside and waited for her request.

"Can you help me up?"

I laughed because I had known that was what she was going to ask. The lawn chair sat way too low to the ground and gave no support, so I knew she wasn't going to be able to get up. She was sharp and she was healthy, but she wasn't Sylvia.

I put my hand out and helped her up. As we were walking across the lawn, I saw a woman approaching us. I knew that I should have known her, but I couldn't place the face. She grabbed me by the arm.

"Can we speak somewhere, please?" she asked.

I studied her face. She was in her late sixties, had dark brown eyes and was about my height. I had seen her before. I should have known who she was, but I could not remember.

"Sure," I said. I turned to my grandmother. "Gert, Rudy is standing right over there by Tobias. You go on over by him."

I then gestured to the Santa Lucia Church. The woman led the way, and within a minute we were standing inside the church. There was nobody else inside. She walked up to the front, genuflected and sat down in a pew. I wasn't sure what it was that she wanted, so I just sat down next to her.

"You have no idea what you've done, do you?" she asked.

"What?" I said. "Do I know you?"

"I am Lanna Petrovic. Used to be Ward. I'm Patrick's sister."

And one of the six cousins.

Now I recognized her. She was a native. I'd seen her before on several occasions. "Of course," I said. "I should have known you. What have I done?"

"You found the blanket," she said. She moved her hand up to cover her mouth. A tear ran down her cheek.

"Tell me what happened," I said.

"You have no idea of the number of lives you are going to ruin. What will my grandchildren think of me?" she asked.

"You were just a kid," I said.

"How did you find it?" she asked, ignoring what I'd said.

"You mean you didn't know where it was?"

She shook her head no and swiped at a tear. "Aunt Catherine found it. She hid it as blackmail."

"What?" I asked. "Wait. Start at the beginning."

Lanna said nothing, she just picked at her thumbnail.

"You guys went out in the woods to catch a fairy, didn't you?"

Her eyes registered surprise. "How did you know?"

"The stained-glass window. The books. The fact that Catherine believed in the existence of fairies, so I assumed that her children would, too. Why else would Byron be outside during a storm?"

"Patrick didn't want to go. It had been storming, but he wasn't worried about lightning. Who would have thought in a million years that something like that would happen? He just didn't want to get caught out in the rain, because then we'd get in trouble," she said. "Hugh and Cecily insisted. So we all snuck out after everybody was asleep. It was a typical summer storm. It stormed and then it stopped. Only we didn't know that there was another front moving in. Hugh convinced us that the storm was over and that we'd be fine."

I never said a word. I tried not even to breathe because I didn't want to bring her back to the present. I just sat there and listened.

"So, we picked Byron up, blanket and all, and headed out to the woods. It was the woods between Aunt Catherine's house and the town limits. We found the spot that we'd picked out days before on another visit, and laid him down on the ground. It was a clearing, a meadow. There was one solitary tree in the meadow. We put him under it. We thought he'd be safer there because we could see him. And we'd be able to see the fairies when they came," she said. More tears rolled down her face. "The storm came up fast. When we realized that it was a new front coming through, we all ran into the clearing to get Byron. Before we could get to him . . . the . . . light . . . lightning—"

She broke down into a fit of sobs. For a full minute she just sobbed and heaved, her body racked by every one of them. I was imagining a lone tree in a meadow, with the wind blowing and the lightning licking across the sky. And six scared children. I shivered.

"It was horrible," she said finally. "The smell . . ."

I hadn't thought about there being a smell. I didn't want to think about a smell.

"We didn't know what to do. We panicked. We were standing in the middle of a field with a storm raging all around us. Hugh was yelling above the storm. 'We have to get rid of him. We have to get rid of him.'"

"Oh, God," I managed.

"Aurora was screaming, 'You killed my brother.' Over and over. Hugh didn't really kill him but to Aurora he may as well have. Finally, Hugh just picked him up and carried him toward New Kassel. Aurora was screaming the whole way. She was totally against it. Totally against putting him in the wall. But what else were we going to do? We were all afraid that we'd go to jail. We were too young and too naive to know any better. Plus, then Cecily reminded us that Byron was her mother's favorite child. And that life in our family would be hell if Aunt Catherine knew that all of her nieces and nephews, and her two daughters, were responsible for the death of her favorite child."

I sat there stupefied. Hearing the story from her was more horrifying than anything I could have conjured up.

"Patrick and Aurora were totally against putting Byron in that wall. But Hugh and Cecily insisted. Hope and I were at the point where we didn't care. We just wanted it over with. We were petrified that we were going to be hit by lightning, too," she said. "Then, on the way back through the woods, Aurora found Byron's blanket. We were all afraid to leave it there. So, Aurora picked it up and took it home. She hid it under her mattress."

But that wasn't where I found it, I thought to myself.

"Hugh and Cecily came up with this idea that we heard nothing, we saw nothing. We were in our beds the whole time. Hope said that it was a pretty smart thing to do because the authorities would assume that Byron was kidnapped. Which is exactly what happened," she said, staring down at her hands.

"So," I began, "what about the blanket?"

"Aurora and Cecily had every intention of getting rid of the blanket, but they couldn't find a time when their house wasn't crawling with the authorities. Finally, on a day when they thought they could get rid of it, when they went to get it, it was gone," she said.

"Catherine found it?"

"That's what we assumed. Only she never, ever spoke of it," she said. "I think she was waiting for her daughters to admit to her what they'd done."

"That makes no sense," I said.

"Why?"

"Because later, when Hector Castanza came along, she believed so completely that he was her son. If she'd found the blanket, how could she have believed that Hector was her son?" I asked.

Lanna wiped at her eyes. "I don't know," she said. "All these years we assumed Aunt Catherine had found it and hid it."

"So, who killed your brother?" I asked.

"I don't know," she said. "Torie, you have no idea what you've done."

"I didn't write that article in the *Post*, nor did I leak the information," I said. "I've done nothing."

"But you have. Even if you didn't leak anything. You're the one who found the blanket and turned it over to the authorities. We all knew that someday, when the Yates house came down, they'd find Byron and that most people would assume it was Byron. We kept hoping it wouldn't come down until after we were dead. Or that the floodwaters would just wash the house away. That I don't blame you for. What I blame you for is finding the blanket and giving it to the sheriff. And for confronting Hope on television about the whole ordeal. My children and grandchildren all want answers. My neighbors are looking at me differently. I think people are talking about me when I go shopping or to church," she said. "It's awful."

"Well, what happened to Byron was pretty awful."

"Don't you think I know that?" she screamed. Her voice echoed off the walls of the church. "Every single day, I have thought about that poor beautiful baby rotting in those walls. Every day. I have paid more dearly than if we had just admitted it the night it happened. People would have talked for a while, but then they would have gone on to something else. But having to think about him every day and not being able to talk about it has been a sentence much worse than anything anybody could have done to me back then. And now, having it come out when I'm an old and respectable woman—"

She sobbed again. "I'm very sorry," I said. "It must have been horrible to live with that."

"You have to do something," she said.

"What do you mean?"

"You have to make a retraction or something. You have to do something," she said, panicked.

"Lanna, I don't think there is anything I can do. The damage is done," I said. "I don't mean to sound pompous, but everything we do we have to answer for. Eventually."

"I was just a child."

"I know," I said. "But you grew up eventually, and still did nothing about it."

She just stared up at the crucifix. She didn't blink, but the tears still ran down her face, dropping off her cheeks.

"Lanna, it's very important. Why do you think your brother went to that house the night he died?"

"I think he went there to remove the skeleton," she said. "Somehow he found out that Bill was going to tear down the Yates house, and he wanted to get the skeleton out of the wall so that nobody would ever know what had happened."

"And if he hadn't died there, it would have worked," I said. "But how did he know the house was going to be torn down? Did you tell him?"

"No."

"Anybody else in New Kassel that Patrick kept in contact with?"

"Our family. Umm . . . Elmer Kolbe," she said. "And the Pershings."

Thirty-four

After leaving the Santa Lucia Church, I felt a little over-whelmed. It was as if the world were different when I stepped out into the sunshine. Lanna Petrovic's words haunted me. Every time I closed my eyes I saw that lone tree standing in the meadow, with the lightning snaking across the sky. And then I'd see the window with the fairies dancing and playing. An innocent child-hood adventure that turned horribly tragic.

Sheriff Brooke had arrived. Only he came as a civilian today. Tomorrow was his day to be on duty. He was standing by Tobias, ordering some kettle popcorn. I made a beeline straight for him and barely noticed when somebody said, "Hey, Torie." I waved to who-ever it was and kept the sheriff in my view.

"Sheriff!" I called out.

"Torie," he said. "What's up? You look upset."

"I *am* upset," I said. "And since when did you start noticing when I'm upset?"

"Jalena says I need to be more in tune to others," he said.

I couldn't help it. I cracked up laughing. Tobias gave a smirk, but wiped it off his face as soon as the sheriff looked at him. Our eyes had connected, though, so I know what Tobias was thinking. The same thing I was thinking—what the hell?

"Did my mother also tell you that you're an insensitive cad?"

"No, she neglected to mention that," he said. "Don't push it, Torie. What's up?"

"I just had a long talk with Lanna Petrovic," I said. "She confessed everything to me."

"Why? I didn't realize that you knew her that well."

"I don't," I said. "She thought I was the one responsible for the leak. And since I found the baby blanket, she's sort of holding me responsible for the fact that her neighbors are freaking out because they're living next door to a possible killer."

"Yeah, well, that'll do it," he said. "Funny thing. I just had a conversation with Hope Danvers and she admitted everything to me."

"She did?"

"Yes. She said that she had talked to Patrick on the phone and that he was going over to the Yates house to remove the skeleton. He wasn't trying to blackmail her," he said. "It seems at least the two of them had stuck together. Patrick knew that, out of the six cousins, Hope had the most to lose if the wall-baby story came out. He was watching her back, that's all."

"If you can believe her story," I said.

"Well, there is that," he said.

"So what about the Finch sisters?" I asked.

"It looks to me like they both have an alibi for the night Patrick Ward was killed as well," he said.

"But then that just leaves Lanna and Hugh Danvers," I said. "Call me gullible, but I don't think Lanna killed her own brother. I just don't."

"I'm waiting for Deputy Miller to call me right now," he said. "He's supposed to have the alibi information on Hugh Danvers. So we'll see what he comes up with."

"Okay," I said. Rudy walked over to us and planted a kiss on my forehead. He had Matthew in the backpack carrier. Matthew was sound asleep and drooling all over Rudy's shoulders. It didn't seem to bother Rudy, which sort of made me feel really lucky that I had such a great guy. I mean, think about it. He doesn't care if his son drools on his shoulder. I know that may seem minor, but at that moment in time, it was a big deal to me.

"So, you guys talking murder and mayhem and all that morbid stuff?" he asked.

"You got it," I said.

"Your wife is seriously disturbed," Colin said. I jabbed him a good one. "Oof."

"I do have one thing that's bothering me," I said.

"What's that?" Colin asked and rolled his eyes. He saw the look on my face and immediately knew I was serious. "Sorry."

"The blanket."

"What about it?" he asked and finally took his kettle popcorn from Tobias. He shoved a handful in his mouth.

"Lanna says that Aurora brought the blanket home and hid it under her mattress. They were going to dispose of it, but couldn't get the chance because the place was crawling with the authorities," I said.

"Okay. So what?"

"So, when Aurora went back to finally dispose of it, it was gone. Lanna swears that Catherine took the blanket and hid it."

"Why would she do that?" Rudy asked. The sheriff and I both looked at him suddenly, because we had forgotten he was standing there.

"That's what I want to know," I said. "If she found the blanket hidden underneath her daughter's mattress, then she had to have known that Hector Castanza was an impostor. But she didn't."

In the distance we heard the next band come onstage and start playing. I scanned the crowd quickly, and found that Chuck Velasco had helped my grandmother back to her lawn chair. And my mother was seated next to her this time, instead of me.

"It can only mean one thing," I said to the sheriff.

"That Catherine isn't the one who found or hid the blanket," he said.

"Exactly," I said.

"So, then who did?" Rudy asked.

"I don't know," I said. "All six of the cousins thought that Catherine had done it all these years. They've all been holding their breaths, waiting for her to drop the bomb."

"What do you mean?" Colin asked.

"They all assumed that Catherine was going to use it at a later date for blackmail or to try and have them all thrown in the slammer," I said. "The fact that she never did also confirms my suspicion that she wasn't the one who hid it. She never knew it existed. Which is why Hector Castanza was able to play to her sympathies. She'd never seen any blanket that would indicate foul play within her house."

"Then which one of the six cousins hid the blanket?" he asked.

"You're assuming one of the cousins found it and hid it," I said. "What if it was somebody else?"

Thirty-five

The firehouse was nearly as old as the city of New Kassel itself. Made of red brick, it stood three stories tall and had originally been used as a boardinghouse for the railroad workers. Then, around 1910, they turned half of the building into a big garage for the fire vehicles. Out front was a fire wagon from the horse-drawn era, and a fire truck from about 1930 was next to it. They were on display year-round, and Elmer spent a great deal of time waxing and polishing them.

Elmer Kolbe was the fire chief and had been since what seemed like the dawn of time. He's been saying he's going to retire, but he never does. For the past ten years at the annual Christmas Ball, he's announced that this was his last year, and then the next year he'd say he had been drunk and hadn't meant it.

I went into the firehouse and was instantly mauled by Gretchen the Dalmatian. Gretchen seems to have more spots than most Dalmatians, but Rudy assures me that it is just my imagination. She is also a bucket of slobber, which isn't my imagination. I petted her and laughed, because one cannot help but laugh when a big-spotted, slobbery dog is trying to lick one's nose. "Down, girl."

Peter Holstein sat behind the desk with his sunglasses on top

of his head, reading the latest issue of some NASCAR racing pub-
lication. He looked up at me and winked. "Hi, Torie." Peter winked
at everybody. He was built like a bodybuilder, but not the kind with
those nasty veins sticking out all over the place. Just the kind with
the huge muscles bulging beneath his shirt.

"Hi, Peter," I said. "Is Elmer around?"

"Yeah, he's out back watering his flowers," Peter said and smiled.

"Oh, okay," I said. I petted Gretchen again, pried myself loose
from her, and went back out the door and around the firehouse,
rather than going through it. I felt weird about going through the
place, unless I was on a tour. Elmer was in back watering his flowers,
just as Peter had said. Elmer spent so much time at the firehouse
that it was his home away from home. And one of the things Elmer
loved was flowers.

"Elmer," I said.

He turned around and nearly splashed me with the hose. "Why
aren't you at the Pickin' and Grinnin' Festival?" he asked. His gray
eyes were small and beady, but they sparkled when he smiled. He
was at least sixty, although I've never asked him his exact age.

"I was," I said. "I'm taking a break."

"Are you about ready to go back to doing the tours?"

"Yes," I said. "I think I can just about fit into at least one of my
dresses."

"Good," he said. "It hasn't been the same without you."

"Aww, thanks," I said.

"So, what brings you over this way?" he asked.

"Well . . . this is going to sound strange. But your dad was the
sheriff when the Finch kidnapping occurred, right?"

"Yeah," he said. "I've had reporters calling me like crazy, all of
'em wanting to know what I thought my father would think about
the skeleton in the wall. Stupid people. How do they think he
would feel? The same as all of us would feel. Only probably a little
worse."

"Because it was right under his nose?" I asked.

"Yeah, I think so. That would just crush him, I think." Elmer said nothing more. He just raised the hose, causing a higher arc of water to splash down on his sunflowers. A rainbow appeared in a cloud of mist for just a second and then it was gone.

"Well, I want to know about the night of the investigation. Do you have any memory of it at all? I mean, I'm not sure how old you are, so I'm not sure you can help me."

"I wasn't born until the year after," he said. "Momma used to tell me that my dad wouldn't let me out of his sight until I was three."

"I can imagine how that would have made your father be overprotective. It certainly has made me look at Matthew in a different light," I said. Actually, the whole situation was eerie. I had two older daughters, just like Catherine. And then I had a younger son, just like Catherine. I just couldn't imagine my children doing something like what Aurora and Cecily had done and not telling me. It's not that I couldn't imagine some horrible accident happening because of something my children were involved in. That I could imagine. I couldn't imagine how my children could keep it from me. Had Catherine been blind to the signs? Were the children that estranged from her because Byron was her favorite?

Imagining Rachel, Mary and Matthew as Cecily, Aurora and Byron was what fueled me to find the truth. Talking to Elmer just made me realize it.

"Well, I was curious; do you remember your father talking about it at all? I mean, what was his overall impression?"

Elmer sort of smiled at me. Then shook his head. "You don't want to know what Dad thought," he said.

"Yes, I do."

He paused a minute, internally weighing if he should tell me or not. I had to wonder if when he did tell me, it would be the complete truth or not. I always wonder about when people hesitate before telling me something. Finally he spoke. "Dad thought it was the kids. His gut feeling was that the kids either did it or knew who did it," he said.

"Then why didn't he say something?" I asked.

"Because it made no sense. Why wouldn't the kids tell? And if they did kidnap Byron, why? What did they do with him? Was he alive or dead? A body never showed up. I can remember Dad telling me once that it just didn't make any sense, and until he could come up with some motivation or some shred of proof, he couldn't say anything."

I knew the kids had taken Byron. And I knew why. And I now knew why a body was never found. I thought I'd go with the next question anyway. "If the kids knew something, what did your father think it was?"

"Dad said that the adults in the household acted weird."

"What adults? Catherine and Walter?"

"Catherine, Walter, the two servants; also the Pershings . . . I think that was it."

"How did they act weird?"

"Well, Catherine was hysterical. He said Walter was like stone. I don't necessarily think that was weird. But he said the other adults all acted scared and very protective of the children. Like they knew something they weren't telling. But none of them ever changed their stories."

"Hmm," I said and chewed on my lower lip. "The two servants . . . are they dead now?"

"Yes. One of them died in a car accident back in 1972. You've heard the story. I'd been fire chief for about six years. We got the call, and when we got out there, this Mustang was wrapped around a telephone pole. Virgie was in the backseat. Her grandson had been taking her to the doctor," he said. "Pretty weird, being the one to scrape her out of there, knowing that she'd been involved in the case that nearly caused my dad to retire."

"I think I remember that," I said. "I was just a kid. We were coming back from Progress and the traffic was stopped for like two hours."

"Might have been it," he said. "The other servant, Ruthie, died in a nursing home . . . oh . . . around 1988."

So neither one of them could have killed Patrick Ward. But one of them could have hidden the blanket.

"Ruthie's granddaughter lives over on New Bavaria," he said. We were both quiet a moment. "Aren't those Impatiens beautiful?"

"Yup," I said. "They are so colorful."

We stood there in the brilliant sunshine a few more moments and then I turned to leave. "Hey, Elmer. One more thing. Did you know that Patrick Ward was coming to town?"

"Yes, I did."

"You did?" I asked, surprised. "How did you know?"

"Sylvia told me."

"Sylvia."

"Yeah," he said. "I was shocked to find out that Lanna didn't even know he was in town. Because a couple of us knew it. It didn't make any sense. But then, nothing about the whole Finch scenario has made any sense."

It made more sense than he knew. But I couldn't tell him any of it. "Well, thanks, Elmer. Are you off tomorrow?"

"Yeah."

"You gonna come hear some music?"

"Yeah, probably."

"I'll see you there."

Thirty-six

It was early Sunday morning and the sun was just above the tree line as I drove down the outer road toward Wisteria. It was the last day of the Pickin' and Grinnin' Festival, and if I didn't get out to see the sheriff early I wouldn't get to see him at all, because I had to work at the festival today.

A misty low-lying fog snuggled close to the fields, with the trees and hills in perfect clarity. We often had fog in this part of the country because we were so close to the river.

Eventually, I pulled in front of the sheriff's station and went inside. A dampness clung to my skin, making me think that today was going to be even more humid than the weatherman had predicted. Deputy Miller nodded to me as I entered. "Good mornin', Torie. What brings you out so early on a Sunday?"

"I need to see Colin," I said.

"He'll be right out," he said. I nodded that I understood and watched out the window as the sleepy town of Wisteria slowly woke up. A rusty fifty-year-old truck clanked down the street, a station wagon met it the other way. And so I watched as the townsfolk made their way to church or breakfast or wherever until the sheriff came out of the back room.

"Hey," he said. "Want some coffee?"

"No, thanks. You know I don't drink coffee," I said.

"Oh, yeah. Want some . . . I don't have anything else," he said. "Guess you can never work here."

"I need to talk to you," I said.

"What about?" he asked. He noted the seriousness in my voice, and the smile fell from his face. Smile? Had he actually smiled when he saw me?

"The estate," I said and cut my eyes around to Deputy Miller, who was very much paying attention to what we were saying. I smiled at Deputy Miller and then looked back to Colin.

"Oh, sure," he said. "Come on back."

He led me to the makeshift kitchen with its two hot plates, microwave, half-size refrigerator and metal table with two chairs. He pointed to one of the chairs. "Have a seat."

I was sure there was an interrogation room somewhere, but I was assuming he didn't want it spread around that I was in the interrogation room. As it was, I had been asked by several people what exactly it was that I had been doing in Bertha. Seems the sheriff's employees might be loyal, but they still liked to gossip. I mean it's not every day the sheriff throws somebody in jail. I guess they couldn't help themselves.

"What's up?" he asked.

"I need to look at the file again."

He sat there for a minute and then crossed his arms. He didn't lean back in his chair, which was so common for him to do. Probably because he knew it wouldn't hold his weight and he'd end up on the floor. "What for?"

"I only had a few hours with it before. In order for me to actually look at each page, I just skimmed some of them. I'd stop and read when it looked pertinent," I said.

"So what?"

"Have you read the file?"

"Most of it," he said.

"There's something not adding up," I said.

"We know what happened to Byron. What's not adding up?"

"The blanket, for one thing. And who killed Patrick Ward, for the other. What came in on Hugh Danvers's alibi, anyway?"

"He was in Springfield, Missouri, campaigning for his sister. Solid alibi," he said. "He couldn't have killed Patrick."

"How can all of the cousins have solid alibis? Somebody had to have killed him, right?" I asked.

"Maybe because of the connection to Byron, we've been assuming he was killed over Byron. Maybe he had other enemies and his death is not related to the Finch case in the least," he said. "It could be that simple."

The kitchen sink dripped, making a *bloink* sound every thirty seconds or so. The sheriff's department was in serious need of taxpayer money. The indoor-outdoor carpet was worn through to the concrete floor in several areas. "It could be that simple," I repeated. But I doubted it.

After a moment or two of reflective silence, the sheriff finally spoke up. "What is it you're hoping to find, Torie? You think there's something in that file that's going to say, 'In the future, this is the person who's going to poison Patrick'? I'll let you look at it, Torie. But I'm not sure what good it's going to do," he said.

"I need to know who was in the house the morning after. I think whoever was in the house the morning after may have witnessed something between the kids," I said.

Colin stopped for a moment. "In other words, you think this person, whoever it was, knew from the get-go that the kids did it?"

"Yeah," I said. "I'm not sure how, years later, that will help us with who killed Patrick, but I guess it depends on who it was."

"Okay," he said. "Sit tight. I'll go get the file."

•

The sheriff put me in his private office and shut the door. An antique frame holding a photograph of my mother graced his desk.

It was a sweet picture of my mother seated on the deck of a boat, a beautiful red-orange sunset behind her. I assumed it had been taken on their honeymoon. I was surprised to find, right next to it, a photograph of my kids taken at his wedding. My kids' picture sat on the sheriff's desk. I'm not sure how I felt about that.

Just when I thought I had him figured out, he'd surprise me.

Of course, I noticed that there was no photograph of *me* anywhere. Maybe he was saving that for the WANTED poster.

"Here," the sheriff said, coming back into the room. "I might be able to help you with this. I know what to look for."

"Okay," I said. I wasn't going to argue because I did have to work the festival today, and I knew I could be here for hours scouring the papers in that box.

A few minutes later, Colin sat back in his chair and pinched the bridge of his nose. "Well, I think I've found what you're looking for. But, it's not going to do you much good. Everybody on this list is dead, except Sylvia."

"Everybody?"

"Everybody except Sylvia and the cousins, of course."

"Let me see," I said and held out my hand.

"See," he said and pointed to a list of names. Sheriff Kolbe had written down the names of everybody who had been in attendance every time he went out to the Finch house to interview people or ask questions. Walter Finch's mother had arrived at mid-morning to comfort her son and daughter-in-law. She, of course, was long dead. Catherine, Walter, Wilma, Virgie and Ruth—they were all dead. The only one who wasn't was Sylvia.

And Sylvia had told Elmer that Patrick was coming into town.

"Torie? What's the matter?" Colin asked. "All the color just drained from your face."

The room grew suddenly hot, and Colin's voice seemed to trail off in a tunnel somewhere. A prickly feeling crawled up my neck and my throat turned into cotton. I swallowed hard. "Um . . . you know what? I think I was wrong. I'll talk to you later, Colin. Thanks a lot."

I left his office without hesitation. I didn't give him a chance to ask me anything further. When I made it to the front desk, I waved to Deputy Miller on the way out the door and never looked back.

Thirty-seven

I entered the Gaheimer house with both trepidation and determination. There was a certain amount of confusion reeling within me. I only hoped that I could see the truth. As I stood in the middle of the ballroom, with its glistening marble floor and the sky-blue-painted ceiling, I heard voices coming from the stairs. The tour was ending and Helen Wickland was at the head of the group of tourists.

"Thank you," she said. "This concludes our tour. Have a great time in New Kassel. Enjoy the festival."

With that, the dozen or so people exited the Gaheimer house and Helen shut the door behind them. She turned and jumped when she saw me. "Lord, when did you get here?"

"Just now," I answered. "Where's Sylvia?"

"Upstairs. Last time I saw her she was changing the bedding in one of the guest rooms. Not that anybody ever actually sleeps in any of these beds. Why does she change the bedding so often?" Helen asked and rolled her eyes.

I truly didn't know the answers to the questions about Sylvia, although I probably knew more about her than anybody else in town. But it was still just the tip of the iceberg. "Habit," I said. "When's the next tour?"

"Forty-five minutes," she said, glancing at her watch.

"I need to talk to Sylvia," I said. "I'll see you later."

I went upstairs, as I have done a thousand times. The ninth step creaked, just as it had a thousand times. But somehow, this trip was different from the other thousand times. I could just chalk it up to being older and wiser, but there was more to it than that. I was afraid. I was actually afraid to go up the steps.

"Sylvia?" I called out.

"In here," she said.

I reached the landing and took a deep breath. She was in what we called the brown room. I knew this because it was Sunday. And every Sunday morning after the first tour, she began to change the bedding. And she always began in the brown room, worked her way down the hall and finished up in Mr. Gaheimer's old room. As sure as the sun came up, this was her routine. Maybe there was security in doing familiar things. Or maybe her character was just so unbendable that even the smallest of details had to be done in a certain way. And in her mind, her way was the right way. It always had been. Ever since I could remember.

"Sylvia," I said.

She pulled the earth-tone-colored Log Cabin quilt up to the head of the bed and put the pillows on top of it. Then she put the ivory crocheted shams on top of the pillows.

"What are you doing here?" she asked. "Aren't you working the festival today?"

"Yes," I said. "I need to talk to you."

"About what?" she asked.

"About Wilma," I said.

"What about her?" she asked, raising her chin a notch.

"You didn't tell me that Wilma was there that morning," I said. "She came with you when Catherine called. Didn't she?"

"What are you talking about?" she asked. She picked up the old linens and set them on the edge of the bed.

"The morning that Catherine Finch called you and told you that Byron had been kidnapped in the middle of the night. She asked you to come, and Wilma went with you. Didn't she?" I asked.

"Yes," she said. "What of it?"

"What did she do while you were there? Did she stay with you?"

"No," she said. "She went to find the children. Wilma always had a soft spot for children. All children."

I ran my hand along the top of the cedar chest at the foot of the bed. "So . . . when she got there, she went to comfort the six cousins," I stated. "The six children."

"Yes," she said. "Can this wait until some other time?"

"No," I said. "It can't. Did she ever talk to you about what the children told her?"

"You're assuming they told her something?" Sylvia asked.

"Sylvia, the cousins took Byron out into the woods that night. He was killed by the storm and they got afraid. They hid him in the wall of the Yates house," I said. "I need to know if Wilma mentioned this to you."

"Yes," she said and looked out the window. Just like that. Yes.

"So you knew all along," I said. She said nothing. "Sylvia! You knew all along! Didn't you?"

"Yes."

"All this time you knew that Byron was in that wall? You let Catherine suffer like that?"

"Yes."

"Oh, Sylvia," I said. A sob escaped from my lips and it surprised me. I hadn't realized I was so emotional about the whole thing. A tear rolled down my cheek and I swiped at it, hoping that she wouldn't notice. Sylvia hated tears. They were a sign of weakness. "How could you?"

Sylvia steadied herself and sat down on the edge of the bed. "My sister pleaded with me. She convinced me that the children's lives would be ruined if we told," she said with a shaky voice. "And she was right. Catherine was my best friend. But once Byron was born, nobody else existed. Not even her two daughters. It was as if they were just the practice run for the real child. If she had found out what her daughters had done, she would have never forgiven them. Never. Aurora and Cecily were right to keep it from her."

"You don't mean that," I said. "Surely not."

"Oh, I do," she said. She reached over to the table and straightened a vase full of fresh flowers. It didn't need straightening.

"So . . . the blanket. Did Wilma find it and hide it?"

"Yes," she said. "Wilma told me the only thing that could link those kids to the disappearance of Byron was the blanket. She hid it somewhere in the house and said that she wasn't worried about Catherine finding it because Catherine wasn't the one who cleaned the house. She'd meant to go back at a later date and remove it, but she could never get a chance to be upstairs without Catherine being with her."

"It just makes no sense," I said.

"My sister was very protective of children," she snapped at me. "It was an accident."

"Yes, but poor Catherine . . ."

"There was nothing poor about Catherine. It was a shame that she lost her son. We thought it would be even more of a shame if her children lost her."

"Yes, but they did lose her. They lost her anyway," I said. "Her suspicions pushed them away."

"But at least they were adults by then. They at least got to be raised in a somewhat normal house," she said.

I swiped at another tear and noticed that my hands were shaking. I could scarcely believe what I was hearing. "Sylvia? Did Patrick Ward come to visit you the night of his . . . the night he died?" I asked. I asked the question a little louder than I intended, but I was so afraid that I wouldn't be able to speak the sentence at all that I overcompensated.

"Do you realize what you're asking me?" she asked. She folded her hands in her lap and looked up at me. "I will not lie to you. How badly do you want to know this answer?"

"But—but it makes no sense, Sylvia," I said. I fell to my knees and buried my head in her lap. I sobbed like a child. "Why kill Patrick Ward after all these years?"

"I didn't," she said simply. "I don't know what my sister did."

Still the tears came. "Did you see Patrick Ward that night or not?"

"Yes."

"And Wilma?"

"Yes. She saw him."

Sylvia handed me a handkerchief. I don't know where she produced it from. She was like that. No pockets, no purse, and yet here was a handkerchief. I wiped my nose and my eyes. "Explain it to me," I said. "I don't understand."

"I don't know," Sylvia said. "I'm assuming we'll never know. My sister was not herself. She was becoming absentminded, forgetful. Even reckless, in a sense. She was very ill."

She laid an aged and gnarled hand on mine. It was the simplest of gestures, but from Sylvia it meant the world. It was all I could do not to break down again.

"I think she forgot that all this time had passed. Patrick came here to tell us that he was tired of living with the secret. That his conscience had bothered him too long. He wanted people to know the truth," she said.

"So he didn't come here to remove the body so that when the building came down it wouldn't be found?" I asked. "Governor Danvers—"

"On the contrary. He didn't know the building had been slated for destruction. He said that if Hope Danvers wanted to go all the way with her career that there were things she needed to answer for. The people needed to know the truth about everything in her life."

"He was going to expose her?"

"He was going to expose all of them, and make them all answer for what they did," she said. "Wilma didn't realize that he was an old man now, too. She kept saying that the children needed to be protected. We had to protect the children. In some ways, I think Wilma was as traumatized by what happened to Byron as the children were."

Wilma had thought the children were in danger. In her delusional state, she had thought she was still protecting the children. Only, the children were adults now, with grandchildren of their own.

"Why didn't you tell Patrick that the building was slated for destruction?" I asked.

"You know Bill, he talks and talks," she said. Her voice trailed off and she looked to the window. "I really didn't think he'd ever get it done. I, too, was ready for the truth to be out."

I waited for her to say something else. Eventually she swallowed hard and finished what she was telling me. "It never occurred to me that Wilma would do something . . . dangerous."

"What happened?" I asked. "Tell me what happened after he told you both what he was going to do."

"Wilma asked him to stay for dinner and I went upstairs to watch television. *The Thin Man* was on one of the cable stations. I wanted to watch it. I'd already eaten a sandwich, so I wasn't that hungry. When I came down to eat, Wilma had washed up the dishes. There were no leftovers," she said. "I thought nothing of it—until Patrick was found dead."

"So you don't really know if she poisoned him or not," I said.

"No," she said. "I don't know for sure. But I—"

"But nothing," I said. "You don't know for sure and there's no way to prove it, now. We can never know."

"But I *know*."

I was willing to say that it was a question that there could never be an answer to. At least in my mind. Even if Wilma had poisoned him, she didn't know what she was doing. And she thought she was protecting the children. It seemed to be the thing she lived for.

"How did you know?" Sylvia asked.

"I found the blanket," I said. I was pretty sure that Sylvia had read that in the paper. But there was no way for her to have known that, for me, that fingered either her or Wilma.

Sylvia gave a crooked smile.

I went on. "I knew none of the six cousins had hidden it. I knew Walter wouldn't have hidden it. He would have said something. The two servants would have had ample time to throw it away, and nothing they did would have been questioned. I knew Catherine hadn't hidden it, because she genuinely thought Hector Castanza was Byron. How could she have thought that if she'd had proof that Byron fell victim to a horrible disaster that night? That only left you, that I knew of. But then Elmer said 'the Pershings' when he was talking to me about his father and the case. Lanna had said that the only people Patrick was still in contact with were his family, Elmer Kolbe and 'the Pershings.' Then Colin showed me a list of people who were present and accounted for the morning after Byron's disappearance, and Wilma was on the list," I said. "I knew what children meant to Wilma . . . I sort of figured she was the one who hid the blanket."

"What are you going to do?" Sylvia asked after a long pause.

I found that after several moments of contemplating that question, I could not answer it.

The News You Might Miss
by
Eleanore Murdoch

Thank you, everybody, for making this year's Pickin' and Grinnin' Festival the most successful in the history of New Kassel! We sold all of our leftover berry products, Helen ran out of chocolate, Tobias actually got a blister from making that kettle corn, and the rectory yard received very little damage. We are in the black, fellow citizens!

On a sad note, I'm sure you've all heard the "official" news by now. The skeletal remains found in the old Yates house have been positively identified as those of Byron Lee Finch, infant son of the late Catherine Finch, world-renowned singer. Autopsy results state that he was most likely hit by lightning in a middle-of-the-night rendezvous with his cousins. I don't know about you folks, but the fact that I passed by him every day while he lay in the wall of that house sort of gives me the heebie-jeebies. Not to mention it makes me wonder what all the rest of you may have hidden in your walls! At least we can take some solace in knowing that his remains are finally to be interred in the Santa Lucia Cemetery, next to his mother and father.

And as far as Proposition 7 is concerned, I want to thank everybody who helped Helen Wickland, Torie O'Shea, Charity Burgermeister and myself in our VOTE NO campaign. You'll have to wait until the next issue to find out if all our hard work paid off and we have succeeded in keeping our well-meaning, but-misguided, mayor at bay.

Until next time . . .
Eleanore

Thirty-eight

It rained a steady downpour of big warm drops. If I could have analyzed the raindrops, I would have sworn that they were gray. The sky was gray, my mood was gray, the world was gray. Only the gentle rustle of the trees reminded me that maybe not everything was gray in this bleak void.

I stood at the freshly dug grave of Byron Lee Finch with a single white rose in my hand. The rain pelted off the many umbrellas around me. Rudy held ours above us. Rachel held her smiley-face umbrella over herself and Mary. Aurora and Cecily were both in attendance, as were Hugh Danvers and Lanna Petrovic. The governor had managed to plead previous engagements as her reason for not showing.

The sheriff and my mother were in attendance, located right next to Rachel and Mary. Sylvia was there too, on my left, stoic as concrete. Father Bingham said his "ashes to ashes, dust to dust" thing and then "Amen."

One by one, my family and the townspeople left. One by one, the reporters all left.

I remained. And I wept.

I'm not sure why I cried. I guess I cried for poor little Byron.

He hadn't meant for all of this to happen. He was just an innocent baby sound asleep in his bed, and then carried through the woods, and then he was dead. I cried for his sisters, who had never wanted anything to happen to him. They just wanted to see the miraculous appearance of a fairy. They wanted to see the thing they'd read about and been told about by their mother. In a sense, it was for her approval that they had begun the adventure in the first place.

I cried for the other four children who had lost their innocence that night. With a flash of lightning, a life without nightmares was gone. They would never sleep soundly, they would never feel guiltless again.

I cried for Catherine, who had lost a child, the thing that had spurred me to solve this mystery in the first place. And I cried for Sylvia and Wilma, who had kept a secret all those years. I wasn't sure if what they'd done was good or bad. Mostly, I wept for Aurora and Cecily, though. In a sense, they had lost their brother *and* their mother on that night. But I think the real reason I cried for them was because they had never really had their mother in the first place. I could not imagine having a favorite to that degree. Oh, sure, I may like the way Rachel handles a situation better than Mary, but Mary always rebounds and makes me laugh at something so goofy that Rachel could never manage. I couldn't imagine giving birth to three children and only living for one.

Catherine Finch had been so cruel in that sense that I'm not sure she ever really knew what she had lost. That was the saddest thing of all.

"Torie?" a voice said.

I turned to find my husband Rudy standing in the rain. He'd left me the umbrella, and so he was nearly soaked. "Are you going to stand here all day?"

"I think I might," I said.

He walked over to me and gave me a big hug, getting me wet in the process. "Okay, what is it? There's something you're not telling me."

"I don't mean for there to be something."

"Come on, tell me. What are husbands for?" he said. I looked up into his chocolate-brown eyes and smiled.

"If I tell you, then there's two of us who know," I said.

"Who know what?"

"Are you sure you can handle it?"

"Bullets bounce off my chest," he said, sticking his chest way out.

I explained to him, as best as I could, about Wilma, and how Sylvia and I suspected that Wilma had been the one to poison Patrick. He listened intently until I was finished. "I don't know what to say," he declared. "Wilma can hardly be held accountable. We all know she wasn't in her right mind."

"Sylvia said that for days after Patrick visited, she'd find Wilma saying things like 'We must protect the children. Nobody can know.' It's pretty obvious that she didn't understand that they weren't children any longer. She'd lived with that secret for so long . . ."

"Remember that," he said.

"What do you mean?"

"If you have any secrets, when you're old and senile you may start confessing to things you don't want me to know about," he said with a smile.

"Yeah, but by then you'll be so old and senile, you'll forget whatever it was I confessed to you five seconds after I confessed to it," I said. We laughed together, and I felt a little better. Which was what Rudy did best. He always made me feel better. Well, there were times when I could just strangle him, but then again I wasn't always an angel, either, so I should just forget about those times.

"What are you going to do?" he asked finally.

"About Wilma?"

"Yeah," he said. "Are you going to tell anybody? I mean, technically, Sylvia knew. She was an accomplice."

"That's the strange thing, Rudy. I finally know what it's like to

222

be the one with information that others want. And I love the person too much to tell the truth. Is that bad?" I asked.

"Wilma's gone. No justice can be done now. So let it go," he said. "And so far as Sylvia knowing about Byron, there really was no crime committed. It's not like she was harboring a murderer all these years. Besides, what could they do to her, besides ruin her name?"

I looked down at the little pile of dirt.

"I should still tell the sheriff," I said. "It's really up to him to decide if anything should be done. Not me."

"What?" He felt my forehead. "Torie, are you feeling all right?"

"I just feel funny keeping it from him," I said.

"Because he's your stepfather now?"

"No," I said. "Because he's my sheriff."

Thirty-nine

"Where are we going?" Sheriff Brooke asked from the passenger side of my van.

"We're going to Aurora's house," I said. "To give her those boxes." I pointed to the boxes that I had stacked in the very back-seat of the van.

It was a week after the funeral of Byron Finch. The sun was shining but it was starting to get cool. Autumn would set in in full force in about three weeks. My favorite time of year.

"So, what am I giving her?" he asked.

"All the photographs I could find. You know, her and Cecily's baby pictures were still in the albums. I thought they'd appreciate them."

"All of those boxes have photographs?"

"No, there's a set of china, a tea set, some jewelry—oh, darn it," I said.

"What?"

"I keep forgetting to call that guy about the necklace. I've never found anything resembling the necklace that he asked about," I said. "Probably just a rumor."

"I wish it had been true. I might have been able to retire," he said.

"Or at least make another trip to Alaska," I said.

"Oh, no. I promised your mother that our next trip would be back to West Virginia. She wants to see her homeland," he said.

"That's sweet," I said.

"I thought so," he said.

I rolled my eyes and wondered if there would ever be a point in time when he wouldn't irritate me, even just a little. "I thought maybe you could give them the two big oil paintings in the house, too. And if they make a special request, you might consider giving—"

"You're going to bankrupt me," he said.

"It's the right thing to do."

He nodded.

"Speaking of the right thing to do," I said.

"Uh-oh."

"Shut up," I said. "Just shut up, okay? I'm trying to do something here and it's hard."

"If it helps you any, I'll meet you halfway," he said. He placed his hands on his chest and cleared his throat. "I'm sorry about . . . well, you know. Throwing you in Bertha. You're an okay kid, but, well, you just irritate the hell out of me most of the time. That's all. I know you mean well."

"My mother put you up to that, didn't she?"

"No, she didn't."

"Oh, yes, she did," I said, smiling and pointing at him.

"No, she didn't. Now what was it you were going to tell me?"

"Sylvia and Wilma knew where Byron Finch was the whole time. The kids confessed to Wilma, because they knew she'd help them. She was the only grown-up they could trust. Wilma told Sylvia, and neither one of them ever did anything about it."

I looked over at him, and his mouth was open. "You're kidding," he said.

"No, I'm not. And there's more."

"There's more?"

"Sylvia said that she agreed with Wilma. That if Catherine had known that the children had been involved, it would have been far worse. Byron, evidently, was Catherine's favorite and everybody knew it. I mean, he was the favorite to the point of the other children barely existing in her eyes," I said.

"Oh, jeez."

"I'm going to tell you the next part only because I think it's the right thing to do. It seems Wilma and Sylvia were the last people to see Patrick Ward alive," I said.

"Oh, jeez!"

"Hope lied to you. Patrick was going out to the Yates house to finally remove Byron from his prison and expose them all. He was tired of the lies, and wanted the truth out. Especially when he realized that Hope was going to try and climb all the way to the top of the political ladder. In a way, he would be doing her a favor. Imagine if she became President and then the truth came out," I said. "But I think he was doing it more for himself."

"What do you mean?"

"He was coming to the end of his life, too. He was in his late sixties and he knew his time on this planet was getting short. I think maybe he thought if he was the one to break the silence and make things right, that maybe Saint Peter might think so, too. If you know what I mean."

"Yeah, yeah . . . I do."

I turned onto Aurora's street and parked in front of her house. I turned the engine off and stared at the sheriff. "Sylvia said that Wilma acted very funny for days after Patrick was there. That she kept talking about having to protect the children. I just wanted you to know, because I think it's up to you to decide what to do about it."

"What?" he asked and grabbed his heart. "You mean, you don't think it's your business to decide the fate of our law-breaking citizens? When did this revelation occur?"

"Don't be an ass, Colin. I loved Wilma, almost as much as I do my own grandmother," I said. "That's the great thing about a small town. It's as if everybody is related to one another. I'm lucky to have such a large extended family."

He said nothing. We both looked up at the house of Aurora Guelders.

"You're no fun when you're all serious," he said.

"Well, you're never any fun."

"So what do you think I should do about this?"

"Why are you asking me?"

"I value your opinion."

Since when? "I would do nothing. But then I'm very close to the subject. I think that keeping the secret all those years was wrong on one hand, but on the other . . . I don't know. And if Wilma did do something to Patrick—"

"Do something? You mean kill him, don't you?"

"If she did kill him, you can never prove it. And I don't think she was fully in her right mind, anyway. She was a sweet, sweet woman," I said. "In her right mind, she would never have committed murder. I believe that."

"Well," he said after a long pause. "We'll never know, will we? Wilma's gone. And with her went the truth."

"What if she didn't do it? Then Patrick Ward's killer is still out there," I said.

"That's the problem with you, Torie. You're too critical. Sometimes you don't win them all. Sometimes, cases go unsolved. And sometimes, believe it or not, some cases are better not solved," he said.

I appreciated his words, more than he would ever know. Basically, because I would never tell him. "Let's get this stuff unloaded," I said.

"Okay," he said.

"By the way," I said. "Rudy told me that you found out who had been trying to scare me that night in Catherine's house. Who was it?"

"No surprise, really. It was Hugh Danvers. Some of the cousins were worried about what you were going to find in the house. Hugh thought if he could scare you, maybe you wouldn't go back. The silly thing is, eventually I would have gone through all of Catherine's things, and what if I had found the blanket?" he asked. "I'm convinced that if people really thought their actions through, they'd never do most of them. But people don't think. They think they're thinking, but they're not. They're thinking from a biased position. What's best for *them*."

"So, are you going to do anything about it? How'd you find out, anyway?"

"After the funeral he confessed it to me. I'm not going to do anything about it. Unless you want me to," he said. "It was you who he was scaring."

"No," I said. "There was no harm done, really. He was scared."

"I figured you'd say that," he said.

We got out of the van and walked around to the back. I looked up at Aurora's house and wondered what sort of reception we would get. This was my peace offering to her. I hoped she would forgive me.

"So, when are you going to make me a bona fide deputy?" I asked as I unlocked the door.

"When hell freezes over."

Keep Reading for an Excerpt from
Rett MacPherson's
Latest Torie O'Shea Mystery:

BLOOD RELATIONS

Available in Hardcover from
St. Martin's Minotaur

The Gaheimer House is one of the oldest houses in New Kassel, dating back to the mid-1860s," I said. I was back to giving tours of the house, and I could finally fit into all seven of the reproduction dresses that my boss, Sylvia, had made for me several years ago when I started this job. I wish I could say that having a baby last year had added the extra pounds to my rather short frame, but it really hadn't. It wasn't my son's fault that I had eaten too much and reduced my exercising to chasing my chickens around the backyard. No, it was mine. All mine.

But a year later and about thirty pounds lighter, I could fit into the reproduction dresses and was giving tours twice a day. I wore my favorite, the 1870s deep blue polonaise gown with an open front that revealed an underskirt of the same color. It was trimmed with chenille-ball fringe in a deeper, almost navy blue.

I moved the tour of about eleven people into the dining room, my stiff and itchy crinolette swishing as I went. "For those of you who aren't from the eastern Missouri area, New Kassel was founded by a group of German immigrants in the 1830s. The Mississippi River was an excellent way of importing and exporting, and the town was located not too far from the Missouri River junction. The

Missouri River is important because before the great railroads were built west of the Mississippi, the Missouri was the main route west. Unless you went by wagon."

On this particular tour, I had a young couple with twin girls, an elderly couple, a threesome of mid-forties women, an ancient-looking man who could have passed for a midwestern version of Rasputin, and a solitary female about thirty.

"I want to remind everybody as we enter this lovely room filled with delicate china and silver that all of the items in the Gaheimer House are antiques, so we ask that you refrain from touching them," I said, more for the couple with the twin girls than for anybody else. I'm the mother of three kids; I know how things accidentally get broken. Kids are great. I had been thoroughly amazed at how much I could love a little creature when Rachel was first born, but that didn't change the fact that kids live to touch things expensive, old, or irreplaceable. And if the twins on this tour were anything like my middle child, Mary, something would get broken.

"The wainscoting that you see here is made of sycamore. Mr. Gaheimer went to Connecticut on business in the late 1880s and brought back this dining table, which seats twelve. If you'll notice, the chandelier matches the gilt convex mirror. . . ."

I could say this stuff in my sleep. I've been doing this for almost ten years. I'm also the archivist for the town, compiling things like marriage and land records for Granite County. Sometimes I even write biographies, and I'm usually the one in charge of any displays we put up, as well. I know this town inside and out, and I know the job inside and out. Every now and then, though, if something distracts me, I forget my monologue and end up staring out at the tourists, stammering and stuttering. Just like today.

The solitary female, whom I mentioned before, was staring back at me. Not staring at me like you'd expect someone might when listening to a tour guide, but *really* staring at me. She was about my height, maybe an inch taller, and had brown hair and hazel eyes. Something about those hazel eyes disturbed me, beyond the

230

fact that they were boring through me as if she were trying to read my soul. There was a . . . familiarity, but I couldn't place it. Dark lashes and eyebrows stood out against her rather pale face. She hung on my every word, my every gesture. And soon it became very difficult for me to speak.

"And uh . . . um, this punch bowl at the end of the room was a gift from . . . from . . ." Who was it a gift from? I couldn't remember.

"Torie," somebody said.

"No, not Torie. Susan B. Anthony, that's it!"

"Torie," the voice said, more persistent now. I snapped out of my stupor and realized that *my* name was Torie and somebody was calling me.

"What?" I looked over to the entrance, where I saw my boss, Sylvia Pershing, standing there. Sylvia must be close to a hundred by now. Of course, I've been saying that for the last twenty years. I just knew that she was old when I was a kid, and now she seems immortal. She's thin, frail, bony, and full of piss and vinegar. She has never cut her silver hair in her life, and she braids it into twin braids every morning and wraps them around her head. She is the president of the Historical Society, where I am employed, and she owns half of the town, including the Gaheimer House. Her sister Wilma died last year, and Sylvia has not been quite the same since. She can still do more than half of the people in the town, and she can still cut you with her razor-sharp tongue, but it's as if she doesn't enjoy it anymore.

"Yes, Sylvia . . . what is it?"

"I hate to interrupt the tour, but when you're finished, you need to call the school," she said with a slight tremor caused by age.

"Oh, all right," I said. I resumed the tour, wondering just what Mary had done that would require me to go and bail her out. The rest of the tour went much like the first part had, with me stumbling over words and finding myself stealing glances at the woman staring at me. I found myself doing things like wiping at my nose to make sure there were no errant boogers, and cleaning my teeth with my tongue. I mean, was there something gross about me? What was her problem?

Finally, the tour was over. I headed down to my office as fast as I could. I put sixty cents in the soda machine, got a Dr Pepper, and went to my office. I shut the door and took a long, fizzy sip of my soda. Then I dialed the school, whose number I've had memorized since Mary started kindergarten.

Of course, New Kassel is a tiny town. There's one school for kindergarten and all twelve grades, and the graduating classes have about forty students each. And so when Francine answered the phone and I said, "Hi, it's Torie," she knew exactly who was calling.

"Yeah, Torie," Francine said. "We got a problem with Rachel."

"Rachel?" I asked. My oldest. This, I hadn't expected. "Are you sure?"

She laughed a little. "Of course I'm sure."

Rachel. Hmmm. "W-what's the problem?" I asked. I would have sat down, but you can't sit down in a dress like the one I was wearing. Potty breaks are an event that take as much organization as the invasion of Normandy. And nearly as much time.

"She got into a fight," Francine said.

"A fight?" I asked. "Francine, this is Torie O'Shea. Are you sure you got the right kid? Rachel O'Shea. You're sure?"

"Yeah, I'm sure. She gave Davie Roberts a bloody nose because he flicked her bra strap."

"Oh jeez," I said. Yes, it had been one of the great emotional moments of my life when my prepubescent daughter became pubescent and had to go out and buy her first training bra. She was still a kid, for crying out loud, but boobs are boobs. She was humiliated beyond belief, no matter how many of her friends I could name who were wearing training bras already. It also didn't matter when I pointed out that usually she couldn't wait to wear what everybody else wore, so why was this one item of clothing any different? But it was, and she didn't see my logic at all.

"It's pretty bad," Francine said.

"What do you mean, 'pretty bad'?" I asked.

"I mean, I think she broke his nose. His eyes turned purple within twenty minutes."

My first reaction was to say, "Well, then Davie should keep his hands to himself," but that didn't make what Rachel did right. I don't know how many times I've told my kids, "I don't care who throws the first punch, it's the kid who throws the last one—the one who retaliates—whom I will punish." Yes, Davie should have kept his little twelve-year-old perverted hands to himself, but Rachel should not have broken his nose. "I'll be right there," I said to her.

"Okay," Francine said.

"But, hey . . . are you guys going to do anything to Mr. Frisky Hands?"

"Yes, he's getting detention. That is, as soon as he returns to school."

"Oh jeez," I said again, wondering just what Davie's mother was going to say to me at the next PTA meeting. There was a knock at my office door just as I said good-bye and hung up the phone.

"Come in," I said.

The door opened and in walked the woman from the tour. The one who had kept staring at me. I was a little surprised, but yet . . . was I really? "Can I help you?" I asked. I sounded a little defensive, maybe even hateful. The woman flinched.

"Um, I was wondering if I could . . . I can come back at another time," she said.

"No," I said. "I'm sorry. It's just that I have to go to the school to get my daughter. There's been a . . . disagreement with one of her classmates."

"Oh."

"Could you . . . I'll listen to you, if you'll help me out of this stupid dress," I said, turning my back to her and exposing the buttons.

"Oh, sure," she said, and began undoing the buttons. There was an underslip, chemise, and crinolette, so I knew she wouldn't actually see any flesh. Women in the nineteenth century were packaged in layer after layer, so the only person who could ever glimpse their bare skin was the person who was supposed to. A satin and lace prison, if you will.

"What can I do for you?" I asked as I unbuttoned the sleeves.

"I understand that you trace family trees? You are Torie O'Shea, correct?"

"Yes," I said. "I wouldn't wear these tombs if I weren't."

"Well, I was wondering if I could hire your services?" she asked.

It was January. No major holidays or projects coming up. No marriages or births. There was no reason I couldn't take on this job. I just wasn't sure I wanted to, though. I always react this way. I am a historian. A genealogist. And yet when somebody actually asks me to do my job, I always balk.

"It might take me awhile. And even then, I can't say that I'll have every branch fleshed out as far back as it will go. What I'll do is establish a certain number of generations and try to fill that in. If I get more in the time allotted, then that's a bonus for you."

I turned around and began looking for my car keys.

"How many generations do you go back to?" she asked.

"When were you born?"

She looked around the room, self-conscious suddenly. It was as if she wasn't sure if she should answer. How could I trace her family tree if she wasn't even willing to give me her birth date? "Nineteen seventy."

"Then I'll try and finish eight. That's about two hundred years. Is that okay with you?"

"Sure," she said, and shrugged.

"All right," I said. "What's your name?"

Again, that semifrightened bunny-rabbit look. Her eyes darted from the Rose of Sharon quilt hanging on my wall, to the window, to the poster advertising all of New Kassel's charms, to the floor. Finally, she spoke. "Stephanie."

"Stephanie . . ." If I hadn't been so rattled over Rachel, I would have asked her more questions, like why she had been staring at me so intently during the tour and why she was acting so weird over simple things like her name and age. But my anxiety about Rachel mounted with each moment that passed.

"Connelly."

"Nice to meet you, Stephanie Connelly," I said, my dress hanging on my shoulders. "I'll leave you a form to fill out as best you can. And my rates are on there as well, so you can see how much this is going to cost you. But right now, I need to get down to the rest room and change my clothes so that I can go and pick up my daughter."

"Okay," she said, putting her hands in her jean pockets.

I pulled a form out of the top desk drawer, set it on my desk, and put a pencil next to it. "Just fill it in, leave me your phone number and e-mail address, if you've got one, and I'll get back to you. I'm sorry. I have to go."

"Sure, that's fine."

Realizing that my keys were in my jean pockets—where they always were—I picked up my jeans and shirt and tennis shoes from the chair next to the door. "Thank you so much for undoing these buttons. You have no idea how difficult it is to get in and out of this dress."

"Oh, you're welcome," she said, and smiled brightly.

Immediately to the right was the kitchen. I walked through it to the rest room that Sylvia had built for staff use. Nobody could see me walking through the kitchen with the dress unbuttoned to the small of my back, unless Sylvia happened to be there. But since Sylvia was usually the person to help me out of the blasted things, I didn't really care if she saw my slip-covered back or not. As soon as my clothes were changed, I was out the door and on my way to the school. But I couldn't help feeling a little weird as I left. I remembered an occasion a few years ago when a tourist had approached me after a tour and had hired me as a genealogist. She had ended up dead.

•

"I just think you should say something to Rachel, other than 'Good shot, honey!'" I said to Rudy.

Rudy, my ever lovable and generous-hearted husband, was leaning up against the countertop in our kitchen. He was eating an Oreo, the inside first, and teasing our dog Fritz with any possible crumbs. He wore his long-sleeved blue oxford shirt and khakis for work, but he hadn't put his shoes on yet, so our wiener dog kept licking his toes, trying to find crumbs.

"And why are you eating Oreos for breakfast?" I asked, irritated in general.

"I'm not eating Oreos for breakfast. I had eggs and waffles for breakfast. I'm just eating the Oreos because I want to and I can eat them anytime," he said. "Lighten up."

"You know . . . our daughter broke another kid's nose."

"I know," he said, glowing.

"You're seriously missing something here, Rudy."

"What? Davie got too friendly with her and she put him in his place," he said.

"Look, I agree that I want our girls to be able to defend themselves in case they are ever attacked," I said. "But we shouldn't condone Rachel's actions because a kid flipped her bra strap. I mean, self-defense is one thing, but if we condone this, then who's to stop her when the next kid just *looks* at her breasts?"

Rudy stood up straight. "Hey, that is my daughter you're talking about. And I don't want to think about any kid *looking* at anything but her face."

Rudy was having a difficult time dealing with the fact that Rachel *has* breasts, much less that they are growing. He had equal difficulty with the fact that she was no longer that little girl who used to wear ribbons in her hair and big pleated dresses with gigantic bows. Now, she wears bell-bottom jeans with yin/yang symbols on the rear-end pockets, and her straight hair is parted in the middle—a *crooked* part, for that's the in thing—and hangs shaggily around her shoulders. She is still a kid in many ways. She still loves boy bands and Harry Potter, and on occasion, if nobody is looking, she'll still play Barbies with her sister. But in another year, she'll be a full-fledged teenager, complete with pimples and boys. Rudy was in denial.

"Boys are going to look at her, Rudy. And someday they'll—"

"Don't go there!" he said, and held a hand up and shut his eyes. "I can't deal with this."

"Why not?"

"Because I was one of those sweaty, hormone-driven teenagers once, and I know what I used to . . . She's not dating until she's thirty. That's that. Can I just enjoy my cookies, for crying out loud?"

"Look, we don't have to worry about her dating, not just yet anyway. We've got a few years. My point is, she'll be leaving broken bones in a path from here to Arkansas if we don't do something about this now."

"And there's a problem with that?"

"Rudy!"

"All right, all right," he said. "You're right."

"I'm just saying that she should have gone to the teacher or the principal first, and then if he did it again, she could have taken more drastic actions, but we can't just condone the violence. Because if we condone it enough, someday she'll be the aggressor and we'll be getting phone calls from the school telling us to come get our bully. Not to mention we'll have to deal with the parents of all the wounded children. As it is, I'm not looking forward to seeing Davie's parents anytime soon."

"I think you're overreacting," he said.

"Probably. But, I just—" I took a deep breath. "One of my New

Year's resolutions was to be more tolerant and accepting. And to be kinder, more forgiving. In this world where people shoot other people for having a soda bottle in their hands, we need to practice and teach tolerance and forgiveness."

"Okay, I hear you," he said, putting his hands up in surrender. "Did *you* talk to her?"

"Yes," I said. "I let her know that I was happy she could take care of herself and that Davie was a jerk. But I also told her that if she ever busted a kid's nose again for something like this, I would ground her until her wedding day. I mean really, Rudy, was his behavior that bad?"

Rudy shrugged. "I used to do the same thing." He blushed. "Sometimes worse."

"Exactly. Davie's parents need to teach him to keep his hands to himself, and we need to teach Rachel not to take any crap. But not to go beating people up over every little thing. We're lucky she didn't get suspended. If it hadn't been for the fact that she's never been in trouble a day in her life, they probably would have suspended her."

"I know," he said. "But I was just so proud of her."

I couldn't help myself. The thought of my waiflike daughter hauling off and slugging Davie Roberts was just too surreal for me not to laugh. "Me, too," I said. We laughed together a minute and then I straightened up. "But only for a moment."

My son, Matthew, came toddling into the kitchen with his sippy cup in one hand, a plastic velociraptor in the other. He wore his Batman pajamas, but the cape had come off somewhere in his bed. Rudy picked him up and gave him a big hug. "No flicking bra straps when you get older," he said to him with a stern face.

Right, like that was going to work.

"I gotta go," he said, giving me a kiss and handing off Matthew. "I'll talk to her tonight."

"Okay," I said.

•

I was late getting to my office. First, I had taken Matthew to my mother's house for the day, then dropped Rachel and Mary off at school, where I'd had a talk with the principal about yesterday. I'd asked him to please stress to Davie's parents that their son's behavior wasn't entirely acceptable, either.

I had barely sat down, when there was a knock at my door. "Come in," I said.

"Hi," a woman said. I stared at her for the longest time and then realized that she was the woman who had been on the tour yesterday. Stephanie . . . Connelly. Surely she didn't think that I had her family tree finished already.

"Ms. Connelly," I said, and stood.

"I was just wondering if you had a chance to look over the form I filled out."

Well, she was certainly a tenacious one, I'd give her that. She wore jeans and a pink sweater, no jewelry except a wedding band, very little makeup. "No," I said. "I just got in. Ms. Connelly, I won't be able to have anything for you to see for at least a week."

Her expression fell. "Oh, well, I know that. I just thought you'd at least have looked at the paperwork."

"No, not yet."

The phone rang then. I held a finger up to her as I answered it. It was my mother. "Hi, Mom," I said. Mom's voice was pleasant on the other end of the phone, asking me if we'd come to dinner later that evening. "Sure. I don't think we have anything else going on. We'll see you about six. Look, I have to go. There's somebody in my office. Love you, too. Bye."

Stephanie Connelly just stood there, picking at her thumbnail with her fingernail and biting her lower lip. What was her problem? Her gaze fell to the photograph of my children that I had sitting on my desk. It was one I had taken just two weeks ago—all three of them out in the snow with the lopsided snowman they'd spent the whole day making. Rosy cheeks, red noses, glistening eyes. They looked the picture of happy, healthy children.

"Are those your children?" she asked.

"Yes."

She just smiled and leaned a little closer to get a better look.

"Ms. Connelly—"

"Could you just look at my paperwork?" she asked. "It took a lot for me to come here and actually do this, and . . . I want—no, I *need* for you to at least look at it."

I fished out the Advil from the top drawer in my desk and put two in the palm of my hand. It was going to be a long day. "Just a minute," I said. I went to the soda machine and got a Dr Pepper, then chased down the Advil with one swallow. Back in the office, I seated myself, cleared my throat, and made a big production of retrieving her file from the top of my desk and opening it.

Name: Stephanie Anne Webster Connelly.
Birth: 26 June 1970, St. Louis, Missouri.
Married: Michael Norman Connelly on 10 May 1995,
    St. Louis, Missouri.
Children: Julia Victory Connelly, born 5 October 1996.
Mother: Julia Anne Thatcher
Father: Dwight Keith

I read that last line again. Dwight Keith. I looked up at her sharply, and she flinched. Then I looked back at the paper and read her daughter's name again. Julia *Victory* Connelly. My name. Victory is my real name; Torie is my nickname. Dwight Keith is my father's name. A chill settled in my chest as I looked up at her once more.

"Is this some kind of joke?" I asked. "I . . . don't understand."

The phone rang again. I picked it up. It was Eleanore Murdoch. "Not now," I said. "No, no, Eleanore, I'll talk to you later. Bye."

Tears welled in Ms. Connelly's eyes as she shoved her hands as deep in her pockets as they could possibly go. "I shouldn't have come," she said, and turned to leave, but I didn't let her go.

"What is this all about? What's the meaning of this?" I asked. What was she trying to say? What was she trying to accomplish by filling out her forms falsely?

Taking a deep breath, she just blurted it out. "I'm your sister."

I took another two Advil.

I didn't know what to say to her. I mean, it was preposterous. My father . . .

My father.

No, it was silly. I would have known if I had a sister, for crying out loud. I just sat there, blinking, not really sure what to say to her. She obviously expected something from me, but I didn't know what. And I'm sure my silence was not at all welcome.

"I . . . I think there's been a mistake," I said finally.

"No," she said. "There is no mistake. I am Dwight's daughter."

I am Dwight's daughter.

Her words echoed around in my head. My mind reeled and spun. A roaring in my ears blocked out all sound, so that I found myself in a vacuum, silent except for her words bouncing around. It was my turn to fight back tears. The familiarity in her eyes . . . They were my father's eyes. She was looking at me with my father's eyes. My eyes. But then, that could only mean . . .

My parents hadn't divorced until I was twelve. She was only five years younger than I was. The betrayal was like a bitter pill, too big for me to swallow. I felt as if a knife had been shoved in my heart.

"You can call him and ask him," she said.

Call him and ask him? Then that would mean that he knew about her. The fact that he would know about her and not ever have told me hurt me even more. How could he keep this from me for thirty years? Knowing how I felt about family, knowing I hated being an only child. When I was a kid, I would ask Santa for a sibling. Every single year. Wasn't it just like him to keep something to himself that I had always wanted? It was as if somebody had just twisted the imaginary blade that had penetrated my flesh moments ago. Just call him and ask him. That simple. With one phone call, shatter my whole world.

"I don't think so," I said.

Call him and ask him. Did she know his phone number?

"But . . ." she began, unsure of what to say. "I . . ."

"You what? What do you want exactly?" I asked, trying hard not to be too angry.

"I want a relationship with my sister." She shrugged.

"Right," I said, pushing my chair away from my desk and then standing. "Well . . . I'm not your sister."

Before I could ask her to leave my office, Elmer Kolbe came bursting through the door. He's our fire chief, way past retirement age, and all-around good guy. "Torie, you gotta come see this."

"See what?"

"You know how the river's been down so low?"

"Yeah?"

"You can see the wreck."

"The wreck."

"*The Phantom,*" he said. "The steamboat that sank back in 1919."

"You're kidding," I said. But I found myself at odds with how I wanted to feel. Any other time, I would have jumped over my desk and taken off to the river like Tom Sawyer or Huck Finn. The legend of *The Phantom* is something told on every bar stool of every pub and diner in New Kassel. I'd grown up with the legend. I'd grown up, like everybody else, wondering if there would ever be a time that Old Man River would be low enough that we could actually view the wreckage. And it had finally happened. But now, with Ms. Connelly standing there with her news so fresh in the air, I was just sort of numb.

I was happy for Elmer's interruption, I decided. Because it saved me from any further discussion with Ms. Connelly. It saved me from having to kick her out of my office.

"Come on," he said, waving a hand at me. "Come and look."